CHALLENGE the DARKNESS

Dirk Greyson

Published by
DREAMSPINNER PRESS

5032 Capital Circle SW, Suite 2, PMB# 279, Tallahassee, FL 32305-7886 USA
http://www.dreamspinnerpress.com/

This is a work of fiction. Names, characters, places, and incidents either are the product of author imagination or are used fictitiously, and any resemblance to actual persons, living or dead, business establishments, events, or locales is entirely coincidental.

Challenge the Darkness
© 2015 Dirk Greyson.

Cover Art
© 2015 Reese Dante.
http://www.reesedante.com
Cover content is for illustrative purposes only and any person depicted on the cover is a model.

ISBN: 978-1-63476-481-0
Digital ISBN: 978-1-63476-482-7
Library of Congress Control Number: 2015943917
First Edition August 2015

Printed in the United States of America
∞
This paper meets the requirements of
ANSI/NISO Z39.48-1992 (Permanence of Paper).

Readers love

Day and Knight

by DIRK GREYSON

"I really did enjoy this book…
a terrific read"
　　　—Rainbow Gold Reviews

"I had a hard time putting this book down… very captivating… I
hope to see these characters again in the future."
　　　　　　　　　　　　　　　　　　　—Hearts on Fire

"This is a great start to… a new series."
　　　　　　　　　　　　　　　　　—The Blogger Girls

"…this author knows how to tell a story no matter what name he
goes by. Thank you for another excellent tale, sir."
　　　　　　　　　　　　　　　　　—The Novel Approach

To Kate Douglas, for inspiring the story in the first place. You are an amazing author, and I hope I do you proud. Thank you for everything. This story wouldn't exist without you.

CHAPTER 1

MIKAEL VOLOKOV stood at the edge of the ring, his gaze, like those of the dozens of spectators—both human and wolf—glued to the two people inside. They circled each other again and again, sizing each other up before an announcement was made for them to begin the fight to the death. Anton Romanov was the bigger wolf without a doubt, but Gregor was wily and smart, a brains versus brawn match if there ever was one. Normally Mikael would put his money on Gregor, but there was something about Anton—maybe his reputation for brutality or the way he exuded all the confidence in the world. This was going to get ugly, and fast.

"You both know the rules," Mikael said in his loudest alpha-male voice. He would brook no argument. Gregor had requested his presence to help ensure the outcome was fair and to serve as his safety net. Packs rarely mingled freely, and alphas didn't usually spend any time with each other. They had a tendency to want to rip out the throat of any perceived threat, and another alpha in their territory was most definitely a threat.

"There aren't any rules," Anton sneered.

"Then we'll all go home, and you can walk away with your tail between your legs," Mikael snarled back, prepared to step in if needed. He knew he had the backing of most of the wolves around them. It seemed none of them were in favor of this challenge from the neighboring pack alpha, but this would have to be settled the old-fashioned way. What startled Mikael most was that apparently Anton had insisted as part of his challenge that Gregor's family be present to see the challenge and its outcome. Brutality was one thing; instilling terror was quite another. "A challenge between alphas is a fight to the death, and neither of you is to leave the circle until there is a victor. At stake is leadership of both packs." God help them all if Anton was victorious.

1

"We know. Get on with it," Anton snarled.

Gregor simply looked at him and nodded his agreement. Mikael had known Gregor since childhood. They hadn't spent any time together since they both realized their abilities and alpha natures. But the old ties never went completely away. Mikael knew when Gregor got quiet there was going to be trouble. He hoped it was the kind that would kick Anton's ass.

"On my mark," Mikael said. "Fight!" The word echoed across the clearing. Mikael saw worry on Gregor's wife Anna's face and near terror on the faces of their two boy pups. They looked about five and seven, but they were old enough to understand the stakes—they could end up without a father.

The two men stared at each other, tension building between them. It wasn't a surprise that Anton attacked first; it was his nature as a brute. He caught Gregor's leg and twisted to avoid Gregor's swipe with his shifted arm. Anton hit the ground and completely shifted to his wolf form, snarling and leaping right back at Gregor, who managed to shift as well, but just barely. Damn, Mikael had seen very few wolves who could shift that quickly and be instantly ready to go. The two wolves clashed in midair, with Anton barreling into Gregor, sending both of them crashing and rolling to the ground in a tangle of legs, teeth, and black fur mixed with gray. They were moving so quickly both wolves blurred together.

Mikael was supposed to remain neutral, but inside he wanted Anton out of the picture for all their sakes. Gregor got a good tear into Anton, who snarled his pain and dug into Gregor's hind leg with his teeth, clamping his jaw closed. Gregor managed to shake him off, but he would need to shift to heal that wound, and there was no time for that. Anton rolled once and came up on all fours, baring his teeth, ready to strike. Gregor was hurt and in pain, Mikael could feel it deep in his bones. He knew his old friend was in trouble. Anton leaped, and Gregor dodged, but he was just a hair too slow. Anton caught him in the side and tumbled Gregor off his feet. He went for the throat, and instantly blood spattered all over Anton's gray coat.

Mikael had seen enough of this that it didn't bother him. Shifter society could be violent at times, but what caught his attention was Gregor's two pups looking on as their father breathed his last. Mikael knew who the victor was and what Anton was doing, but the look on those pups' faces was enough to make him hate Anton. Sure, a challenge was one thing, but making sure his opponent's family, as well as his own, was there to witness the final brutality was beyond the pale as far as Mikael was concerned.

"That's enough!" Mikael roared with all the power he could muster.

Anton stopped, and after one final snarl, he stepped back, turned his head skyward, and howled his victory. The members of his own pack who were present joined him, while the members of Gregor's pack wondered what kind of hell would happen to them now. Anton continued his howl and then grew silent before shifting back to his human form. Wolves had no qualms around nudity, but one of Anton's betas brought him a robe—trimmed with ermine as though he were Czar—and draped it over his shoulders.

"This pack is now mine, and it will be integrated with my own. There will be no separate pack structure. Those of you who wish to keep your position may fight for it, just like I fought for mine." Anton turned to Anna. "You may join my household, along with your pups."

"I'd rather die," she spat and gathered her pups to her. Gregor and Anna had been true mates, ordained and joined by the Mother herself. Anton's disregard of tradition and their beliefs would not go down well with anyone.

"That can be arranged."

Mikael stepped forward. "Anna and her cubs have petitioned to join my Yellowstone pack, and I have accepted them as members. If you wish to challenge that, you can fight me here and now." Mikael had had enough of this self-aggrandizement on Anton's part.

Anton was breathing heavily, but he still seemed to consider it. "No. I will not. They are weak, and I don't want that bloodline mixing with mine and those of my pack." Anton turned, the robe fluttering behind him as he walked from the circle. "No others are free to leave, however," he pronounced, turning back to face the group. "I will not have it, and my retribution will be swift and final." He swirled back around and walked away like the king victorious.

The other members of Gregor's pack silently turned and left the area. They had to be wondering what the future held for them, and

Mikael wished he could help them, but he'd been lucky to save Anna and the two boys from having to live with and around Anton. That was the best he could do at the moment.

"I want to go home," the smallest pup said softly to Anna. "Why isn't Daddy getting up?" he asked, turning back to where Gregor lay on the ground.

"Daddy's dead," the older boy said, fighting tears.

"What do we do now?" Anna asked.

"I have my car, and we'll get you back to your house as fast as we can. Hopefully Anton will celebrate his victory before he decides to lay claim to the house, and by then you can have your things and be gone."

Mikael herded the small group to his Volvo station wagon. Yeah, the car wasn't very alpha-ish, but it worked well for the pack. Mikael was all about doing what was best for his pack. They were his family, after all, and he treated each of them as such, the same way he'd now treat Anna and her pups.

He got the small group to the car and buckled in. Anna directed him, and he drove as fast as he could to the house, what had once been their home. It was dark.

"Okay." Mikael turned to face the two shell-shocked pups. "What are your names?"

"I'm Alexi, sir, and this is Misha," the older pup answered.

"Excellent. What I need you to do is to be big boys and go right up to your rooms and pack your suitcases and toys. I'll help you if you like." He turned to Anna. "Take everything that's important. Clothes can be replaced, but special things from Gregor cannot, and I doubt you will ever be able to set foot in this house again."

Anna nodded and got out. She helped the boys out of the car, and Mikael lifted Misha into his arms and carried him into the house. Anna turned on lights and sprang into action. She could grieve once she and her pups were safe. Mikael took the boys upstairs and found suitcases. Alexi began pulling clothes out of his neat drawers and placing them inside one suitcase, his packing haphazard. Mikael helped Misha do the same, then found a plastic toy box on the floor of the closet. Once the boys' suitcases were packed, he instructed the boys to pack their favorite toys in the box.

4

Mikael then looked around the room. He spied pictures of each of the boys with their father. He grabbed them and wrapped them in bedding, then put them on top of the toys in the box. Then he closed the toy box and instructed the boys to find their mother while he started loading the car.

It didn't take long. As Mikael stood by the Volvo, his ultrasensitive hearing picked up vehicles heading their way—still a few minutes off, but they had run out of time. "Boys, get in the car," Mikael said as soon as he stepped inside the house.

Neither argued; they just raced outside. Mikael heard the car doors slam closed—*thunk, thunk*—and called to Anna, "We have to go."

"This is it," she said, coming into the room with a suitcase in each hand. Mikael grabbed the boxes from the sofa—damn, they were heavy—and followed her outside.

"Don't stop to turn off lights or even close the door." Mikael put the boxes in the back and grabbed one of Anna's suitcases, which he wedged in, and then he closed the overhead door. Anna put the other case at her feet, and as soon as they'd both closed the car doors, Mikael started the engine and took off, turning away from the house and Anton's men. It wasn't the direction he needed to go, but he explained to Anna that there was a turnoff they could take to circle back to the road that would take them in and through Yellowstone National Park.

"How far is it?" Alexi asked.

"You boys settle down and try to go to sleep. We're going to be driving for a while." The park was huge, but Mikael had grown up there and knew every inch of it like the back of his hand. He knew the route that would take them to their new home, and after making a few unnecessary turns to ensure they weren't being followed, he made a beeline for his own territory.

Occasionally lights could be seen in the distance, but mostly it was just them, the stars, and the occasional cry of one of the full-blooded wolves drifting on the wind. The wolves knew something major had happened and that the environment around them had changed. It was clear in their cries. The instinct to stop and answer tore through him, but his wolf understood they had a task to do and cooperated. Mikael gripped the wheel, retaining control of his wolf, and drove as fast as he dared.

The pups were asleep in the backseat by the time Mikael reached the main road. Anna had said very little for hours, and he knew the grief of losing her mate must be beginning to overwhelm her. The acrid scent of fear combined with the pungent acidity of anguish filled the car. Mikael didn't need to ask how she felt; his nose told him everything. "I know what you're going through," he told her. "My mother lost my father when I was a few years older than Misha. She told me the only reason she survived were her three pups. You have to go on for the boys."

"But he's gone," Anna mumbled. "The other half of my soul has been ripped away from me. We've lost our home and our family. All of it was taken from me in the instant Gregor died." Her voice remained steady, though, and Mikael knew she'd keep it together. She was the mate of an alpha, and that alone would sustain her.

"I know. But the boys will need you, and your new pack will need you."

She turned to him. "You lied to Anton."

"In a way. When Gregor asked me to come to ensure the fight would be fair, he told me if anything were to happen to him, he wanted me to take care of his family. You and those two boys were important to him. So when Anton tried to claim you, I had to step in." He glanced in the backseat and saw that both boys were asleep, lying down on the seat, curled together just the way he'd slept with his siblings, Karl and Catherine, when they were pups. "What he was doing violated everything I believe in, and if I could have, I'd have helped everyone in the pack, but I can't. They are beyond me, but not you and the boys." He had to save a piece of his old friend. If Anton had taken the boys, odds were good that at some point they would end up dead too. Gregor's blood in Anton's pack would have been a threat to him, especially if they grew to be as strong as their father.

"What if they grow up to challenge you or your sons?" Anna asked with a touch of pride.

"They won't. I won't have children."

"You'll find a mate," Anna said.

"I might, but I know my mate will be another man. The Mother told me so in a dream when I was eight years old. She showed him to me—another eight-year-old boy. I remember his blond hair, fierce eyes, and the way he looked back at me. It was like we could see each other for a brief time through the ether. Then he was gone, but I always knew he was my mate. I just haven't met him yet."

"What about your brother and sister's children?" Anna asked.

"You'll see. Karl is my beta, and he's fantastic at it. He always has my back, and Catherine is an enforcer. No one messes with her, including her husband, Stan. My younger brother, Christopher, is away at college." Christopher's role in the pack was up in the air at the moment, by his choice. He'd always seemed to go his own way and follow his own drummer. "They are my support, always, and I couldn't be the alpha I am without them. We're not a large pack, only about twenty in all. The core of the pack is my family—my siblings and their spouses, their children, and my uncle and mother. And now you and the boys. So if they grow up and follow in their father's footsteps, as long as they care for their pack the way Gregor always did, they'll have my blessing and support."

Anna didn't say anything right away. "Thank you, Alpha," she finally said softly.

"Mama, are we there yet?" Alexi mumbled.

"No. Go back to sleep." She reached behind and stroked his head until he went quiet once again. "We'll really be welcome?"

"Of course. The rest of the pack is my family, but I am still the alpha, and they will do as I say. Besides, Catherine is going to love you, and her pups will welcome yours. We're a family, and you're going to be part of it. It won't feel like it did before. You were the alpha mate, but you won't have that rank in this pack. Still, you'll be regarded, and I think you'll fit in well." God, he hoped so. His pack was harmonious and happy, and Mikael wanted it to stay that way.

"I'm grateful for the chance you're giving us," she whispered and then turned to watch out the window, staring into the same inky blackness that surrounded the car, with only the headlights to pierce the night.

Finally Mikael exited the park and then turned almost immediately onto a road that seemed little used. He purposely kept it that way so his pack would be left alone. He continued driving for nearly five miles, then pulled into a small compound of homes surrounded by trees that soared toward the sky. Mikael pulled to a stop and turned off the engine. He opened the door and got out, scenting the air of home. Everything was just as it should be.

"You're back," Catherine said from the porch. Mikael knew the instant she scented the other. Her eyes narrowed and her entire frame went rigid.

"You can stand down. I have three new pack members with me."

Catherine didn't move, as tense as Mikael had ever seen her. "All right."

Mikael motioned for Anna to get out of the car. She opened the door and stood straight and tall. "This is Anna. Her mate, Gregor, lost the challenge. Her boys, Misha and Alexi, are in the backseat, asleep. Show her inside and make sure they have something to eat. Then put all three of them in the guest cabin." That had been the family joke for years. They never had guests, but his mother had always maintained it, just in case. "That will be their home. We can introduce them to everyone in the morning."

"If you say so, Alpha," Catherine said, and Mikael growled a warning at her. He knew that tone, and he was in no mood for it. She didn't do change well, never had.

"I do, and you'll do as I ask without question." Mikael strode up to her and stared her straight in the eyes. She tilted her head to the side, baring her neck in submission. That sort of act wasn't usually his thing, but she needed to be reminded of her place every once in a while. "These three need a home. They've lost everything, and given what I've seen, we could be in danger of the same fate." He hardened his eyes and saw fear tinge the edges of her expression. Fear was something his sister rarely showed. She was an enforcer, strong as hell and damned near as fearless, but she could be headstrong.

"What do you mean?" she asked, this time much more humbly.

"We'll talk tomorrow." He smiled slightly and put his hand on her shoulder. "Let's get them settled and then go to bed. Do your best to reassure everyone. They're going to know that something is wrong, and we need to keep the pups calm." Mikael lowered his voice. "Anna and her family need time to grieve, and we'll give them that. She lost her mate and the pups their father."

"I understand."

"Good." He turned, walked back to the car, and opened the back liftgate. "We'll help you take your things inside," he said to Anna.

"That isn't necessary, Alpha. I can do it," Anna said.

"Let's get the boys to bed." He looked at Catherine, who started unpacking. Mikael opened the passenger door and gently lifted Alexi into his arms. The youngster curled to him, resting his head on his shoulder. Mikael was instantly filled with anger and grief. Gregor should have been putting his pups to bed. Anna lifted Misha into her arms, and Mikael led her across the compound to one of the smaller buildings. Mikael had helped his father and the other men build it when he was a teenager. It was really just a large cabin, with exposed beams and wood-paneled walls.

Inside, he made his way to the second bedroom with its double bed. It hadn't been made up, but he settled Alexi on the mattress, and Anna laid Misha next to him. The two brothers curled together and settled right back to sleep.

"I'll make up everything in the morning," Anna told him. "You've already done more than I could ever expect." She lowered her eyes and tilted her head to the side. "Thank you."

"You're welcome," he said as calmly as he could. Mikael took one last look at the pups and left the room, meeting Catherine as she carried in the last of the bags and things from the car. At the door he turned back to Anna, nodded to her, and then stepped outside.

He inhaled the woody, sweet scent of home. He walked back to his house and stood on the porch. The call of the trees and wind echoed in his ears. Without thinking, he shucked his clothes and shifted before his feet hit the bottom step. Scents, familiar and strong, filled his nose, and the rustling of a rabbit hundreds of yards away reached his sensitive ears. But he wasn't interested in food. He needed to run to let his baser self be free. In this form, his human half was still present, only freer, and he was able to think and let go while instinct took over the rest of him.

His paws tore over familiar ground—every leaf, tree, and twig was his, and he knew them all. With very little effort or sound, he covered miles, making a huge loop around his home, ensuring that all was as it should be. For the millionth time in his life, Mikael wondered what it would be like to make these runs with someone at his side. He always did them alone. They were his time, but what would it be like to have a mate with him on these runs? After hours, tired, but his mind clear, he loped back home, shifted back on the porch, and walked inside.

His home was a larger version of the guest quarters. Exposed beams, paneled walls, heavy, masculine furniture—it was the home of a man. His mother had done her best to soften the place when she and his father had lived here, but she knew the battle was lost once Mikael took over. He liked things simple and didn't do fussy. However, that didn't mean he hadn't let his mother help him decorate. The walls were filled with pictures of his family and pack. This great room was the center of the pack and where everyone spent a lot of their time.

Mikael threw his dirty clothes in the hamper and went right to his bathroom, where he brushed his teeth and took a shower before crawling into bed, envying the boys who had someone to curl up with at night. He'd slept in a pile with his brothers and sister until they'd found mates and had families of their own. Now, as alpha, he slept alone, just like as leader he alone made decisions and accepted the consequences that affected his entire family. He hadn't really understood what his father had done and how effortlessly he seemed to do it until Mikael had taken over for him after his death. He had known he was expected to lead, and he thought he'd been prepared for it. But after five years, there were still times when he wondered if he was strong enough to protect his family. After tonight he wondered that even more. Could anything protect them from Anton should he turn his sights in the direction of Mikael's family?

The meadow was unlike any he'd ever seen or smelled before. Wait... yes he had. Somewhere from deep inside, a long-faded memory, one nearly dead, sprang to life. The sky was bluer, the wind fresher, the trees more pungent, the breeze perfect. He stood with nothing between his skin and the kiss of the breeze. This was her domain, and he remembered the first and only other time he had been here.

"Your fears are well-founded." She stepped from behind a tree, the sun forming a type of halo. Her eyes were as dark as a night sky with stars transforming the blackness from menace to beauty, for that's what she was—beauty personified, with lips the color of the strawberries that covered the small glen near the compound in early summer, and hair the color of summer wheat.

"I understand."

She didn't need to explain. Her meaning was clear as an image of Anton in wolf form filled his mind.

"The last time you were here I showed you your mate. Remember him, and remember that you will need each other far more than you will initially realize."

Mikael lowered his gaze. "I understand," he repeated.

"No, you don't, but you will eventually. Remember that I have chosen him for you."

"I will," Mikael said because he had no choice. She was his goddess, the one who had seen the pack through the decades of darkness and eventually found a way for them to rejoin the light. He owed her everything.

She chuckled, and her eyes danced, galaxies whirling in their depths. "It may not be as easy as you think." She was clearly taking some enjoyment in this. "You will need to face him." Anton as a man flashed in his mind. "But how you face him will be up to you."

"Why are you telling me this? Isn't Anton one of your children too?" Goddesses were a mystery, but it seemed they should play fair.

"No. He is definitely not one of my children. He is not of the light." She turned as birds glided down to her head, landing gently in her hair. "I must go, and you must return."

"Why tell me this?" The light faded, and the meadow with its trees and green disappeared into the darkness.

"So you will know."

Mikael opened his eyes and breathed in the familiar scents of home. He was back in his own bed. Damn, goddesses were flashy.

"Don't complain—I could have taken you to the North Pole."

Gentle laughter filled his head and then faded away. He lay still and hoped she was gone as he shivered slightly at the thought. He got up and walked to the window, pushing the curtains aside before staring out into the darkness. Whatever that dream had been, the message was clear. He'd already known he had a mate out there somewhere, and he assumed that the experience he'd just had meant he was going to meet him soon. After a few minutes, he turned, pulled the curtains, and went back to bed. He needed his sleep for what he was going to have to do tomorrow.

CHAPTER 2

"HOW DID it go?" Mikael's mother asked when he stepped into the kitchen, and he was thankful he'd put on a robe. Nudity was no big deal, but he still didn't want to be running around naked in front of his mother. Some things were just wrong, and he wasn't interested in seeing her naked either. He might have to bleach his eyes.

"It was worse than I suspected." He accepted the mug of coffee she offered. "As you probably already know, we have new pack members in the guest cabin, which I suppose we're going to have to find a different name for now that I've given it to Anna and her cubs."

His mother didn't ask why, which was a testament of her respect for his role as alpha. "That's... unexpected."

"Anton said he'd take her into his household. I couldn't have that. She'd just lost her mate and...." The ruthlessness made him angry all over again. "I accepted her and her pups into the pack. I wish I could have helped them all."

"Then they're going to need breakfast." She turned away and got busy. Sometimes his mother really shocked him. She was the best, and while she offered advice, sometimes before he asked for it, she never once questioned the decisions he made.

"We're also going to have a pack meeting at noon in the cave." He lifted his mug and turned away as she gasped softly. He stopped. "Yeah, Mom, it's that serious." Mikael took his mug of coffee and, as calmly as he could with his heart racing a mile a minute, walked back to his bedroom to dress. The full meaning of what the goddess had told him the night before hit him like a blast of winter wind off the Yellowstone plateau. Their conversation hadn't been about his mate as much as what he was going to have to do. The Mother had been sending him a message to be prepared and ready for battle, so yes, it was that serious. By the time he reached his bedroom door, he could already hear his mother on the phone.

It took him half an hour to clean up and dress. By the time he was done, the house was full. He could tell by the overlapping voices of his entire family and the occasional whispers of the names Anna, Misha, and Alexi. The great room quieted instantly when he walked in. The men all bared their necks and the women lowered their eyes. Even the pups quieted. Everyone knew something important was happening and seemed to be holding their breath.

"Eat your breakfast. We'll talk at the cave." Mikael turned to Catherine's oldest, Jane, who was fourteen. "You'll be in charge of the pups." He looked at each pup with a stern look that said they had better behave. They nodded even with their mouths full of Grandma's pancakes and bacon. Alexi had syrup dripping down his chin, but he too nodded seriously and then turned to his mother.

Mikael went into the great room and sat down. He wasn't hungry, not even for his mother's breakfast, which seemed crazy even to him. He sipped his coffee and stared out the large window to the woods outside. Mikael wanted to run again, but he wouldn't find the answers he needed out there. Fuck, the answers might not even exist. Contrary to what he wanted to believe, not every problem had an answer; some had to be endured and others accepted.

"Excuse me, Alpha," Anna said as she came into the room. She stood with her eyes down and sat when Mikael gestured toward the other chair. "I'm not sure of my place here and...."

"You are a member of this pack, the same as anyone else," Mikael said. "That's your place. What would you like to know?"

"Should I go to the cave?"

"You would be welcome," Mikael said. "But I'm going to urge you to stay here with your pups. It isn't because you're being excluded. You aren't. But...." He knew the topic of discussion and wanted to spare her additional pain.

"I understand. What happened yesterday—" She swallowed, hurt and loss filling her large eyes. "—will be discussed."

"Yes. And I think it's more important that you spend time with the boys. They need you. I lost my father long before I was ready, but at least I was an adult. Be there for them—that's all anyone will ask of you for a while. Grieve as openly or as privately as you wish." Mikael saw movement out of the corner of his eye—Catherine, remaining close. He was well aware that with their sensitive hearing, the others were able to listen to their conversation, so what he said would be taken as law by everyone. "No one will think any less of you, and I daresay this pack, your new family, will support you in every way they can."

"Thank you," Anna whispered, and then a soft whimper reached his ears. Anna turned her head and stood up, knowing one of her pups needed her.

"I was just playing, Mama," Catherine's son William said plaintively.

"I know. Misha is having a hard time, so you need to play gently," Catherine told him. She could be tough as nails but was incredibly gentle yet firm with her children. It was one of the things that had both surprised and delighted Mikael. He had expected her to be hard on them, but Catherine somehow managed to strike a near perfect balance, at least in Mikael's opinion.

"Sorry," William said, and Mikael smiled to himself. His pack might be small, but it was healthy and prosperous. Mikael was determined to keep it that way.

THE MORNING flew by in a fog of contemplation for Mikael. He kept rolling ideas through his head. He left early and ran deep into the woods, until he came to the familiar place on the far side of the property. When he was a child, he'd asked his father why they hadn't built their house right here. A small stream ran along the base of a shallow ravine that passed directly in front of the cave, providing water that nurtured the wildflowers that grew on both sides. In wolf form, Mikael breathed deeply, pleased to be home—for this too was his home and would be to the entire pack. He crossed the stream and easily climbed up the rocky face to the small opening in the rock. He crouched low and slid inside and along the short passage until the ceiling heightened.

Mikael shifted, his muscles changing, bones reconfiguring until he stood as a man in the nearly complete darkness. Not that he needed to see. He knew this place. Every rock and stone was as familiar as old friends and as sacred as any altar in the grandest cathedral in the world. He walked to a much smaller side room and touched the battery light they left in the cave. He turned it on and opened one of the plastic containers of clothes. He dressed in a long, flowing robe that had been used by his father and grandfather, and then set he about making sure everything was ready.

Mikael spread robes like the ones he was wearing, plus heavy blankets, on the ledges and floors, long-ago gifts from native friends who had passed through the veil to the Mother many years ago. He had just finished when the others began to arrive, familiar wolves passing into the cave. He knew each and every one, including his sister, gray and black, with her mate, nearly all gray, right behind her. They settled on the blanket next to the one where Mikael sat cross-legged, still in human form. If either of them was surprised, they made no indication and simply sat in their places to wait while the others gathered. Mikael's brother Karl came next, taking his place next to Mikael. Then Mikael's mother and uncle joined them, all still in wolf form.

"As you know, this place is sacred, but it's also where we conduct our most important business." Mikael stood. "This is the domain of our wolves, and it's the reason all of us are here. Our wolves took refuge in these caves when humans killed off our full-wolf brothers. We prayed for help for decades until the Mother was able to facilitate our reentry into her light. It was this place that provided succor and refuge to our wolves in a world where we could no longer exist." Mikael looked at each of his family members. They all knew the story, but Mikael wanted to tell it to the pups once again. "We reentered the light not long ago, once humans reintroduced wolves for us to hide among, and packs reformed. But this has resulted in something none of us foresaw, and we must discuss what we are going to do."

That was their cue to shift. Mikael waited as one by one, the wolves transformed into their human counterparts. After they did, they slipped on the robes that Mikael had set at each place. For wolves the cave was ideal, but it was cold for humans.

"What's going on?" Karl asked as everyone settled down.

"Patience," Mikael admonished with no heat. Karl was always in a hurry to get nowhere in particular. Karl nodded and grew quiet once again. "As you know, I was present at Anton Romanov's challenge, and I'm very concerned. He has no respect for our traditions."

"But Gregor lost the challenge. Was it unfair?"

15

Mikael turned to Karl. "He insisted that Anna and her pups be present as well as his own pups. Misha and Alexi saw Anton kill their father." Even Karl flinched and turned to Maddie, his wife, who seemed on the verge of tears. Karl could be a hardass, but he'd married the sweetest person Mikael had ever met, and Maddie was a moderating influence on his brother.

"None of us would never do that. We respect our traditions," his mother said, and everyone in the room nodded. Mikael and his siblings had all been taught that by both their parents.

Mikael continued, "I've come to believe, given everything I saw and given what the Mother shared with me...." A soft, collective gasp filled the space. "Anton is not of the light."

"If he comes here, I'll rip him apart," Catherine growled. Damn, Mikael was glad she was in his corner. Oh, he could growl louder and longer than she could, but it was good he didn't have to often.

"You might not get the chance," Mikael said. "He's the biggest wolf I have ever seen, shifter or not. He's also a brute with no remorse or conscience. Anton takes whatever he wants and is willing to kill to get it. Gregor and his pack were no threat to Anton. He challenged Gregor because he wanted his territory, nothing more."

Everyone began talking at once, and Mikael raised his hand. The silence was immediate.

"Are you saying you think we're next?" his uncle Viktor asked calmly.

"I don't know. But I incurred Anton's wrath when I gave Anna and her pups a refuge."

"You did what was right," his mother said without hesitation, and the others nodded their agreement. She stepped forward. "What are you proposing?"

"That we contact the Evergreen pack to our north and arrange a meeting with their alpha." Conversation broke out once again, and this time Mikael snarled, the sound echoing off the cave walls. Silence fell instantly.

"Alpha, that isn't our way," Catherine said respectfully.

"I know the traditions, same as you, and if you think I want to do this, you're out of your mind. It's completely against my nature. But I think we need to contact the Evergreen pack and talk to their alpha. I've heard, as we all have, that he's reasonable."

"Are you proposing we merge packs?" Karl asked.

"No. I'm saying we talk with them, form an alliance of sorts. If what I suspect is correct, Anton isn't going to stop until every pack in this area of the country is under his control. He wants it all, and as he gets stronger, we'll fall one by one." The very idea made him sick to his stomach. This was more than a pack, and being alpha wasn't some power trip. This was his family, and it was his job to keep them all safe. The thought of them under Anton's thumb scared him shitless, but he couldn't tell them that. Part of being an alpha was taking care of his entire pack, and while he might experience fear, he knew never to show it.

They remained quiet, and Mikael met the gaze of each pack member. "Karl, I want you to contact the beta of Evergreen and talk to him. Set up a meeting at a neutral location, preferably for lunch."

"Why lunch, Alpha?" Karl asked.

"It's easier to act civilized and talk over food," Mikael said. "All I want to do is meet with their alpha, talk to him. Expressly state that I am not interested in, and have no intention of, challenging his authority and will stand for no challenge to mine. The two of us have a common threat we need to discuss." Mikael raised himself to his full height and width. He was a formidable man, strong as hell, but he knew brawn wouldn't get him what he wanted, not in this case. There were times when it worked for him, but this… this required finesse and brains.

"We're all behind you," Catherine said, her gaze unwavering. "I want my children raised by this pack and in this family."

"Me too," Karl echoed. "I'll call a buddy I know in Evergreen. We met a few years ago. I'll see about making the contact we need." Wolves were social even though they moved in packs that were solitary and very territorial. Some packs went years without meeting another wolf outside the pack. That was part of the problem and what helped make them vulnerable to a power-hungry guy like Anton, who understood those weaknesses and used them to his advantage.

"Excellent. Are there any questions?"

His uncle stepped forward. "Did you really speak with the Mother?" he asked with a sense of awe.

"I believe so, yes. She came to me last night." Mikael decided that the rest of what she'd told him was meant for his ears only. "She's done it only once before, and that was long ago." He would say no more.

The others looked at each other and then back to him expectantly. "What do we do now?"

"We thank the Mother for all she's given us and continues to provide." Mikael stepped down, and one by one, his family took off their robes and placed them back in the plastic containers, then shifted to their wolf selves. Mikael did the same, his robe falling to the floor around him. He easily shook it off and called to his pack to follow him outside. By the stream, they all lifted their heads. Mikael howled, giving thanks for what he had, and one by one his pack members joined in until a chorus of overlapping cries echoed out over the land and then died away to silence. Seconds later, a single cry reached his ears, and then a group of higher, younger voices joined in, the rest of the pack answering them.

ALL THE pups gathered on the huge rug in the center of the great room. Most were in human form, but Misha and Alexi had shifted and were curled together away from the others. Karl had left to get right on the task Mikael had assigned, but the others were hanging around.

"Long ago the woods all around us were filled with wolves," Mikael said.

"Some like us, right?" William asked, eyes wide, and Jane shushed him right away.

"Yes, some like us," Mikael answered him, and William turned to his sister, sticking out his tongue. "No more of that," Mikael scolded lightly before returning to his story. "This country was filled with wolves, and some of them were our ancestors who could shift from the world of men to the world of animals. We were held in high regard by the people who lived here, and many of us lived among them. But then other men came, and we realized we needed to be wary of them. They killed wolves for sport, and many of our kind were shot along with them, but we survived."

"How?" William asked with childish enthusiasm.

"Well, some of us became men and didn't shift anymore, while others stayed away from the men with blond hair and white skin and lived in remote areas, where they had yet to go. Still others became what the easterners knew as mountain men." Mikael smiled. "They existed off the land, and people often wondered how they could live in such remote areas for such a long time."

All the pups shared a smile except the two boys, who lifted their muzzles, sniffed slightly, and then lowered their heads again. Mikael knew they were listening, nonetheless.

"What happened then, Uncle Mikael?" William asked when Mikael took too long to continue.

"Well, as the easterners moved west, they created farms and ranches and saw the wolves as a threat. They killed them off until they were all gone. Many of our kind left and went up to Canada and Alaska, where they still live today. But some of us stayed." Mikael paused. "Those were hard times. There were no wolves to hide among, so we had to live as humans." He lowered his voice as though sharing a secret. "We couldn't shift, or if we did, we couldn't be seen. There weren't any other wolves. But… my great-great-great-granddaddy met and married a hearty woman from Russia who was a Siberian wolf who came down from the cold of Alaska. He took her last name, and they homesteaded the land where we live now. He found the cave and knew that was a place where we could be close to nature and be our wolf selves."

The pups all smiled, thinking that was the end of the story. "He was really smart," Maria, Catherine's younger daughter said. She was just a little older than William.

"Yes, he was, but can you imagine—we could be wolves, but we couldn't call or howl. For a very long time, we had to be quiet, and we nearly lost our ability to call. Many pack members left, and we got smaller and smaller. Our wolf halves were very unhappy and grew quiet and in some cases died away. Others joined their brothers and sisters up north and left this land completely."

"That's sad," William said.

Mikael stood up and moved down onto the rug, and the pups gathered around him. Misha and Alexi slowly approached, and Mikael gently held each of them as they rested their heads on his leg. "It is.

19

But the Mother hadn't forgotten about us, and she put the notion in some men's heads that wolves needed to be brought back. Not all of them were happy, but in 1995, men reintroduced wolves into Yellowstone Park."

"Yay!" the kids said in unison.

"Exactly. And do you want to know something funny?" Mikael asked. They all nodded, and the two pups yipped with excitement. "The men were all surprised at how fast the wolves rebounded. In a few years there were a lot more of them than they expected there to be. Cries could be heard from the remote areas of the park."

"Those were us?" William asked proudly.

"Yes," Mikael answered. "I remember my dad taking me out one night. He and I climbed a hill and looked up at the sky. That night he turned his head to the full moon and howled his joy at the top of his lungs. From all over the park, the cry was echoed."

"I heard them and answered from down by the cave," his mother added from where she'd been sitting, listening. "That was a magical night, when we knew we were truly free once again."

"Yes, it was. That was the night he taught me to howl like a wolf, and someday I'll take each one of you up to the top of that same hill and show you how to cry your happiness to the full moon just like your grandfather showed me." Misha whimpered softly. "Misha, Alexi, I'll show both of you too. I know you'll make your daddy proud." He lightly touched their backs to try to comfort them, even though he knew their grief couldn't be soothed away.

"The Mother helped the transplanted wolves thrive so we too could live." He turned to his uncle, who nodded his agreement. "The humans are very concerned about the wolves. They went to a great deal of expense to help bring them back to these lands. But you have to be careful, or one of the humans will tag you." He reached out and lightly grabbed William's ear for just a second before releasing it. The little boy skittered away and transformed into a wolf pup, growling at Mikael, baring his sharp little teeth. Mikael growled back, transforming only his hand and arm, pressing William to the floor until he rolled on his back, showing his belly. "I didn't hurt you, and you need to be good." He released William, who joined Alexi and Misha in their pup pile. The two welcomed him and curled together. "Uncle Viktor got tagged a few years ago. He came back with a yellow tag stuck through his ear."

"Did you take it off?" Jane asked.

"Yes, but we had to do it well away from the compound. There was a tracker in it, so we removed it far away from here."

"I tried to shift, but the tag stayed in my ear," Viktor said. "It hurt like crazy." The pups all rubbed their ears, and the three in the pile all put their heads down with their little paws over their ears.

"So humans are bad," Maria said.

"No," he answered as his gaze went to the adults. "There are good humans and bad ones, just like there are good wolves like your mama, uncles, and grandma…."

Misha shifted to a boy, but didn't get up, lying naked with his brother and friend. Even in human form, the pups needed the camaraderie of the pack, especially when they were hurting. "And bad wolves like Anton."

"Yes," Mikael said gently.

Anna came over and lifted Misha into her arms. "Come on, sweetheart. Let's get you dressed."

"I wanna be a wolf," Misha said and struggled to get back down. Anna held him so they were at eye level. Then, after a few seconds of silent communication, she put him back down. Misha shifted back to his wolf pup form and rejoined the pup pile.

"I know it seems easier for you to be wolves and to not think about your dad, but that won't help in the long run. Your dad has joined the Mother in a place where it's always spring, and there are lots of rabbits and buffalo for him to hunt, with your grandfather and everyone from your pack who went before you." Alexi and Misha blinked up at him. It was obvious they were listening. "You have a family here who will love and care for you. I promise."

Anna lifted both of her pups into her arms, and Catherine picked up William. "The three of them can stay together tonight," Catherine told Anna, who was clearly concerned.

"Are you sure?" Anna asked.

"Catherine and I have an extra room if you'd like to stay too," Stan said. He was a kindhearted wolf who adored Catherine. He also tended to be submissive but had his own inner strength and an

21

intelligence that was clear in his bright eyes and ready smile. He also had a wicked sense of humor that livened the entire pack. But when it came to making decisions, he left that up to Catherine. "You're welcome to it. Some grieve alone while others need a pack around them."

Anna turned to Mikael, silently asking his permission.

Mikael nodded to her. "I want you to be comfortable."

"Thank you."

"The guest house will remain yours if you want it." Or they might need to put an addition onto one of the existing homes, and maybe it would be Catherine and Stan's if Anna decided to stay there permanently.

"Come on, let's put the young ones to bed." Catherine left the room, and Stan followed her without a word. Anna followed behind with a wolf pup head on each shoulder, eyes already falling closed. Mikael had little doubt the three of them would be as inseparable as he, Catherine, and Karl had been when they were that age.

Maria and Jane got up, and Jane took Maria's hand and led her away to bed.

"I'll tuck them in," their grandmother said with obvious joy.

Mikael wandered over to the window but couldn't see what he wanted, so instead he stepped outside and walked to the edge of the porch, where he could see the stars. He heard and scented Karl long before he actually approached.

"I got in touch with my buddy in the Evergreen pack, and he said he'd contact Kaiawa, their beta, and get back to me. Apparently they've all heard about the results of the challenge, and some of them are concerned as well. He had no idea how their alpha would react to your offer to meet, but Conrad did say their alpha tends to be of the mind to hunker down and wait things out."

"Damn," Mikael muttered as he clutched the railing, his fingers shifting to claws, leaving marks on the wood.

"I stressed that we were all at risk and what you were proposing. Conrad said he would pass on the message."

"Thank you," Mikael said as calmly as he could, his hands shifting back. There was nothing to be gained by ripping his home apart.

"I'm not really surprised. Packs tend to keep to themselves," Karl said without heat.

"I know. I'll go it alone against Anton if I have to, but there's strength in numbers. I know that and so does Anton...."

"Maybe Evergreen's alpha will figure it out too." Karl sounded hopeful, but Mikael looked up at the stars and hoped the Mother saw what he was doing and would aid him in his endeavor. Alphas generally met each other for one of two purposes: to resolve an interpack dispute, which was often handled through force or strength, or a direct challenge, which resulted in one of the two having Gregor's fate. Mikael knew what he was proposing was unprecedented since the packs had come out of hiding and into the light.

"We'll have to wait and see." It was the only answer Mikael could give. Karl left him alone after a few minutes, and Mikael stared at the stars until he figured he might as well go to bed. He stepped back inside and closed the door. A small streak of light gray darted out of the hallway and toward the kitchen. Mikael took two steps and scooped him up. "Where do you think you're going, Alexi?"

Big wolf eyes blinked up at him.

You need to shift so you can talk to me, Mikael told Alexi by placing the words directly in his head. The little wolf's eyes widened, and he whimpered. "Do you remember how? You have to think of yourself as a boy. Remember what you look like, and it will happen." Young ones often shifted without thinking or control and then seemed to have trouble shifting back. Mikael set Alexi on his feet, and a few seconds later, he went through his shift and smiled up at Mikael.

"I forgetted for a minute," Alexi said.

"That's okay. Now where were you going?"

"I have to pee, and I want a drink of water," Alexi answered. Mikael didn't think it would do any good to point out that the one thing was related to the other. "I was going outside to use the tree."

"How about you use the bathroom because it's so late, and I'll get you a drink of water. Then you can go back to bed." Mikael paused. "Didn't your mom put you to bed at Catherine's?" Alexi nodded and walked over to where Mikael indicated the bathroom was. "Then why are you here?"

"I wanted to mark the trees out there, and Mama says I'm not supposed to go through the woods alone, so I came from that house to this house."

Mikael shook his head. The logic of children was going to give him a headache. "Go potty, and then I'll take you back to your mama." *Who's probably having three fits and a hemorrhage right about now.* Alexi nodded and went into the bathroom. When he came back out, Mikael got a blanket and wrapped Alexi in it before lifting him into his arms and carrying him out the back door and across the compound. Anna came out to meet him, looking as frantic as Mikael had expected. "I think I have someone you're missing." He smiled at her to calm her. "The pup paid me a visit."

"Can Alpha Mikael put me to bed?" Alexi asked with a yawn.

"I don't think you've been good enough to ask for anything," Anna scolded. "You scared me half to death and probably woke up your alpha. Now you need to say you're sorry and go to sleep."

Alexi looked up at Mikael. "I'm sorry, Alpha Mikael," he said, extending his lower lip just a little.

"It's okay. But you need to stay with your mother."

"I will," he agreed.

"Now go on in to bed," Anna said.

"But I said sorry." He looked plaintively up at Mikael. It was the most pathetic expression he'd ever seen.

"Okay, pup, I'll put you to bed, but no more running outside at night."

"But you runned last night. I heared you."

"It's different for grown-ups. You can run at night when you're older, and I'll take you with me. But for now, you need to stay inside." He lifted Alexi to his shoulder and carried him down the hall to where the other two pups lay asleep. Mikael lay Alexi on the bed and covered him with the blanket. He wasn't sure if he'd stay in his human form or sleep as a pup. It didn't seem to matter. The others shifted closer, and Alexi seemed to fall asleep almost immediately.

Mikael left the room and pulled the door nearly closed before turning to Anna. "He's going to be a handful."

"Gregor always thought Alexi was the one most likely to be an alpha." She turned away, and Mikael felt and smelled her grief like a rotten stain that spread through her. "I'm sorry."

"There's no need to apologize. You take all the time you need, and if you want to talk, I'm here and so is everyone else." He patted her shoulder lightly and waited to see if she wanted to talk, but Anna thanked him and went into the room next to the boys, closing the door quietly. There were a lot of things he could do as an alpha, but healing a broken and longing heart was not one of them. He stood outside her door, purposely not listening as he wished like hell there was something he could do for her. But there was nothing other than making Anton pay for what he'd done when the time came.

Catherine poked her head out of her room and raised her eyebrows in silent question. Mikael nodded to her, and she went back inside. Then, as quietly as he could, Mikael went back to his house and got ready for bed.

An urgent knock woke Mikael the following morning. He'd spent much of the night tossing and turning. He got up and pulled on a pair of boxers before yanking the door open.

"Jesus, you look like hell," Karl said.

"So, Captain Obvious, what do you want?"

"I heard from the Evergreen beta this morning. Kaiawa isn't a man of many words, but he said his alpha has reluctantly agreed to meet you tomorrow at noon. A single beta can come along, but that's all, and he said if there's any sign of aggression…."

Mikael tuned the rest out. The usual posturing. He expected nothing less from another alpha. Hell, it's what he would have said if the situation had been reversed. "Is that all?"

"Isn't that enough?" Karl asked.

"More than enough," Mikael answered. It was all he could have hoped for. "Where does he want to meet?"

"At the restaurant near the Old Faithful Inn in the park." It was a very public place with plenty of people around. Mikael would have worried if the proposed location had been secret or secluded. He might have proposed the meeting, but he wasn't stupid. "Do you want me to go with you?" Karl asked.

Mikael thought for a second. "Yes." He considered taking Catherine, but she was needed here and could both hold down the fort and help take care of the pups. "We'll leave in the morning." The trip would take a couple of hours, and Mikael wanted to get there early.

"I hope you know what you're doing," Karl said. "I'll have your back, but…."

Mikael sure as hell hoped he knew what he was doing as well, but he'd already proposed the meeting and it was too late to back out now. It was either full steam ahead and take a step toward developing an ally or crash and burn. Either way, he figured he wouldn't be any worse off than he was now. At least he sure as shit hoped not.

CHAPTER 3

HE AND Karl arrived early at the meeting place. Mikael parked the station wagon and got out of the car. He stood still, inhaling deeply and taking in his surroundings. Most buildings did little to impress him. He'd been to San Francisco just before his father died, and the structures of steel and glass had left him cold and his wolf wondering why in the hell they were there. He screamed for open space, woods, and the scent of home. Mikael hadn't stayed long. But the Old Faithful Inn, now that was a building. It seemed to belong to the land, even with the cars around it, and Mikael's wolf breathed easily, happy.

"We aren't supposed to be here for an hour yet," Karl commented.

"I want to scout things out before they get here." It was a power thing. He wanted the other alpha to approach him, and he wanted to make sure the area was safe. But as soon as they passed into the soaring lobby with its massive stone fireplace and beamed ceiling held up by entire tree trunks, he knew that wasn't to be.

"There are two wolves here already." Karl started looking around as Mikael inhaled. "Only the two, so they seem to have kept to the agreement."

"If we can smell them, they can scent us, so we'll stay where we are for a moment." Mikael inhaled again, pulling the scent of heaven from the air. He scented once again, and his nose damn near jumped off his face and did some sort of happy dance. Mikael turned to Karl, wondering if he smelled it as well, but his brother scanned around on his usual protective alert. "Do you smell that?"

"What? All I smell are two wolves, and it's getting stronger but I don't see anyone yet." Karl turned toward the restaurant. "They must be in there." Karl stopped as Mikael stared at him. "What? You look like you do when Mom bakes her wild strawberry pie and you can smell it for miles."

"This is better," Mikael whispered as a surge of energy raced through him, settling in his now aching groin. *Fuck, what the hell is this?* His pants were achingly tight, and his dick was about to shred the seams of his pants.

"What's wrong with you? Your teeth are lowering, and your eyes have gone feral," Karl whispered. "It isn't like you to lose control. What gives?"

"Fuck if I know," Mikael whispered and inhaled through his mouth, trying anything to calm himself. His wolf wanted out badly, and Mikael was seconds from turning his head to the ceiling and howling to the heavens, which was not good and could not happen. He turned away and saw a sign for the restrooms. He didn't say a word, just headed for them with Karl right behind him.

"What's wrong with you? This meeting is important, and you lose control now?"

"I just need a few seconds, that's all. Stand outside and make sure everyone stays away. I'll be right out." Mikael pushed the door open, and the scents of the bathroom, while clean, overwhelmed his nose and blocked out whatever had set him off. Strong scents were always hard on wolves, so none of them ever wore anything but what God gave them. All Mikael could come up with was that the scents the humans were wearing must have short-circuited his nose for a few minutes. He went to the sink and ran the cold water, splashing some on his face. He breathed normally, and his wolf, while active, seemed to settle back down.

"I'm in control, and unless we want a disaster on our hands, I have to stay in control," Mikael repeated to himself and his wolf for a few seconds. Both halves of himself had to be in agreement at a critical time like this. Once he was feeling better, Mikael left the restroom and stepped out into the lobby.

He scented cologne and deodorant from the humans and wrinkled his nose slightly before dismissing it. Then the sweet, earthy scent hit him again: human mixed with wolf, and earth, heaven, water, and fire all at once.

"Are you okay?"

"Yes. Let's go. We have business to conduct." He was going to do this come hell or high water. He led Karl to the restaurant and stepped inside. Instantly his gaze fell on two large men who met their gazes intently. The one had the warm, rich skin of a Native American. He slowly got to his feet and stood to the side of the other man. "Mother, help me," Mikael whispered. The other man was broader, and as he got to his feet, it was obvious he matched Mikael in height, size, and strength. He was also stunning, with blond hair that reached his shoulders in light waves, but as soon as Mikael got a few steps closer, it was the eyes—as blue and deep as the clear summer sky—that damn near touched his soul. Those eyes were familiar; he'd seen them one time before. The Mother herself had shown them to him long ago. This was his mate, and he was truly royally screwed. Two alphas together would be like dropping gasoline onto a forest fire. They did not mix, and they would fight each other tooth and nail. This was totally fucked-up. He inhaled, and his wolf bounded upward desperately trying to come forward. It took all the willpower he could muster to stop him and to keep his expression neutral as he stepped toward the two men.

"I'm Denton Arguson, alpha of the Evergreen pack." The blond man's eyes never left Mikael, and for the love of all that was holy, Mikael could have happily stayed beneath that gaze for the rest of his life.

"Mikael Volokov, alpha of the Yellowstone pack." He extended his hand, and the other man took it. As soon as their skin touched, Mikael felt as though every cell in his body had just sprung to life. Every scent and sound around him heightened for a second before completely fading away to nothing but a steady rhythmic drumming. He wondered for a second if it was his own heart, but no, it was both their hearts in exact rhythm, sounding as loud in his ears as a gale through the trees. He had to keep it together, because if he didn't, he was going to leap at this other man and either rip his clothes off and fuck him through the floor or tear him to pieces if he resisted what Mikael's wolf desperately wanted.

"I understand we have some business to discuss." Denton's dark, forest-deep voice pulled Mikael out of his momentary reverie, and he stared into the other man's eyes. He seemed calm and cool, so maybe he wasn't feeling what Mikael was. Hell, that was a relief. If Denton was his mate, he'd be reacting the same way Mikael was.

"Yes." Mikael released Denton's hand and stepped back.

"I think we can dispense with our betas," Denton said, and Mikael did his best not to breathe, but damn, Denton's scent wrapped around him, and with each fucking breath, he wanted to jump the man.

Mikael kept his expression as dispassionate as he could and nodded before turning to Karl and glancing toward the door. Karl obviously wasn't keen to go, and neither was Denton's beta, but the two men slowly turned and walked off, glaring at each other. It was almost funny to watch.

"Thank you for coming," Mikael said as they sat down slowly, eyeing each other.

"What is it you wanted?" Denton asked, lifting his water glass but not drinking. His gaze bored into Mikael, who stared right back. No fucking way was anyone getting the better of him, regardless of whether his brain felt short-circuited.

"You heard about Anton and Gregor?" Mikael asked.

Denton nodded. "But what does that have to do with me? I wasn't the one who put myself and my pack in his sights by offering Gregor's family a place in my pack." For the first time, Denton's gaze faltered slightly.

"I see you're well-informed. Good. But did you know Anton insisted that Gregor's mate be present at the challenge, along with his pups?" That got mild surprise from Denton. Maybe he wasn't a completely cold bastard. "Anton's pups were there too, in order to see their daddy's victory."

Denton lifted the glass the rest of the way to his mouth and drank. Mikael tried like hell not to watch him swallow or stare at the movement of his throat. "That's...."

"Yeah," Mikael agreed forcefully and leaned across the table, immediately regretting it because Denton's scent intensified, and it took all his will not to pull the other man over the table and kiss the hell out of him. If that happened, Mikael's wolf wouldn't be able to stop, and there would be one hell of an interpack incident. "I bet your sources didn't tell you that he tried to lay claim to Gregor's mate and pups."

Denton set down his glass with what Mikael saw as exaggerated slowness. "Okay. You have my attention. I've heard Anton was brutal, but there are limits."

"I stepped in to stop it. Would you?" Mikael knew he was challenging Denton's integrity, but he needed to know what kind of man he was.

"Don't you go there...."

"Then I take it you'd have done the same thing."

"Damn right I would," Denton said too loudly, and people from the other tables stared over at them. Denton swore under his breath. "Okay, you made your fucking point. But I'll ask you again: What do you want with me?"

To fuck you across the table. That's what Mikael's wolf wanted, and the scent of his own arousal filled the air around him. Luckily he could scent Denton's arousal, as well, and he smiled. The other alpha might not have been willing to acknowledge the attraction, but it sure as hell was there—Mikael could tell from the musky scent he was giving off by the bucketload. "We need to come to some kind of agreement. My pack is my family, and I will not have them under the thumb of a psychopath like Anton. I'm willing to bet you feel the same way."

"What kind of agreement?" The growl was back, and Mikael wondered if Denton would make that sound when Mikael fucked him. Mother help him, he had to get those thoughts out of his head. This was a negotiation of a treaty of sorts, and he needed to keep his head in the game. Hell, what he needed was... he needed this other alpha not to be his mate, that's what the fuck he needed. His wolf leaped against Mikael's control, desperate to get loose.

"A nonaggression pact, or an agreement to come to the other's aid should Anton start sniffing around," Mikael proposed and then went quiet when a server approached the table.

"Can I get you gentlemen anything?" The kid looked half-scared, and Mikael realized he and Denton had probably been glaring at each other so intently the kid must have wondered if they were going to attack each other. Mikael relaxed his posture slightly.

"I'll have a steak, rare," Mikael said and looked at Denton, who ordered the same. The kid then hurried away, smelling of relief and a touch of fear, probably because he was going to have to come back. He reminded Mikael of one of the rabbits on the pack land.

"I'm not the one with his head in Anton's sights, so what do I get out of this?" Denton asked.

31

"We're both at risk. Anton isn't going to stop until every pack in the area is under his control, and then who knows...."

Denton scoffed. "You're not serious."

"I'm dead serious. I'm willing to bet he has his people primed to take over any pack and move in people loyal to him and only him." Mikael kept his expression neutral. "Do you want your family at that man's mercy? I sure as hell don't. All I'm saying is that we're stronger together than we are apart."

"So you are proposing a merger, just because...." Denton stopped, and for the first time Mikael smelled something other than supreme confidence coming off the other alpha.

"Because what?" Mikael asked with his best disarming smile. His wolf seemed to settle as he too realized what the touch of doubt meant. Denton felt this attraction between them as well.

"You know damned well what, and nothing is going to come of it." Denton shook his head. "This is so fucked-up," he whispered. "There has to be some mistake."

Mikael didn't look at Karl; he didn't need to, to know that his brother was already sensing that something had shifted between them. To their credit, neither of the betas moved closer to the table, but Mikael knew they could hear every word being said. Then Denton lifted his gaze again, and Kaiawa moved toward the table. Karl did the same, until both betas stood behind their alphas.

"Karl, I need you to take a walk for a while," Mikael said.

Denton nodded and turned to Kaiawa. "Why don't you show your counterpart here some of the sights?"

Both men looked skeptical. "We need to speak privately," Denton explained, and both of them nodded and turned to leave the table, but not until they each turned back to double-check.

Mikael and Denton waited until the betas had left the restaurant. Mikael said nothing until he saw the two men walking away from the building, as stiff and alert as if there had been some threat of attack.

"You have a good beta," Mikael said.

"Kaiawa is my blood brother. We were raised together after he was orphaned as a child. Your beta seems very protective, as a good beta should be."

"Karl is my younger brother, and I think he makes sure nothing happens to me because he doesn't want to be in charge of the pack." With them gone, Mikael felt a little openness would be good. "So what should we do?"

"About what?" Denton asked with a touch of that growl.

"We're mates." Mikael couldn't believe he'd actually said it first, but the drive was too strong to ignore. His body gravitated toward Denton. Even leaning over the table brought satisfaction, and leaning back put more distance between them and felt like a chore.

"It doesn't matter," Denton said flatly. "You have duties and a pack to run, and I have the same. Just like I have no intention of allowing Anton to take over as head of my family, I won't let you or anyone else do it either." Denton's gaze was hard as granite.

"If you think I'm letting you assume control of my family and pack, you're out of your mind," Mikael growled with equal fervor.

"Then it's decided," Denton said. "I'll agree to your proposal and will back you if Anton becomes aggressive, and you'll do the same. That is as far as I will go. As for the rest, I think we should go our separate ways and forget about anything else. I refuse to allow my life to be run by some unknown force playing with my emotions." Denton's voice was no more than a whisper, but the message resounded in Mikael's head as though it had been rung from the largest bell in the land. He had found his mate, but he was being rejected. Not that he was particularly pleased with the situation either, but fuck, it still stung. He did his best to keep his expression from betraying it, though. He'd be damned if he'd let the other wolf know how he felt.

The server brought their plates and, with a slightly shaking hand, set them down. He filled the water glasses and then hightailed it away without another word.

"Fine. If that's what you want." Mikael cut a bite of his steak, slowly brought it to his mouth, and closed his lips around the morsel. He closed his eyes, letting the richness of the meat fill his mouth. He slowly removed the fork and then began chewing. He could scent a spike in Denton's arousal, and it took all his willpower to keep from smiling.

"Bastard," Denton swore under his breath, but Mikael heard it clear as day. "Doesn't mean anything."

Mikael wasn't so sure about that, but he kept quiet about it. As he ate he thought about his dream and the message he'd received from the Mother. She had warned him in her own way that Mikael needed to be prepared to fight for his mate and what he wanted. Her message had been so simple, or at least it had seemed that way on the surface, but Mikael was learning that messages from the gods could have more than one meaning. He'd thought from her message that he'd be the resistant party, but he had been raised that true matehood was sacred and something to be celebrated. Many believed that there was a mate for everyone, but Mikael wasn't convinced of it. His mother and father had mated, but whether they were fated mates was something they had never shared with him. Not that it mattered—they were happy their entire lives together and had raised Mikael and his siblings in an atmosphere of unconditional support and love. That was all that mattered in the end.

Maybe fated mates are for when fate must step in.

The idea popped into his head, and Mikael stared across the table at Denton, but he went on eating and looking at him around each bite.

"Do you really believe in mates being chosen by the gods?" Denton asked. "It's not something I've ever seen in my life. People meet and fall in love, have children, and spend their lives together. Some matches are good and some… not so." The way Denton paused told Mikael there was a story there. "I mean, you're a hot guy, and since I like guys, it's only natural that I'd be attracted to you. But that doesn't mean we're meant to spend the rest of our lives together. It just means that it's been a while."

Mikael raised his eyebrows. "Fine. Whatever you want to believe." Damn, this was going to get painful for both of them. "But facts tend to bear themselves out."

"And sentimental bullshit tends to sit around and stink, doing no one any good."

"Colorful metaphor," Mikael commented as he continued eating. He needed to keep the smile that kept threatening to come to the surface at bay. He was beginning to like Denton, which was a good thing if they were mates but would make things worse if Denton was intent on fighting this.

"I don't believe in blowing smoke."

Mikael nodded. He didn't either, but arguing with Denton wouldn't get him anywhere. "How is your steak?" Mikael took another small bite, noticing that Denton paused to watch.

"Not as good as yours, apparently." Denton leaned over the table. "Are you going to eat that or fuck it?"

"I'd rather fuck you."

"Like that's ever going to happen." Denton's words said one thing, but the way his eyes widened and his breath hitched ever so slightly told Mikael quite a different story. Yes, Denton was an alpha, a true alpha, and he liked to be in control—it was their nature. But as Mikael watched, blocking out the steady stream of refusals and head shaking, he saw how Denton's skin reddened and the way he swallowed. But it was the spike in musky arousal that clinched the deal.

"Like I said, you can believe whatever you want." Mikael had had to learn to be patient. It was most definitely not in his nature… or his wolf's. It was a skill he'd had to master, and he could see that making Denton accept the truth would take patience. Maybe a whole truckload of it.

Denton put down his fork. "Fine. Let's say I believe this whole fated-mates thing. What the hell am I supposed to do? Walk away from my pack and leave them leaderless? Fight you for dominance and the loser becomes the winner's bitch? Turn my family over to a guy I barely know?" Denton raised his eyebrows. "Are you willing to do that?" He stared at Mikael, who stared right back. "I didn't think so." Denton sat back and laughed a full and hearty laugh. It would have been sexy if there had been any mirth in it. "Maybe we could merge the packs, and you and I could be some sort of power couple."

Mikael leaned forward. "I don't have the answers and neither do you. Is that what has you scared half to death? That you don't know all the answers? I'm willing to admit it and be a man about it."

Denton swallowed and stood, drawing himself up to his full height. Mikael did the same and was satisfied that he was just that much larger than Denton. But damn, Denton was hot with his eyes blazing and his breath coming just inches from Mikael's skin, bathing him in sweet-scented warmth. Let him get angry—at least he was talking, and the anger told Mikael that he was getting under Denton's skin. That could only happen if Denton believed in some way that Mikael might be right.

"We should sit down before we scare half the people in the restaurant," Mikael suggested levelly. Denton didn't move at first, and Mikael thought he might storm away. Instead, he slowly sat, and Mikael followed, neither of them taking their gaze off the other.

"Never question my manhood," Denton said just loud enough for Mikael's wolf hearing to pick it up. "I never questioned yours, and you don't know me or have any idea what I want, what I'm afraid of, or just how close you came to being ripped to shreds."

Mikael watched as Denton's eyes deepened and then shifted to yellow before changing back to their usual deep blue. "So you want to play games." Mikael shifted his eyes, and then a finger changed to a claw before shifting back. "That's easy enough to do, but…." *How about this?* Mikael planted his words in Denton's mind and waited for a response. What he got wasn't what he expected. Denton gasped softly.

"How did you do that?" Denton whispered. "I've heard stories that wolves in the favor with the gods could do that, but I always thought it was a myth."

"I don't know about the favor with the gods, but I've been able to communicate with others like that since I was about eight." Right after the Mother first came to him, so maybe being blessed was sort of true. "It used to drive my parents crazy because I could ask for what I wanted without saying anything." Mikael smiled slightly. "Think about it. I was eight and I could ask for a glass of water without making a sound, and I could do it from a distance… and not at the most appropriate times." Mikael grinned, and Denton actually smiled after a few seconds.

"I can imagine," Denton said, and damn if that smile of his wasn't bright enough to light the entire room. The smile remained on Denton's lips even when he chuckled, a deep, rich sound that filled the room, then faded away like the summer breeze. Then his eyes hardened and his lips drew from a smile to a line. "That doesn't change anything. You can be as charming and… it doesn't matter. I'm going back to my pack and you're going to do the same. Yes, I'll back you if Anton comes sniffing around, and I'll make sure it gets back to him that we have an alliance. That should help protect both of us. But that's all."

"Like I said earlier, if that's what you want, I can't stop you. You can believe what you want, but we are mates, and you won't be able to deny that forever."

"Somehow I think I can resist your charms."

Mikael smiled. "So I have charms." He raised one eyebrow and watched as the radiantly handsome man across from him colored slightly.

Denton cleared his throat. "I have responsibilities, and I'm not going to sit here and discuss something that can't happen." Denton slowly got to his feet and dropped a business card on the table. Mikael pulled out his wallet and found one of his cards. He handed it to Denton. When their fingers touched, Mikael had to keep from inhaling at the tingle that passed up his arm. Denton pulled his hand away, taking the card. He motioned for the server and handed the rabbit man some money before thanking him. Mikael stayed in his seat. Part of him wanted to turn to watch Denton go, knowing he might not see him again for a while. But he kept his gaze trained the other way even as dark clouds slowly began to gather inside.

His wolf pranced nervously inside, urging him to get up and go get the one he wanted, the one meant for him. Wolves mated for life, and now that Mikael's wolf had found the one for him, he didn't want to sit still and watch him walk away. "We need to be patient," Mikael told his wolf.

"So is it all set?" Karl asked as he sat down in one of the empty chairs. "I saw them leave."

"Yes. We have an alliance of sorts. He said he'd back me if I'd back him, and he'll make sure Anton knows of the alliance. That alone should be enough to deter him, at least for a while." Mikael finished his water and looked down at what remained of his lunch. He wasn't hungry anymore, and when he pushed away his plate, Karl pulled it away and quickly began cutting pieces off the huge steak.

"What? I'm hungry, and I wasn't invited to your little lunch thing." He ate a huge bite and chewed loudly. "It'd be a shame to let an incredible piece of meat like this go to waste." He ate quickly, and Mikael absently signaled for the waiter to make sure the check was covered. Once Karl was done chowing down, they left the restaurant and walked out to the car.

"So what do we do now?" Karl asked.

"Go back to our lives and keep an eye out around us."

"Is that all?"

Mikael nodded and handed him the keys.

"You want me to drive?"

"Yeah. I know I'm taking my life in my hands, but I have some things I need to do while we're in the car, so you can drive. Just watch out for tourists and don't try to outrun anyone." His brother could be a complete menace behind the wheel. As soon as they got underway, Mikael began to have second thoughts. "You realize you don't get the entire road. You have to share with the cars coming the other way."

His brother scoffed and continued driving like some kind of maniac, while Mikael pondered on the alpha who wasn't willing to believe they were the part of each other's lives that had been missing. Finally, they made it back to pack land, but the tightness in Mikael's throat and the ache from deep in his belly hadn't gone away. In fact, they'd only gotten worse. "Stop," Mikael told Karl. He needed to get out of this car right the hell now.

"My driving isn't that bad," Karl said as he slowed. By the time the car came to a stop, Mikael had his door open. He got out, tore off his clothes, and placed them on the seat.

"Go on home. I'll meet you there." Before Karl could say anything, Mikael shifted and took off into the trees. He heard the door slam closed, and eventually the car pulled away as Mikael continued putting distance between himself and the road.

He knew these woods—every tree and bush was like a signpost telling him where he was. Not that Mikael cared at the moment. Instinct guided him to where he needed to be. After a while, he stopped and climbed a rock outcrop on the edge of a rise that allowed him to look out over a huge valley. Mountains that formed the edge of the Yellowstone plateau surrounded him. He'd been doing his best to let his wolf have free rein. It took Mikael a few seconds to realize his wolf was taking him back the way he'd come, back toward his mate.

Mikael knew he couldn't do that and turned around, facing home. His heart ached, and all four legs pulled him back the other way. For the longest time, Mikael stood where he was, not moving, and eventually he threw his head in the air, howling his heartache and longing up into the sky. His call was answered from far away, and Mikael recognized it as the cry of another in anguish. It came from the direction of home, and while he wasn't positive, his heart told him it was Anna answering his call and adding her song to his own. Mikael lowered his head and turned toward home, descending from the outcrop.

His mate might have rejected him at their first meeting, but he was still out there. Mikael needed to be patient because Denton had to be feeling the same hollowness he was. They just had to figure things out. His loss was, so far, only in his head and to his pride, whereas Anna's was deep in her soul. That put things in perspective. When did he get to be such a drama queen anyway? His mate was alive, and Mikael now knew who he was and where to find him. He'd always imagined that meeting his mate would be this whole thunderbolt type thing where they'd recognize each other, go somewhere, and fuck each other's brains out, and then he'd bring the man the Mother had shown to him home to his pack. He should have known that life wouldn't be that easy; it never was.

Mikael picked up speed, easily covering the distance toward home. His wolf wasn't particularly happy about where they were going at first, but he got happier as the scents of the people and other wolves who formed his family got stronger. He needed *home* right now. He knew his mate now, and he would figure out a way to make him his. He just needed to be patient.

CHAPTER 4

"YOU WHAT?" Catherine asked several days later, her eyes blazing from the other side of his table. She got up so fast she nearly knocked over her mug. "You wait two days to tell me that you met your mate. Who is he? A member of the Evergreen pack? Is that the problem?"

"Sit down," Mikael said. "That whole standing-up thing you do might work on the pups, but it isn't going to work on me." He didn't raise his voice; he didn't need to. Catherine was a great enforcer, but she was also loyal and fully understood her place in the pack. However, she was also his sister, and that sometimes overrode her other roles. "Yes, my mate's a member of the Evergreen pack and...." He looked around and listened intently to make sure they were truly alone.

Catherine sat down. "What's the problem? If he's your mate, he'll leave his pack and come with you. Your status would overrule anything else." She lifted her mug and then slowly set it down again. "Your mate isn't a woman, is it?"

"No. He's definitely all male." He closed his eyes and did his best not to call up an image of Denton or replay the way his scent played with his brain.

"Then what's the problem?" She narrowed her eyes. "Did you do something stupid?"

"That's not the way to speak to your alpha, and no, I didn't do anything stupid." He added some growl to his voice to let her know she was getting close to a line she shouldn't cross. "This wasn't as simple as I thought it was going to be."

"What about relationships is ever simple? But if he's your mate, then he has what you need and you have what he needs. That's how it works. You were brought together by the gods and blessed. You can't turn your back on that."

"Like I said, it isn't that simple." He listened intently, then said, "My mate is Denton Arguson. He's the alpha of the Evergreen pack."

40

Catherine stared at him, and after a few seconds, her mouth dropped open and she openly gaped. When the shock wore off, she grinned. "Okay, you can stop pulling my leg."

"I'm not."

She swallowed. "Two alphas as mates? That's unheard of, as far as I know." She shook her head in disbelief. "Are you sure he's your mate? I mean, it's been a while since you were with anyone. Maybe you found him attractive and—"

"Catherine, I knew my mate the minute I saw him. There isn't any confusion about this. He knows I'm his mate as well, but he has a pack that he's responsible for, just the way I do. Our being mates doesn't change any of that… for either of us. Do you want me to leave here and join him and his pack?"

Catherine gasped. "Of course not. You're our alpha. If anything, he needs to come here."

"And I'm sure his pack members feel the exact same way," Mikael said. "And that's the problem."

"What are you going to do?" Catherine asked.

"I'm not sure yet. I keep wondering how I can miss someone I only met once, but I do. There was such energy in him, and I wanted to touch him. And the way he smelled—" Mikael rolled his eyes. He actually sighed and rolled his fucking eyes like a teenager. "I see him when I close my eyes, and every night when I'm asleep I—" Mikael stopped right there. He couldn't tell his sister about the dreams he'd been having about Denton.

"I think I get the point, and I've never seen you blush like that. Those must be some dreams." Catherine sipped from her mug.

"I want to get to know him."

"Okay. Do you want my advice?"

Mikael shrugged. "Sure." After all, it wasn't as though he was full of ideas.

"First thing, don't go all alpha on him. That might work with some people, but it won't work with him any more than it would work with you. If the two of you are alphas, then you need to treat him as an equal. I would suggest you romance him a little. Make the guy like you, and then once you… do whatever mates do for a while, you can talk and figure out how you can make things work."

Mikael lowered his gaze. "Go all alpha?"

"Yeah. You need to show that you see him as your equal, because he is. In the pack, we all have our roles, and you're the leader. We all follow you because we trust you and know you have our best interests at heart. He doesn't know that, so coming off all strong and in charge is probably not the way to go." Catherine chuckled. "It seems fitting somehow. Even when we were kids, you were always the leader. Now you might need to learn how to follow sometimes."

"So your advice is to romance him and not go all alpha. How do I do any of that when I only met him once and it doesn't seem likely I'll see him in the future?"

"You could call him, but knowing you, that isn't likely."

"Damn right it's not."

"So what's the plan? Wait until he can't do without you because he smelled you once? I don't think so. This is another guy who's as strong and confident as you are, so take the first step. What do you have to lose?" Catherine shrugged. "If you look around, most couples in the pack complement each other. It's true with Stan and me. He's perfect for me. I can be tough as nails, and I tend to act first and think second. Stan is thoughtful and kind. He always takes the time with me and our kids to make sure everything is okay. He tends to be the nurturer because that isn't my first instinct. Yeah, I'm the stronger of the two of us, but he's—"

"Stan is strong, just in a very different way from you. He'd rather you be in charge, but that doesn't mean he doesn't have his own strength. He'd die for you and the kids, I know that."

"Exactly. I know that too. But that part of our relationship was pretty obvious from the beginning." Catherine looked down at her mug. "But what isn't so obvious is that Stan understands me. He knows when I need him to be strong. You know, it's hard having everyone expect you to be in charge and strong all the damn time. Sometimes I want someone to take care of me, and Stan understands that. He does that when I need it."

"Okay." That made a lot of sense to him.

"What I'm saying is that everyone needs something in their relationship, and if you and Denton are fated mates, then you have something he needs in his life and he has something you need in yours.

The trick, and part of the fun, will be when you try to figure out what that is." Catherine stood up and turned to leave. "So you need to decide what you want to do. But don't take too long. If he's your mate, then he has something that you need as well. You may not even know what the piece is right now, but he still has it." She patted his hand and turned to leave the room.

"You know, you're a lot like Mom."

Catherine growled slightly.

"I know. But it's true."

"What's true?" his mother asked as she came in. Mikael hadn't even heard her come in the house. She'd always been slippery. Maybe that was how she'd always known when they were up to no good.

"That Catherine is a lot like you," Mikael answered her.

"That's nice of you to say." His mother beamed at him. "Now I hope you two were done with your talk because I need to make lunch, so unless you're planning to lend a hand...." Mikael left the kitchen double-quick. He hated cooking and so did Catherine. She was lucky, because Stan was almost as good a cook as their mother. Catherine left after a quick good-bye, and Mikael went down the hall to his office and closed the door.

He needed time to think and ended up pacing from one end of the room to the other. His wolf wanted action of some kind, and while his human half urged patience, his wolf was having none of it. Now that he'd met his mate, his wolf had one goal only—to make him his. The need was primal, surging from deep down inside him, and Mikael knew he couldn't put this off any longer. He thrust his hands into his pocket and yanked out his phone, then dialed the number from the ragged-edged card that sat on the desk. "Denton, it's Mikael," he said as soon as the call was answered.

"Hello," Denton answered a little breathlessly. "I was just about to call you."

"Has something happened?" His mind immediately went to Denton being in trouble, and both he and his wolf were on alert.

"No. It's been very quiet. I've...." Denton paused, and Mikael heard soft footsteps come through the line and then the closing of a door. "I keep thinking about you."

"Yeah?" Mikael smiled. "I keep thinking about you too." He managed to stop himself before he entered the realm of giddy teenager, even if he was about ready to do a little happy dance.

"You might be right."

"About what?" Mikael asked.

"You're going to make me say it, aren't you?" Denton growled softly, the tone rumbling through Mikael's ear and through the rest of him until he had to sit at his chair and was about to open his jeans at the waist.

"Yeah. Of course."

"Fine…. There might be something to this fated-mate business after all. Not that I'm saying I believe it fully, but I can't get you out of my mind, and every night I have these dreams about you." He became even breathier, and Mikael nodded softly to himself. He knew exactly what Denton was going through. "Every night and not just once."

"Yeah. I keep seeing your blue eyes wherever I go. I was out for a run yesterday, and when I looked up at the sky, I saw the color of your eyes just about at the horizon, a deep, perfect blue." Fuck, he'd strayed into giddy-teenage territory. Just talking to the man was enough to make his spine zing and his cock burst at the fly of his jeans. Every inch of him ached to get Denton into his arms and in his bed. "Damn, I want you so bad."

"Hold on there…," Denton said, his voice filled with caution. Mikael swore to himself, knowing he'd gone too far too fast.

"All I mean is that I want to see you and get to know you." He backpedaled as fast as he could, though he hadn't meant that. His wolf wanted Denton naked and needy in his bed, and he wanted it right the hell now. "I was calling to see if you'd like to meet me for lunch. I know a great spot."

"Lunch… just lunch," Denton said in his alpha voice.

Mikael had always bristled whenever his father used that tone with him. Mikael knew he was an alpha even when he was young, and it had chafed when his dad used that deep, unbending tone on him. But coming from Denton… he found it sexy and wondered how much fun it would be to fight the other man for dominance, with the prize being some time in bed, alone together. Now that was a challenge he was more than ready for.

"Fine. Tell me your e-mail address, and I'll send you the directions to the place. It's near where our two territories meet, so you may be familiar with it. It's in my pack territory, officially, but I'll host you this time." He purposely didn't mention that Denton could return the favor next time, even if he thought it.

Denton was quiet for a few seconds. "All right. But you'll come alone?"

"Of course." The last thing he wanted was for his brother to be around when he was getting to know his mate.

"Can I trust you?" Denton asked.

Mikael narrowed his eyebrows. "Of course you can trust me." Denton was his mate, and Mikael would never do anything to intentionally hurt him. That was part of being mates. What on earth had Denton been through? Mikael thought everyone understood mates and how sacred matehood was, especially within the pair. He'd have to make sure he set Denton a good example.

Mikael opened his laptop, and when Denton dictated the e-mail address, he entered it and typed the directions, making sure to include scent cues. "I just sent it." He waited for Denton to read it and heard him chuckle.

"I love the scent markers," Denton said.

"I'm sure you'll be able to follow my scent once you get close. So I'll see you there tomorrow at noon? And don't worry about anything. I'll have everything we'll need."

"All right," Denton said warily. "I'll meet you there at noon." He hung up, and Mikael placed his phone on the desk. He wasn't sure if he should be happy or not. The wariness in Denton's voice was probably justifiable, but he heard something else there. His wolf heard it too and wanted to yowl it to his brothers. Mikael didn't want to jump to conclusions, but he got the feeling that someone had hurt his mate pretty badly. Well, Denton had agreed to see him tomorrow, which meant Mikael needed to get busy and make some headway on the current project he was working on. He stood and left his office before heading up the stairs to the topmost portion of the house, where everyone knew not to disturb him unless it was an emergency.

When the door closed behind him, he stared at his current work in progress and then, after a few seconds, got down to business.

THE FOLLOWING morning, Mikael put aside his distaste for cooking and put together a picnic lunch. It wasn't fancy, but he'd made it with his own hands, and he knew Denton would know that because the food would only carry his scent. He'd tasted everything, and while it wasn't as good as his mother's ham salad, it was still pretty tasty.

"Where are you going?" Karl asked as he came inside the house.

"Don't you knock?" Mikael retorted, and Karl scoffed as he eyed the basket.

"Since when…." This house had been their home since they were pups, and neither Karl nor Catherine thought to knock, any more than he had when he was a pup. "What's up?"

"I'm going out for a while," Mikael told him. "I have things to do."

"I should come with you," Karl said.

"No. You need to stay here and make sure everyone is safe and that Anna and the pups are settling in. They've been having a hard time." He needed something to keep Karl busy. "While you're at it, take a look at the van and truck and make sure they're in top shape."

"You expecting something?" Karl asked.

"No. Just want to be prepared." Mikael grabbed the basket and walked toward the door. He didn't plan to answer any more questions. He knew Karl had to be bursting with curiosity, but he wasn't ready to tell anyone where he was going or, more importantly, who he was seeing. His conversation with Catherine had been between the two of them, and she knew how to keep her mouth shut. It was the only reason he'd confided in her. "I'll see you when I get back." He turned to meet Karl's gaze, holding it until his brother nodded. Mikael wouldn't put it past Karl to follow him, and that notion needed to end right now.

Mikael left and hurried out to the Volvo. He put the basket in the back and started the engine, then pulled out onto the dirt road. He knew the way to the spot where he'd told Denton to meet him by heart. He rolled down the window and let the air blow over him. He could find the place in the dark, blindfolded, just by the scent. Up there the air was cleaner, crisper, and carried the scent of juniper, cedar, and this time of year, rich flowers that bloomed in the clearing. It took him half an hour of driving with what had to be a silly grin on his face. He parked and lifted the basket out, carrying it overland toward the spot. He inhaled deeply, scenting for a sign of Denton, but all he got was the woods and mountain air. A rabbit had been through, as had a family of deer, their scents lingering in the area, but that was all.

This was part of his home, a special place. In his dream, the first one he'd had when the Mother came to him, she'd been here when she'd first shown him his mate, so when Denton agreed to meet, he could think of no other place that would be more perfect. He stepped into the clearing and let the sun shine on his skin. He loved nothing more than being outdoors… except maybe the outdoors spiced with the scent of his mate.

"You came," Mikael said without turning to where he knew Denton was now standing.

"Of course I did," Denton said but didn't move any closer. "You're alone."

"Yes. It's just the two of us. As near as I can tell there isn't anyone else out here but us for miles."

Denton sighed. "That's nice. Sometimes living in a house filled with others who can hear everything that goes on everywhere can be a little unnerving."

Mikael chuckled. "Tell me about it. We never got away with anything because my mom has super wolf hearing and my father had a super wolf sense of smell. We didn't do anything without them knowing."

Denton stepped closer, and Mikael let him look around while he spread the blanket on the soft ground. Then he placed the basket on the blanket and slowly walked over to where Denton stood looking over the valley below.

"It's breathtaking here," Denton said.

"It is," Mikael agreed and came close enough to Denton that he could touch him if he chose, but he kept a slight distance between them. "Over there is your pack land, and do you see the outcrop just across the valley? That's…."

"What?"

"When I was a pup, I was visited or had a vision. The Mother showed me this place and showed me that I'd have a mate. When she did, he appeared on that outcropping. Then she brought him closer, and I saw his blond hair and blue eyes. Your eyes."

47

Denton whirled around. "You're saying that you were shown your mate—me—when you were a kid by some…."

"The Mother. Yes, she showed you to me so I'd know you were out there."

"Who is this Mother person?" Denton asked. "My parents talked sometimes about a sort of 'guardian of nature' type deity, but I thought that was just their way of staying in touch with nature."

"Doesn't your pack worship the Mother? We have for a long time. She protected us here when we couldn't be out and about. Then she showed us the way back so we could live as ourselves once again." Mikael was a little shocked. He had honestly thought that all of their kind worshipped the Mother.

"There isn't a pack religion, as far as I know. My father was alpha before me, and he helped guide us out of hiding. I remember when I first heard the cry of a full-blooded wolf. I was just a pup, but my father told us that cry trumpeted our freedom."

Mikael decided he didn't want to have a discussion of religion, at least not at the moment. "Are you hungry?" he asked in his huskiest voice. He certainly was, but he'd make do with food. He stepped away and sat down, then laid out the food. "I brought some water and a bottle of wine, in case you like it." Wine wasn't something his wolf cared for. Alcohol never affected him, and the taste of wine wasn't something he enjoyed. Other pack members imbibed, but not him.

"Water sounds great," Denton said, and he smiled as he took a seat across from him. Denton's smile was nearly as luminous as his eyes. Mikael handed him a plate and finished setting out the food, barely taking his gaze from Denton. He was gorgeous, and now that Mikael could look at him without interruption, he realized just how attractive Denton was. In the sun, Denton's hair shone like gold, and he wondered if that would be reflected in the color of his coat. A golden wolf—now that would be something.

Mikael passed Denton a cold bottle of water and pointed out the various containers one by one.

"Did you make this?" Denton asked, and Mikael nodded. "All of it?"

"Yes. I used some of my mother's recipes, but yes, I made it all." He was pretty proud that he'd managed to get something edible out of the process. "Cooking isn't something I do much, but I wanted to make this for you." He concentrated on Denton's lips, full and red, as Denton took the first bite. He was tempted to lean forward and taste those lips. Mikael was willing to bet they were as sweet and rich as a summer berry.

"In my pack, cooking for someone... like this..." He paused. "...is special."

"Mine too," Mikael whispered. "As I said before, you're my mate. I feel it deep inside, and I think you feel it too. Haven't you been edgy for the past few days? Unusually quick to chastise or rebuke? I know I have, though as soon as you stepped into the clearing that feeling went away. It was like the clouds parted and the sun came out after days of rain. Just because you came closer to me."

Denton swallowed. "I'm not saying I'm not happier and more contented now that I'm with you. But that doesn't mean there's some deity pulling the strings and compelling us to be together. You're a nice guy, I can feel that, and yes, I find you attractive. But who wouldn't?" Denton took a bite and hummed just above his breath. "This is good."

"Thanks." Mikael set his plate down without taking a bite. "Set your plate aside. I want you to take my hands." He held his hands out while Denton did as he asked. When Denton took his hands, energy passed between them. "Do you feel that?"

"Yeah," Denton answered and then swallowed. "It's chemistry, pure and simple."

"It's more than that. But I don't want you to think about me. At least not right now." Mikael released Denton's hands. "Close your eyes and let your hands rest at your sides. Feel the wind and listen as it rustles the trees." He did the same and grew quiet. As usual he felt a slight upwelling from the ground below him. "When I'm alone and quiet, I can feel her."

"Who?" Denton breathed.

"The Mother. She's here, everywhere, like a heartbeat coming from within the earth. An energy flows from her through the trees and all living things. For me it's always been there, and I can feel it all the time. All I have to do is be in touch with the ground and I know she's there."

Denton said nothing. He obviously didn't agree, but he didn't tell Mikael that he was full of crap either.

"Don't open your eyes, but lift your head to the trees and see if you can feel what I'm saying, feel her." Mikael grew quiet once again, and after a while Denton began to sway slightly back and forth like a leaf in the lightest summer breeze. "You feel it, don't you?"

"I feel something, maybe. It's hard to tell just what it is." Denton opened his eyes. "How do you know it's her?"

"Because this is one of her special spots. She was in this spot when she first showed me my mate... well, you. And ever since, this spot has been special for me. It's like I'm closer to her when I'm here. I like to think that's why you can feel her, because she's allowing you to." Mikael shifted closer. "I was taught that everything has to have balance. Night and day, summer and winter, a time to grow and work and a time to rest to prepare for what's ahead. There's a time for pups to be born, and when we get older, we pass on to make room for the young. It's all her plan and her purpose."

"Why would she come to you to tell you about your mate? If she has all this to do, then why... well, you?"

"I don't know. I never considered myself particularly special. But she has some sort of plan for me, and I think for you too. I know it's hard to believe, so all I'm asking is that you don't dismiss it."

"I can try, but I have responsibilities and so do you. We're both pack leaders, and what am I supposed to do? Leave my pack and come to yours? Will you leave your family and come to my pack?" Denton didn't seem to want an answer, because they both knew what it would be. "You can't leave your family any more than I could leave mine. There aren't any easy answers to this one."

"I'm not saying there are. If there were, the Mother wouldn't need to get involved," Mikael explained. But it was expecting a lot of Denton for him to take everything he'd said at face value.

"If you say so. All I know is that I have responsibilities and a role in the pack that I can't walk away from." He swallowed hard.

"Let's not talk about all that right now." Those answers weren't going to come right away. "How about we just spend some time together?" Mikael handed Denton his plate and then picked up his own. Some of the tension around Denton's eyes lessened, and he smiled slightly.

"That's a good idea." He took another bite of the salad and made a yummy sound that had Mikael's wolf thumping his tail in exuberance.

"What do you do besides lead your pack?" Mikael asked as he absently took a bite from his plate. He was quickly becoming wrapped up in Denton. Everything about him pulled Mikael's focus.

"I'm a forest ranger for the National Park Service. My territory is my pack land and the surrounding area. It's my job to make sure the forests are healthy as well as to be on the lookout for forest fires. My ranger station is the one right down there. It happens to be on the border of our pack lands. The funny thing is that I've had the job for four years, but I've never actually been on your territory before. I didn't want to trespass, but I've kept an eye on it from the lookout station on the top of that rise over there. The one just above the outcropping you pointed out." Denton smirked. "Okay, there's no need to be cocky."

"What?" Mikael tried to wipe the expression from his face, but it was too late. "Okay. I knew there was a reason the Mother showed me that spot."

"Just don't get too full of yourself, oh chosen one." Denton's smirk shifted to a full-on grin. "If your head gets any bigger, you're going to float away."

"I'm not that bad...." Mikael paused for a second. "Well, maybe I am."

"I thought so." Denton returned to his lunch, but Mikael saw him glance his way every few seconds. "Can I ask how you got to be alpha of your pack?"

"My father passed away a few years ago, and I was elected to the position. Not that there was much of an election. I knew I was an alpha from the time I was a child. My brothers and sister knew their roles in the pack at a young age too. You met Karl—he's my beta—and Catherine is my enforcer. I have a brother, Chris, who's the black sheep, or in our case, the rogue wolf of the family. Right now he's away at college, but he isn't sure what he wants to do with his life." Mikael did his best not to roll his eyes. "I want him to return to the pack and act as my second beta, but I don't think that's what he wants."

"You could order him back," Denton said.

"Is that what you'd do?" Mikael retorted. He had the suspicion that the answer to this question would tell him a lot about the kind of person Denton was.

"Not unless he was in danger, or if the pack was in desperate need of his help," Denton answered, and Mikael grinned.

"Exactly. I want him to finish college, though it's been hard on him. He's very intelligent, but he's also the one in the family most in touch with his wolf. So being away means he has to be very careful when he lets his wolf run. I expect him home in a week or so." Mikael shifted the food around until he could sit next to Denton. He heard Denton inhale deeply and smelled an increase in his mate's musk. God, that was heady. Mikael closed his eyes and floated on that scent, letting it work its magic on him.

"Mikael," Denton growled.

Mikael was seconds from pouncing. He opened his eyes. Denton had stiffened and was staring at him, shaking his head.

"What? You know I can smell your excitement, and you can smell mine…." He waited for Denton to deny it.

"I know, and you smell really good. But we're here for lunch and to get to know each other."

Mikael set his plate to the side. "Yes, we are." He moved closer, locking his gaze on Denton's. "And I really want to get to know you… all of you. Everything from your favorite foods to what you look like as a wolf…." Mikael inhaled. "…to what that little divot at the base of your throat tastes like when I lick it."

Denton shuddered. "You move fast."

Mikael paused and moved back a little. He could slow things down. "How did you become alpha of your pack?" He needed something to distract him. He picked up his plate and returned to his lunch, but he barely tasted the food. All his attention was on Denton.

"The former alpha was my uncle. He was a great man and an excellent leader. But he had a blind spot for his son, my cousin Collin, who was strong, big, and a bully. Collin had all the alpha characteristics, and he could do a partial shift that the rest of us couldn't. But no one in the pack wanted to follow him." Denton paused and reached for his bottle of water. "We thought Collin would challenge his father at some point, but he never did. Instead, he waited until my uncle passed away and then declared himself alpha." Denton shook his head.

"How bad was it?" Mikael asked.

Denton sighed. "It wasn't good. The pack was falling apart, and members talked openly about leaving. All that did was make Collin even more forceful. My uncle built this pack, my family, from the remnants of what was left after so long in hiding, and we all hated what Collin was doing."

"So you challenged him," Mikael supplied.

"With the backing of most of the pack, yes. Not that Collin had much support, but there were some who didn't want bloodshed, not that way. Collin was stronger and faster than I was, and I know I never should have won, but I did. I was either lucky or…." Denton looked up from his plate, meeting Mikael's gaze.

"Someone guided you?" Mikael supplied.

"I honestly don't know. But it felt like it. At one point when I was exhausted and Collin was ready to strike, I knew I was done, and I swear I heard this whisper, but no one was there. When Collin pounced I knew exactly where to strike. I finished him off and became pack alpha." Denton turned away. "I'm a good leader, and I manage the pack the way my uncle did. We've grown slowly and my family has expanded. We've had pups, and even my aunt, Collin's mother, has… I don't want to say forgiven me, but has accepted that I did what I had to do. The pack has been through a lot, and everything is good right now. I'll fight like hell to keep it that way, and I won't be the source of any additional strife."

"And you see finding your mate as a source of strife?" Mikael asked.

"If it causes them hurt, then yes. I will do whatever I have to in order to protect and care for them." The fierce protection and loyalty in Denton's voice and eyes warmed Mikael's heart.

"I understand," Mikael whispered and leaned closer. He expected Denton to back away. "I really do, and I admire you for that. You're obviously a good leader and they deserve that." In his opinion every pack did. "I like to think I'm a good leader too. But my pack didn't go through what yours did."

"What are you doing?" Denton whispered.

"How long has it been since you did anything just for you?" It sounded to Mikael as though Denton threw everything he had into running his pack, leaving very little for anything else.

"What does that have to do with anything?"

Mikael growled and leaned in, sliding his hand around the back of Denton's neck. He expected Denton to pull away, but instead Denton stiffened, and Mikael had to move to get close enough to kiss him. He started off gentle, with a light touch, but within seconds Denton pressed forward, deepening the kiss and moaning under his breath. Fuck, that was hot, and Mikael thrust his tongue into Denton's mouth, feasting on him, loving the way Denton fought back. For every action Mikael took, Denton had an equally powerful reaction.

Mikael was on fire, and Denton was the flame. Damn, the man was heat personified. He tasted of woods and earth combined with what had to be years of banked passion and enough primal energy to instantly set Mikael's heart racing. He pulled away only so he could breathe, taking the moment to sink into Denton's blue eyes. They told him so much. Denton felt their connection just as deeply as Mikael did, but his eyes were filled with reservation and caution mixed with the same passion that raced through Mikael. He wanted to stop and ask about all those things that were holding him back, while at the same time he wished he could kiss all that away until there was just him reflected in those eyes that were as deep as the sky.

He let his hand slide from behind Denton's neck and lightly touched his stubbly chin. Mikael smiled, and Denton tilted his head slightly in what he assumed was curiosity. "You're an amazing man." Mikael swallowed. "I never thought of myself as being overly romantic. My wolf certainly isn't."

"He's not?" Denton chuckled. "Mine isn't either."

"I suspected as much. But as I was saying, I want to be romantic with you. Or… okay, my wolf is urging me to rip your clothes off so he can lick, smell, and taste every inch of you. I think you know what I mean."

"You're an alpha wolf, a man of action," Denton said.

"Yes. So are you. But you're also worth taking time with." Mikael tilted his head just so and slowly moved in for another kiss. This one deepened gradually, but the energy and excitement were still there, maybe even greater than before. "You're worth really getting to know." Mikael pressed forward a little harder. He thought Denton might topple back, but instead he pressed forward, and they ended up on their sides, face to face, grinning like idiots.

"I hope you don't think I'm going to be that easy," Denton told him. "I'm not a pushover or someone you can charm with your brown eyes and radiant smile."

"You think I'm charming?" Mikael asked with a smirk. "That's a new one. I'm usually compared to the wolf from the fairy tales. I think I can live with the role of Prince Charming."

"God. You're so full of yourself," Denton teased without heat.

Mikael couldn't argue with that and tugged Denton into another kiss that ended way too soon. But then any time this century would have been too soon for Mikael.

"We should finish eating," Denton said.

Mikael reluctantly sat up and looked around for their plates. Somehow they'd managed not to land on them. He handed Denton his and then took his own. He was suddenly ravenous and ate like… well, a wolf, only with better table manners. Mikael watched Denton as he ate, loving the way Denton continued to flush under his scrutiny. The attraction was most definitely there, and now Mikael just had to figure out how to get around Denton's reluctance. He hoped spending more time together would help break down that barrier.

"What do you do? For a living, I mean," Denton said after turning away. Mikael heard him taking deep breaths and blowing them out. "We need to talk about normal things for a while."

Mikael had promised Denton that he was worth waiting for, and he wouldn't go back on his word, so he sat back in his original spot. "I paint, mostly in oils. Landscapes of the area and wildlife. I'm very well-known for my wolves, some of which are family portraits and others are just wild friends who stop in occasionally. The last few winters have been very harsh, so there have been a few packs of wolves that we've helped see through the season. In return they agree to let me paint them."

Denton's fork stopped halfway to his mouth. "You can communicate with natural wolves?"

"On a basic level, yes. They don't have a wide vocabulary, but I can communicate basic ideas to them. It's not that they care if they're painted or not, but if I have their permission and cooperation, then they're likely to stay still long enough for me to get their form on canvas. After that I can usually take it from there."

"Aren't there a lot of artists doing wolves right now?"

"I guess, but each of my wolves is unique, and I attempt to capture their personality. I painted my sister's pups last year and really succeeded. Sometime I'll have you come to the house, and I'll show you the gallery wall. Every one of our pack members has a portrait of some kind there. Well, all except Gregor's family. I haven't started their portraits yet."

"What are you working on now?" Denton asked with excitement.

"Gregor," Mikael answered. "I started right after the challenge, and I can still see him so clearly that I have to paint him before the images begin to fade. I won't show the work for some time, but I have to do it now or I'll never be able to."

"So you'll finish the painting and hide it away?" Denton seemed surprised.

"Exactly. I have one of my father that I've never shown anyone, but for a different reason." Mikael swallowed hard. "I'm not ready to share it with anyone. It sounds selfish, but it's my way of holding on to a piece of him. When I first became alpha, I tried to continue doing things the way he did and I failed. My mom helped me realize I had to be my own leader. So I do things in the spirit of my father. I like to think he'd be happy if he saw the pack now." Mikael shrugged. "But I know he's with the Mother."

"Did she tell you that?"

"No. It's just something I know." Mikael took a bite of pasta salad and chewed absently. There were some things he didn't need to be told or see, yet they were as real to him as if he'd seen them with his own eyes.

"Do you think she'll come to me?" Denton asked.

"I don't know. The times she came to me, I didn't ask her—she just deemed it important enough to give me a message. I've asked the Mother for many things in my life, mostly stupid stuff, though it seemed so important at the time. But all I can say is that she sees the big picture, and she gave me a nudge in the direction she wanted."

"What direction was that?"

Mikael stared at Denton for a second. "To you. I think she knew that our mating would be difficult, so she gave me the push I needed. I mean, had I met you and known you were my mate, I would have moved heaven and earth to be with you. I still will." He thought it best to keep the rest of her message to himself, at least for now. It was clear to him that they had been mated for a reason. He hoped once that reason was accomplished, the feelings and energy between them would remain the same.

"Is that all?"

"I don't know. My father told me the gods have their own time and ways of doing things. But I know she showed you to me, and when she said I'd be meeting my mate soon, she warned me it wouldn't be easy. I figured it would be someone I wouldn't like. I didn't expect my mate to be another alpha or that he'd be resistant to the matehood."

"I'm not resistant, just practical," Denton protested. "My parents weren't mates, not like you say we're mates. They were just together, and I know my dad loved her, but I think he was always looking for his fated mate and that my mom was just second best. She knew it too, I think. Well, knows it. My mom's alive, my dad could be too—I really don't know. He took off when I was a kid. My mom always made excuses for him, but I think he might have found what he was looking for and left the two of us for something better."

Mikael gaped. There was nothing else he could do. He sat there, nearly spilling what was left on his plate as he stared openmouthed like a fish, in utter disbelief. "That's messed up. What kind of person does that to his wife and kid? Mate or not, that's not the way to act toward anyone." Mikael clenched his fists and pressed them into the ground. If he ever met this man, there wouldn't be much left of him by the time Mikael was done with him. He hoped Denton would beat the crap out of him, but damn, he'd do it if it came to that. The hurt expression on Denton's face was more than enough to tell him that the years hadn't dulled the pain of being rejected by his own father.

"Well, that's what happened. My uncle tried to fill the void, but he had a son of his own, so basically it was me and my mom. Of course, I had the rest of the pack, and they were always good to me."

"But it wasn't the same." Mikael finished the last of his lunch and set the plate aside. "I can't imagine what I'd have done without my dad.

He always had time for me and the other pups in the pack. He threw the ball with us and played pounce when we were learning to hunt."

"Pounce?" Denton asked.

"Yeah. We needed to learn to hunt, so he'd play the prey, and we'd pounce on him."

"You played games with your alpha?"

"Sure. He was the leader, but he was also my father, and it was important to him that we all know how to defend ourselves. When I got older he taught me how to control my shift and use it when I needed to. I owe a lot to my dad, and I can't imagine what I'd have done without him, so I can't imagine what you went through."

"I never knew any different. I can barely remember him now." Denton finished his lunch, and Mikael cleared up and placed what was left back in the basket. Then he lay back, staring up at the clouds as they rolled overhead. "I love this place, but summer always seems so short."

"Tell me about it. Where else could it snow any month of the year?" Mikael asked. It was true. He had seen it snow in July before. It hadn't lasted long, but it had snowed. Granted, there were few places to compare with the beauty of this place.

"I know," Denton agreed with a chuckle.

Mikael slowly rolled onto his side, propping his head up on his arm. "So I have a question. It's sort of for my uncle. Are there many of our kind in the forest service?"

"Why?" Denton turned so Mikael could see him. Mikael had hoped he'd lie down as well.

"Well, a few years ago, when he was out…." Mikael tried to keep the smile from his expression and failed.

"He wasn't…." Denton covered his mouth and then began to laugh when Mikael nodded. "Oh my God."

"Yeah. We got the tag off, but it wasn't easy."

"As far as I know, I'm the only one. It comes in handy when we're dealing with an injured wolf. But I'm not part of the tagging program. Though if I had been there when he was trapped, I would have helped him get away." Denton was still grinning. "I can tell you that my job does allow me to keep tabs on what the outside world thinks. They're completely shocked at how fast the wolf population has rebounded, and they can't exactly explain it."

"It must be difficult keeping quiet when you know the answer. Heck, you *are* the answer."

"Exactly. It was in our best interest that the wolves flourished, so my family, and I'm sure yours as well, made very sure they did."

"Yes, we did. I was born a few years before the reintroduction, so for most of my life I was able to be free. But my mom says the first few years were difficult. Everyone still had to be careful because wolves couldn't just pop up everywhere. But I could play, and we kept to ourselves in the back area of the park, so our lives improved and now we're back."

"Yes, we are," Denton sighed. "But so many of our ways were lost over that century while we were just trying to survive, and now we're trying to build some traditions and rules...."

"And Anton is making a grab for power over everything and everyone."

"When I got back home, I confirmed all you told me and more." Denton's expression darkened and his eyes grew nearly black. "You were able to convince me about him, but you knew so much more you didn't tell me. Why?"

"It wasn't necessary, and would you have believed me if I told you that his soul was as black as his coat? The Mother told me he wasn't of the light. I don't know what that means, but it can't be good."

"I know what it means. Have you ever heard of the dark wolf?"

"That's just a legend," Mikael said. "Something parents tell their children so they'll behave."

"And we're stories the humans tell their children and make movies about. Inaccurate ones, but still... stories have a basis in fact, and what's to say that there isn't some basis to that one as well?"

"I honestly never thought about it," Mikael whispered, his mind beginning to spin. "When the Mother said he wasn't of the light, I assumed she meant that he wasn't one of her followers, but what you're proposing is even more chilling." Mikael's good mood evaporated almost as quickly as the clouds covered the sun. He glanced upward as a bank of dark clouds moved across the sky and the breeze turned more forceful and chilly. Mikael hated to leave, but it was going to rain. With each gust of wind, he could smell the humidity growing.

"I think it's getting time for me to go," Denton said.

"I'm afraid so. My brother and sister will be going out of their minds. They don't know where I am, and their protective instincts will be going overdrive."

"I know a few like that," Denton said and got to his feet. Mikael did the same. Then he set everything in a neat stack and slowly moved closer to Denton. The wind, the clouds, dark wolves—all of it vanished as he lost himself in Denton's eyes.

"I'm going to kiss you unless you stop me." Denton didn't, and this time Mikael took Denton into his arms, holding him, feeling his strength—reveling in it. He didn't melt against him; rather, Denton held him too, embracing him with nearly equal power and passion. When their lips finally came together, it was electric, power jolting through him. Denton felt so right in his arms, so utterly perfect.

Denton was his. That's all Mikael could think as he kissed Denton soundly. He felt Denton tremble slightly in his arms, and Mikael responded in kind. How could he not? He had found the one person who made all the pieces fall into place, and all that happened within the span of the kiss. It didn't matter if Denton was the leader of another pack. Nothing mattered other than the fact that Denton was going to be his; he had to be his. Part of Mikael's soul would remain eternally empty if he wasn't.

"You make it hard to say good-bye," Denton whispered when they parted.

"That's what I was going for. We're mates, meant to be together. It should be hard to say good-bye." Mikael didn't release Denton. He closed his eyes, inhaling deeply to impress Denton's scent further into his brain. "I know you aren't ready to believe that yet. All I'm asking for is a chance. Sometimes things work out."

"This is pretty formidable. Neither of us can give up his pack. But okay. I'll keep an open mind." Denton closed the gap between them, kissing Mikael ferociously while he held Mikael for dear life. Regardless of what Denton said, Mikael knew he felt the attraction between them. It was there—Mikael wasn't imagining it.

The wind came up, swirling around them, bringing a chill that forced them apart. Mikael reluctantly stepped back and looked up at the sky. There was no denying it—bad weather was on the way. "You better go before the roads get bad." Mikael picked up the basket and blanket and led Denton out of the clearing. His truck was parked next to Mikael's. He got in and waited until Denton got inside his truck, started his engine, and pulled away before he started down the rough road toward home.

"WHERE WERE you?" Karl asked when Mikael walked inside his house.

"He was worried," Catherine said from right behind him. "I told him you could take care of yourself."

"I'm fine." He handed Karl the basket. "Is everything quiet? Other than the storm?"

"Yes." Karl accepted the basket with a stare, and Mikael heard him sniff slightly. Karl tilted his head and sniffed again. Mikael had left the blanket in his car, but there was probably enough of Denton's scent on the basket—and on him—for Karl to be curious. "You were with another wolf." He smiled. "It's about time."

Catherine snatched the basket away from him. "Don't be nosy. It's not an attractive quality on you."

"For your information I *was* with someone this afternoon, and we had a very nice few hours. Now, since everything is quiet, I'm going up to the studio. I have work to do, as I'm sure you do." Mikael walked to the stairs and paused. "We need to make sure everything is in order and that we are as strong and self-sufficient as possible. Karl, when you can, find someone to take an inventory of all stores on hand. I want enough for at least a few weeks."

"You're expecting a war?"

"I don't know what I'm expecting. But we should be prepared for anything. If necessary, buy another freezer and make sure we have enough fuel to run the generators for days. The weather looks foul." He said no more and began climbing the stairs. He wasn't worried about the weather, but what could be coming along with it.

When he got to his studio, he put the wolf portrait he'd left on his easel to the side and picked up a blank canvas. He desperately wanted

61

to paint Denton, but that would have to wait. The skies outside were a tempest, roiling and rolling as the clouds got lower and lower. He grabbed a pencil and began to sketch what he saw. He wasn't sure what sort of painting he'd use this for, but a sight like this was too good, and unsettling, to let it pass without capturing it.

Mikael was soon lost in his work and his thoughts. He drew and let his spirit get tumbled and spun up in those clouds, even as a part of him replayed the kisses and closeness he'd felt with Denton. Even when the rain finally came and pelted the windows, the warmth inside didn't dissipate. Mikael worked until the light faded. Then he set aside the canvas and stood in front of the windows, watching the storm blow over the peaks and through the trees.

"It makes you realize how small we are, doesn't it?" Uncle Viktor said as he knocked on the doorframe. Mikael nodded to give him permission to enter his private domain.

"Yes, it does. There's a lot I can do as alpha, but I can't control the power like she can with a single storm." Mikael hadn't been surprised by his uncle's approach. He'd heard and scented him minutes before he appeared. It wasn't even necessary to turn away from the windows, but he did, dragging a chair over so the older wolf could sit comfortably. Mikael was too tense to sit.

"What's on your mind?" Viktor asked as he slid into the chair. Mikael glanced toward him and then went back to the windows and his thoughts. "There are rumors you're seeing someone."

"I found my mate, but it's complicated," Mikael said flatly. "I saw him today."

"So there will eventually be another addition to the pack," Viktor said. "You're strong enough to do what you have to in order to win your mate." His uncle touched his arm. "That's wonderful news. You deserve to have someone in your life. I was blessed to have found my mate, and while I had your aunt for just ten short years, they were the best years of my life. She gave me more happiness than I ever thought I deserved, and I'm sure it will be like that for you."

"Like I said, it's complicated. To make a long story short, the Mother showed me my mate and told me he was near. What she didn't tell me is that he's the alpha of the Evergreen pack. I'm trusting you to keep this to yourself, although around here, the walls have ears."

"I sent them all out to their own dens, so you and I are alone in the house." His uncle paused to think. "You know that the Mother never gives us more than we can handle. Finding your mate is a source of great happiness." Mikael glanced at his uncle and saw a tear in his eye. "Do you think your aunt made it easy on me? Sure, she was my mate, and I knew it instantly. So did she, but she still made me prove that I loved her. That what we had went deeper than matehood to true love."

"That's almost a miracle," Mikael commented as the wind whipped the rain against the windows, water running down them in sheets, nearly completely obscuring the view outside.

"If something comes easy we take it for granted, so fight for your mate and do what you need to be happy. You'll never regret it."

Mikael nodded slowly and thought about Denton, unable to help the small smile that broke out. He knew his uncle was right. His mate was worth fighting for. "I want you to tell me what you know about a dark wolf," he said, changing gears after a minute.

"Those are stories my parents told me to make sure we behaved, just like we told them to you."

"Maybe, maybe not. A lot of stories have a basis in fact, and I need you to tell me what you know."

"You think they could be real?" Viktor asked.

"What if Anton is one?" Mikael retorted, and his uncle grew quiet for some time, with just the sounds of the wind and rain on the roof filling the room.

"You know we worship the Mother," Viktor finally said. "She represents order and life. We don't know everything or the whole picture, but she brings order to the world. The snows come in winter, the rain in spring, heat in summer, and then we prepare for winter once again. Everything has its time. Order and light. That's what my dad used to tell me."

"Mine too."

"Yes. He did. But for everything there is balance. So with order comes chaos. That's the darkness. The Mother rules by day, and chaos rules at night. That's how my dad explained it, but I don't think that's true. The night isn't dark for us. True darkness, that's what can descend over the spirit. That's where chaos rules. So if a wolf lets the darkness into its spirit, then it becomes dark and the wolf takes over." Uncle Viktor stood up and walked to the far side of the room. "My dad used to tell me that being bad let some of the darkness into your spirit, so if we were bad enough we'd turn into dark wolves and our human side, the part that kept us from being completely wild, would lose power. We wouldn't just turn into wolves, but rogue, feral wolves, always hungry and looking for something we couldn't have. No pack and no friends."

"That's what my dad told me. He also said that dark wolves hurt the Mother, and that's the worst thing we could do." Mikael turned toward his uncle. "So, the Mother is real, I know this. If that's true, then the darkness—chaos—must be real as well."

"Like I said, it's just a story."

"What if it isn't? The world is always about balance—life and death, good and evil. The Mother has to have a counterpart to keep the balance. If we are the light, then there has to be the darkness. And what if that darkness has been sitting just waiting for us?"

"You can't think this is real? That a dark wolf exists? That's too much for me to believe. I mean, we have always had wolves, and the humans have always had people, who lusted after ultimate power. It happens, but it doesn't mean anything more sinister than that. Anton is after more power than any wolf can handle, and someone will bring him down."

"Not this time," Mikael said flatly. "You weren't there. You didn't see how black Anton's eyes were, or how carelessly he considered everyone around him. It was like he had no soul, no life." Mikael thought for a second. "You remember Aunt Xavia and how she could always tell about people?"

"I'll never forget her," Viktor said. "And yeah, she could always tell a person just by looking at them. She knew instantly if she liked you, and if not, she hated you for life. Though there were very few people she hated."

"Aunt Xavia would loathe Anton from a hundred feet away. I hated being anywhere near him, and I barely spoke to him or got close to him. His eyes are black, like his soul is trying to get out. There's something not right about him, and his wolf is jet black. There isn't a fleck of white or gray anywhere. He's perfectly black. That isn't natural either."

"But you're talking fairy tales," Viktor whispered.

"No. I'm saying that those tales were told to scare us. And I doubt that something bad is going to turn anyone into a dark wolf any more than there are monsters under the bed. But if a wolf aligned himself with the forces of darkness, or chaos, then, yeah, I think a dark wolf is more than possible. I think it's reality, and I saw him in action."

"You've given this a lot of thought, haven't you?" Viktor asked.

"In a way, yes. And I don't know for sure about Anton, but I'm saying what if it's true? He's already taken over a number of packs. Those wolves aren't going to know what hit them. Their lives were peaceful, ordered, and happy. Now they've plunged into hell. I got Anna and the pups away from him, but Anton has the rest of Gregor's pack. Denton brought up the idea that there might be some truth in our stories, and I wanted to ask you if the stories said anything about what to do if someone became a black wolf."

"I'm sorry. If there was anything, it's been lost, at least to me."

Mikael hadn't expected much more, and he nodded. The rain was letting up, and he once again turned to the windows, staring out at the wet, dripping landscape as the clouds slowly lifted and began to move on. "We needed the rain."

"Yes. But you know that everything is going to grow because of it, and when the summer comes, there will be more grass and shrubs to dry out and burn."

Mikael did. That was part of the balance. He thought about Denton once again. What Mikael needed was some balance in his life, and yes, he intended to take his uncle's advice and fight for his mate. He wasn't sure how to do it yet, but the Mother would show him the way. He only hoped he recognized her guidance.

CHAPTER 5

MIKAEL SPENT most of the next week working, but every evening, before he came down from his studio, he picked up his phone to call Denton. It was becoming the highlight of his day to hear his voice. Sometimes he was just getting home from work, and other times he was leaving. Once, Mikael had to leave a message, and he paced the room for an hour like he'd been put in a cage until Denton returned his call.

They talked about everything and nothing. Just listening to Denton's voice both comforted and excited him at the same time. Mikael would sit in his chair, legs thrown over the arms, and laugh at a story Denton told him about the people at work. It didn't matter that he didn't know them. Denton did, and that was enough.

The light was fading as Mikael finished the last brushstrokes on the portrait of Gregor's wolf. He took a step back and admired his work before setting the canvas aside. The last few days it had filled him with sadness, and all he wanted was to make sure he hadn't included the sadness in the picture. As time went by, it got harder and harder to conjure up memories of happier days, but he'd done what he'd set out to do. Anna and the boys would have something to remember their father by when they were ready to see it. There wasn't enough light to work any longer, so Mikael packed up and cleaned everything carefully before reaching for his phone. He was about to make his regular evening call when his phone chimed. He smiled when he saw Denton's number and answered.

"Hey, it's nice of you to call."

"Hey. Sorry, but I'd love to be calling for one of our talks. But something's happened. I'm not sure how to explain it or what it means. But I think you and your sister should come down here right away. You have to see what I think is some sort of gift from Anton. I don't really know what to make of it, but…." The confusion and frustration in Denton's voice would have had Mikael running even if he hadn't asked.

"I'll get Catherine and we'll be over as soon as we can. It'll take an hour or so."

"Hurry," Denton told him.

"I will." Mikael hung up, already headed out the door. "I need Catherine right now," he yelled and instantly small feet jumped to.

"Yes, alpha," Alexi said, and by the time Mikael reached the bottom of the stairs, Catherine was hurrying his way.

"Get Mom or Stan to watch the pups. I need Karl to stay here and keep everyone together. Something is going on at Evergreen, and you and I have been asked to come over. We need to be on the road in five minutes, faster if you can." He turned and headed to his room to get out of his painting clothes, and everyone else in the house raced to spread the word. By the time he returned, the entire pack was in the den, watching him as he entered.

"What's going on?" Karl asked.

"I don't know. But I got a call from Denton, and he asked me and Catherine to come over. I need you to watch over everyone here. Our borders are well marked. He said it was some sort of message from Anton, but he wasn't sure what to make of it. I want to make sure everyone here is safe." Mikael looked over all the faces that stared at him, old and young. "Stay here and stay together. If anything happens, call me. Karl, call Chris to make sure he knows to be careful." Mikael went through the room and touched each and every one of his pack mates to reassure them. The young ones he lifted and held briefly. Then he turned and stepped outside. Catherine followed him a minute later.

MIKAEL DROVE as fast as the roads would allow. Thankfully, the weather had been fairly dry, the rain of a week earlier becoming a memory on the landscape. The land wasn't bone dry, but the summer thunderstorms and their lightning that would roll over the region would have plenty of dry grass to ignite when the time came.

"I know you're in a hurry, but you're driving like Karl," Catherine said.

Very few things fazed her, but she seemed on edge. Somehow he didn't think it was his driving.

"Are you and Denton getting closer?" she asked.

"Yes." Mikael accelerated on one of the few stretches of long straight road between them and their destination.

"It hurts you, doesn't it? To know he's your mate and be unable to be together."

Mikael growled and concentrated on the road ahead.

"I'll take that as a yes."

"Of course it does. He's my mate. Do you want some sort of blow-by-blow on how much I want him with me all the damned time? The last time I saw him was a week ago. My wolf has been pacing like he's in a cage. The only time he stops is when we talk on the phone, and then he paces once again. It's like I want to jump out of my own skin. But there's fuck-all I can do about it. At least this very second."

"You're worried about him," Catherine pronounced.

"Where in the hell do you get that?"

"Maybe by the way I expect the steering wheel to snap off in the claws that seem to appear every few miles. You don't lose control often, and knowing you're going to see him is sending you into overdrive."

Mikael eased off the accelerator and loosened his grip on the wheel. "Of course I'm worried. We're going because he said there's something we need to see. If this were a social call, I doubt he'd ask my enforcer to come along." Mikael smiled. "I doubt he's really interested in scaring half his pack to death."

"Please. I'm a sweetheart," she said with a smile that belied all her strength. Catherine was so many things it was sometimes hard for Mikael to keep them straight. She could be as gentle as anything when she was with her pups, but at other times she was strong and fearless— Mikael had seen her kick the ass of a bear that was threatening to get too close to her pups. Sometimes Mikael felt sorry for the bear; the poor thing didn't know what hit it. She was no small woman, and she was certainly no shrinking violet. The strength, fortitude, and loyalty inside her were enough for any two men, and yet she wore her power with ease.

"You can be," Mikael retorted. "You can also be the bitch from hell, and I thank the Mother that you're *my* bitch from hell." He smiled, and she bared her teeth playfully in return.

"Let's get there and find out what's going on."

Mikael went as fast as he dared as he followed Denton's directions down the old mountain logging paths and backcountry roads. He turned into a drive, and they coasted to a stop next to a small collection of what looked like vacation cabins. At least they appeared to have been that at one time.

Mikael got out and stood by the truck, sniffing. The scent of at least a dozen wolves filled the air. He sniffed a second time and was immediately assaulted in the best way possible by his mate's scent. It took all his strength to keep from shifting and letting his wolf run off to find Denton. He sensed stress and a touch of fear in the scent, and that was nearly enough to snap his control.

"Welcome," Denton said as he came around from the dark side of one of the cabins. He slowly approached, and he and Catherine eyed each other. Catherine was magnificent, tall and erect, staring straight at him. She bent her neck, slightly and quickly, in deference to Denton's position. "You must be Catherine," Denton said after a few seconds. "It's a pleasure to meet you." He extended his hand, and Catherine shook it. This was no social handshake. Mikael was sure Denton got the full-on grip of steel from his enforcer.

When Denton released Catherine's hand and turned to him, Mikael went warm inside for a brief moment. He wanted to pull them together and kiss the life out of Denton, but he knew he had to follow Denton's lead. This was his land and his territory. Mikael was a guest, and Denton's pack mates would interpret any act of aggression as a challenge to their alpha. Oh, Mikael wanted to conquer Denton and his territory, but in the bedroom, and most definitely not with claws and teeth. Well, not primarily, anyway.

"What is it you'd like us to see?" Mikael asked almost gently.

The tension in Denton spiked, his scent becoming slightly acrid. Whatever it was, it was more stressful than meeting Mikael's sister. "Please follow me." Denton turned, and they carefully followed him back the way he'd come. They went around the side of one of the cabins to an outdoor communal area surrounded by cabins. A fire ring blazed with dancing light, sending shadows on all the buildings. It would have been perfect except for the fact that it was empty. Chairs lay turned on their sides. A table sat resting on its top. It seemed everyone had scattered and raced for cover. "I had to tranq him, and we managed to cage him while he was out, but it didn't last long."

The rattle of metal, sharp and clear, rang into the night. It was followed by a bang and then a brief silence before the sounds repeated. Three men, wolves by their scent, including Kaiawa, stood around the cage. They parted as Denton approached. A wolf was inside, pacing and then throwing himself against the door. Mikael wasn't sure how long the cage would survive. They stood back, and Mikael scented the wolf before taking a step back.

"What is it?" Catherine asked. "He smells strange."

Mikael nodded. Catherine was an excellent enforcer, but Mikael's sense of smell was much stronger than even hers. "He's enraged and a shifter, but the human scent is driven way back, almost to a hint. Like his human part hasn't been in contact for some time."

"At first we thought he was a natural wolf, but something seemed off," Denton said as he came to stand next to him. "You sense more?"

"Yeah. He's definitely part human. Do any of you recognize him?"

The wolf stopped moving in the cage and stared at Mikael, head tilted slightly. Then he hunched back and bared his fangs, but made very little sound. The others turned to stare at Mikael. "Get out your phone and snap some pictures," he said to Catherine. "He's not familiar to me, but send the pictures to Karl and see if anyone in the pack recognizes him. It's a long shot, but we need to know where he came from." Mikael never took his eyes off the wolf, who seemed to calm somewhat.

"Maybe he's controlling him," someone breathed.

"No. I'm not," Mikael said in an equally quiet tone, knowing the other wolves would hear.

"You're not what?" Denton asked. "No one said anything."

"Yes, they did. Someone in one of the cabins asked if I was controlling the wolf. I answered them." Mikael's hearing was especially good when he was on alert.

"I didn't hear anything," Denton said.

Mikael nodded, still staring down the wolf in the cage. Catherine snapped a few pictures and worked her phone. After a few seconds, the caged wolf turned back to the door and lunged for it. The metal snapped, and the wolf barreled out of the cage, zipped around one of the men, and made for the woods.

"I'm on it," Catherine said, and she was on his tail before anyone else could move. Clothes flew, and within seconds Catherine had shifted, and Mikael saw she was already closing on the other wolf. They reached the tree line, and Catherine leaped, landing on the escaping wolf, bringing him down. Growls and snarls followed, but that ended within seconds with a high-pitched yip and then a low rumble.

"I believe Catherine has him," Mikael said proudly as he and Denton made their way over, with Kaiawa following as well.

Catherine had the wolf pinned to the ground, his throat in her mouth.

"Do you think we should tranq him again?" Kaiawa asked.

"I don't think it'll do any good. I don't want to kill him, and the dose we'd need could do that," Denton said. "I think we need to tie him up good, and then we'll figure it out."

Catherine got up and shifted back to her human form once the others secured the wolf.

Mikael noticed some of the males looking at her and then turning away. "Are you hurt?" Mikael asked her.

Catherine rolled her eyes. She walked back to her clothes and pulled them on.

"I take it that was a stupid question," Denton said with a touch of awe in his voice.

"Yeah. But if I hadn't asked she'd have been pissed and said I didn't care." There were times when it was much easier to do what he had to, even if he didn't always understand the reasons why.

Denton's pack members tied up the wolf, probably a little excessively, but after that display of strength they weren't taking any chances.

"I sent the pictures. Karl said he'd show them around," Catherine said.

"Tell him to be sure to show Anna. She would know different wolves than the rest of us."

"Will do," Catherine told him, and after texting, she put her phone away.

Mikael turned to Denton. "Where did you find him?"

Denton looked at his men and then back to Mikael. "That's what I really wanted you to see." Denton glanced at Kaiawa. "Stay here with him and try to keep him calm if you can. Alpha Volokov and I will be back."

Denton turned and motioned with his head toward the woods. Mikael followed. He shifted his eyes and could see very well in the dark.

"It isn't far," Denton said.

"How was he able to get so close to your compound?"

"He didn't. We scented him and went to drive him away but ended up capturing him after we saw this." They stepped into a clearing, and Mikael blinked trying to make sense of what he was seeing.

"It's a deer… or what's left of it," Mikael said.

"That's just it. It's the whole deer. Nothing has been eaten or removed. Near as I can tell it was split open while it was still alive and splayed open."

"Why?"

"That's why I called you. I can't figure it out. We kill for meat and to live. We don't kill for sport or cruelty. This was done for both reasons." Denton walked slowly through the grass. "The heart is right there, and the other organs are spread out in a circle. There is some kind of message here, but I don't get it. But it's by design, and I doubt that wolf back there is the one sending it. He was just delivering it."

"You're right. There isn't enough cognition for him to have developed it. He's all instinct and something else. He smells very off, even for a wolf. It's almost like that part of him has somehow been altered." Mikael turned to Denton. "Did you take pictures of this?"

"Yeah. I snapped a few."

Mikael nodded and tried to puzzle it out but didn't get anywhere. "Let's head back. If you're okay with it, I'd like to see if I can communicate with him."

Denton put his hand on Mikael's shoulder. "Are you crazy? There's nothing there but an out-of-control animal."

"I'm not so sure," Mikael said quietly. "His human portion is still there, it's just been sublimated. I don't even think his wolf portion is really his. There's something else at work here, and I'd like to try to see if I can contact what's left of him."

"As long as you don't put yourself or anyone else at risk, I'm fine with it." Denton's voice rang with caution and concern. They were too close to the others for Mikael to say what he wanted, so he smiled and bent his head slightly in agreement. Then he followed Denton back to the fire circle, where the others waited for them.

"What was it?" Catherine asked.

"We agree it's some sort of message," Denton said to the group. "Alpha Volokov and I feel that he might know something, and Alpha Volokov is willing to try to contact his human half. Everyone is to remain on alert and be ready. If we have to, we will kill him. I want weapons ready, but only use them on my or Alpha Volokov's command. Under no circumstances are you to take action on your own." Denton stepped back and signaled the others to make a circle around the bound wolf. He was still snarling, even with rope bound around his muzzle.

Mikael was about to get into position when a phone rang. He paused and growled at his sister, who held up her hand even as she snatched the phone out of her pocket with the other. "It's Karl." She answered it and listened, speaking only once to say yes, and then she hung up. "Can I speak to both of you?"

Mikael and Denton joined Catherine and moved well away from the others. "Anna recognized him," Catherine said softly. "He was an orphaned teenager from her former pack. She said he left about a year ago without word to anyone as far as she knows. His name is Vadim."

"Thank you," Mikael told her and looked to Denton. "Please know that the reason for the secrecy isn't your pack mates." Denton nodded, and Mikael moved back toward the others. They took up the circle once again, and Mikael took a deep breath, considering the best way to handle this.

"I am Alpha Volokov," Mikael said, quietly, but filling his voice with power and authority. The wolf stopped snarling. "You will listen to me. This is not your territory, so you are under our authority. Do you understand?"

The wolf began growling and struggling.

You will listen to me. I have the ability to put words directly into your head.

The wolf stilled. That got his attention.

I want to speak directly with Vadim. I know your human half is still here, even if he's been pushed aside. I'm calling on Vadim to come forward. It isn't necessary to shift, but I want to speak with him. Mikael stroked the wolf's coat, slowly and gently, the way his mother used to do for him when he was a cub. He hoped that would rekindle some old, nearly forgotten memory. *I am Alpha Volokov, and I'm stronger than you. You will submit and you will do as I ask.* Mikael shifted his other hand, then rested his claws on Vadim's neck but made no move to hurt him. *I have a great deal more power and strength than you, and you can see and feel it. Now I'm asking you to let Vadim come forward.*

He continued stroking Vadim's back and moved his paw away from his neck and let him see it shift back to human. *I can shift all of myself just as quickly, but I don't need to because you are going to let Vadim come forward. I can feel him inside you, and he's as much a part of you as the wolf is.* Something changed slightly in Vadim's scent, becoming more shifter, but Mikael also got the acrid scent of fear mixed with acidic guilt. *You have done nothing wrong thus far. No one has been hurt. Nothing's been done that cannot be set right and fixed, but, Vadim, you must try to communicate with me.*

Just like the wolf was inside them when they were in human form, so the human was inside when in wolf form. The "consciousnesses," for lack of a better term, melded, blended together into one. One was more dominant than the other based upon physical form, but neither completely disappeared. Vadim would not be able to talk to him in wolf form, but he would be able to communicate in a humanlike way. Mikael waited so see what would happen. He continually monitored the wolf's scent to see if it changed again, but it remained the same, and other than lying there, Vadim did nothing.

Then the wolf's tail began to slowly and rhythmically beat against the earth.

Vadim is that you? I want you to move your tail three times and then stop.

The tail beat the ground three times and came to a stop.

All right. Wag once for no, two for yes. Do you know who I am?

Thump, thump.

Are you prepared to shift back to human form?

Thump, thump.

Can you control your wolf?

Thump.

Can you shift?

Thump thump.

But you can't necessarily stay in human form.

Thump thump.

We can help you, but you must agree to cooperate. I know a friend of yours, Anna. She is now part of my pack. She's very concerned about you. He didn't know that for sure, but knowing Anna she'd probably been worried sick about her missing pack member. *Will you agree to cooperate?*

Thump, thump.

Mikael stood up. "I have been able to reach Vadim," he told Denton.

"I was hoping those tail thumps were communication."

"They were. He has agreed to shift, but to do that we need to untie him." Mikael knew what he wanted to do. At home he could have made the decision instantly, and his instinct was to do just that, but instead he looked at Denton and waited.

"You can't be serious," Kaiawa said. Even Catherine bristled slightly, but she had enough sense to keep quiet.

Mikael did his best to keep his expression neutral. He didn't want this to come across as a challenge to Denton. It was his decision to make, and Mikael would abide by whatever he chose. After a few seconds, he turned back to Vadim, who lay still and seemed to have relaxed. Some of the tension and frenzied attempts to escape had quieted.

"It seems risky," Denton finally said. Mikael could hear his indecision and conflict.

"I know it is. We'll form a circle around him and be prepared for an attack or an attempt to run, but his energy levels are low, and as long as we aren't aggressive but remain strong, he should be able to shift, which is what he needs to do if he's ever going to regain some kind of control over his human side." Mikael would have been impatient at home but here remained patient.

"All right," Denton agreed, and Mikael flashed him a quick smile.

"I can't believe this," Kaiawa said, and Mikael shifted his gaze, glaring at him hard, and let some of his fire show in his eyes. He also growled under his breath, knowing the others would hear it. No one was going to publically disrespect his mate. Denton did the same, which pleased him. Kaiawa backed down quickly and even took a step back. Mikael shot him another glare and then returned his attention to Vadim.

We will untie you, but if you challenge us or try to run, she will come after you, and this time she won't stop. You will be destroyed. Do you understand?

Thump thump.

"Good. Now hold still."

Mikael slowly unfastened the ropes from around Vadim's body and legs, and he made no move to get up. The tension within the circle was palpable, rolling off the others in waves. Catherine looked ready to pounce at any second. Mikael knew the moment of truth would come when he removed the muzzling ropes. If Vadim was playing possum, he'd show his hand at that moment. Mikael slowly loosened the ropes and then let them fall to the ground. Then he cautiously got to his feet and joined the others in the circle.

"Okay, now shift," Mikael said and sent the same command silently into Vadim's mind.

At first nothing happened, and then the wolf began to struggle, legs churning but getting nowhere. The wolf got to his feet, and Mikael began to think he'd made a mistake and that he was going to run, but then a slight shimmer surrounded the wolf, and slowly the fur vanished in favor of smooth skin. Paws transformed into hands, and then legs and arms appeared. It took longer than it should have, but eventually, a man, quite slight and smaller than Mikael would have expected, lay on the ground.

"Get a blanket," Denton commanded, and one of his men stepped away as Vadim began to shake and fear rolled off him in waves.

"You're fine," Mikael soothed quietly. "None of us will harm you."

"It's... it's been so long," Vadim whispered as he continued to shiver and try to cover himself. When the man returned, Mikael took the blanket and knelt down, placing it over him.

"You're warm. No one will hurt you. I know what you can sense, but it is tension because of what happened earlier, nothing more." Mikael looked at the others, who took small steps back.

"The wolf is very strong," Vadim said shakily.

"You need to keep yourself in control. Your wolf has been stronger for quite a while, and your human has been pushed back. The wolf isn't going to be happy to lose control, but you need to fight him and regain your strength." Vadim nodded, and Mikael helped him into a sitting position. "We need to get him someplace warm," Mikael said to Denton. "The night air is cool, and he isn't used to not having his wolf's fur."

Denton nodded and pointed to the building closest to the woods. Mikael helped Vadim to his feet. He stood, but faltered. Mikael scooped the small man into his arms and easily carried him toward the cabin. A soft growl from Denton reached his ears, making Mikael smile. His mate was jealous; that was good. Catherine got there before he did and opened the door.

The cabins were single rooms and very rustic. A small bed with a bare mattress stood against one wall. That would do for now, and Mikael laid Vadim down. "You need to rest and build up your strength. Someone will stay here with you so you won't feel alone." Mikael stepped back and looked at each of the gathering people. "Catherine can stay with him, if that's all right with you," Mikael told Denton, who nodded, and then Mikael's gaze fell on a confused Catherine. "He's going to need your strength as well as your compassion. Be gentle when he needs and fierce if that's what's called for."

"Aren't we going to get some answers?" one of Denton's pack members asked.

"He's too weak and scattered to give us much information right now. Once he's had a chance to rest and get used to being in his human skin once again, he'll be able to tell us a lot more. All I did was break through to his human side, but that hasn't changed any of the reasons why he's been in wolf form for so long." Mikael turned to Vadim, watching as Catherine settled into the wooden chair next to the bed. "We'll get more and better information from him in the morning, I suspect."

"All right," Denton said. "I think we have things under control. I need someone to clean up that mess out there, and then we can settle for the night."

"Should we bury it?" Kaiawa asked.

"Burn it," Mikael said. "Then, when the fire is cool, spread the ashes on the meadow to help fertilize it. That will give the deer back to the Mother and help the meadow grow."

Denton nodded to his men, and the men left the cabin. But Kaiawa stayed close to Denton, and Mikael's dislike of the man continued to grow. He stood too close and seemed to be trying to exert influence over Denton, and that was not acceptable. Still, this wasn't his pack or his territory. He glared at Kaiawa, who finally took a step back. Mikael was getting tired of the man, and when he bared his teeth, Kaiawa finally got the message and left the room.

Denton motioned toward the cabin door. "I believe your sister has things well in hand here."

"She does." Mikael shared a look with her and then followed Denton outside. "She's tough as nails, but she's also a mother and knows when someone is truly hurting." It was what made her a champion enforcer.

"So what are we going to do? It's very late, and Vadim needs some rest. It doesn't make any sense for you to go home only to come back first thing in the morning."

Mikael nodded his agreement, as a jolt of energy fueled by possibilities shot through him. He didn't need to be told which cabin was Denton's. The largest one was undoubtedly the alpha's place, and he followed Denton across the open space and up to the door. Denton pushed the door open and stepped inside. As soon as the door closed behind them, Mikael turned Denton around and yanked him close, crashing their mouths together. Mikael couldn't hold back. He wound his hands through Denton's light, soft hair, and he growled slightly when Denton resisted. He pushed Denton back against the door, using all his power, working a leg between Denton's.

A soft whine made Mikael hold Denton closer. Fuck, he loved that sound. He kissed him harder, cradling Denton's head in his hand as he deftly opened the button at the waist of his jeans. He'd been waiting for this for so damn long, too fucking long, and when he pulled at the fabric, the rest of Denton's buttons popped open. Mikael slid his hand down Denton's lower belly and past the waistband of his boxers. Denton's breath hitched and a shiver ran through him. "How long has it been since someone took care of you?"

"Well...."

"I don't mean sex. I mean since someone really took care of you?" Mikael slid his fingers along Denton's shaft and then closed his hand around the throbbing heat. Damn, he felt good, and Mikael pulled slightly, delighting in Denton's sharp intake of breath.

"It's my job to take care of everyone," Denton gasped.

"No. It's your job to lead, and right now it's my job to make you feel good." Mikael kissed Denton hard, drawing a little blood, but he wasn't going to listen to Denton's argument. "I've waited since I met you to get you in bed, and now…." Mikael manhandled Denton toward the closed door at the back of the cabin. He hoped like hell it was a bedroom because he needed one…. No, *they* needed one, right now.

Mikael turned the knob, looked in the room, and saw the bed inside. That was enough. Within seconds he had propelled Denton to the edge of the mattress and then down. Denton bounced once, and Mikael already had the cuffs of his pants in hand, tugging them off and dropping them on the floor. Mikael growled and shifted his hand. The boxers didn't stand a chance. Denton yanked his shirt off, and Mikael stared at the golden-skinned wonder laid out on the mattress, a light dusting of hair on Denton's strong chest.

"Is this what you were hoping for?"

"Better," Mikael grunted as his eyes shifted to black and white. In his excitement, he was losing control. Only this man had ever tested the limits of his control over his wolf. "You are so much better than I ever hoped for." Mikael climbed on the bed, his gaze raking up Denton's body as he inhaled deeply, further imprinting Denton's musky male scent on his mind. "I want to taste you." Mikael licked Denton's chest, capturing a nipple between his lips and then licking it.

Denton quivered, and Mikael grinned, licking again as his mate's salty sweetness, spiced with sweat, burst on his tongue. This felt so right. Mikael whimpered and pushed back the notion that tomorrow he would have to return to his pack and he and Denton would be separated once again.

"What?"

"Nothing," Mikael whispered. He opened his shirt and shrugged it off, tossing it on the floor without taking his gaze away from Denton's. "I get lost in your eyes."

"The kids used to think I was a freak because I didn't have wolf eyes like others in the pack."

"They didn't appreciate how amazing your eyes are." Mikael sank into their depths, like riding the waves of the deepest ocean. He leaned closer and stilled.

Denton lifted his head, bringing their lips together. "These pants need to go," he growled when they broke the kiss.

Mikael didn't want to put any distance between him and his mate, so they fumbled for a few moments until the rest of his clothes ended up on the floor and nothing came between them. Thank the Mother, it was glorious. Mikael petted and stroked, sucking a spot just behind Denton's ear until he groaned and quivered under Mikael's attention.

"What's with me?" Denton gasped after a few minutes. "I want you, everything, all at once."

"That's how it is with your mate. If you're together forever, you still can't get enough, and when they aren't with you, it feels wrong, like something's missing." Mikael wound his arms around Denton's back, licking trails down his skin. The flavor got stronger the lower he went, and Mikael followed the intensity. "Am I teasing you?"

"You know you are," Denton answered shakily.

Mikael licked the head of Denton's cock before slowly sucking him deeper. "Damn," he mumbled as the flavor of his mate burst on his tongue. God, it was like fireworks in his mouth, and Mikael sucked deeper, taking all he could get.

Denton pulled away, to Mikael's surprise. He blinked a few times, and then Denton pounced on him, pushing him back on the mattress. Mikael chuckled and growled when Denton pressed a hand to his chest, holding him in place while he licked up Mikael's shaft. "You're not the only one who gets to have the fun." Denton sucked him into wet heat, and Mikael's vision blurred as he was filled with intense, eye-closing, jaw-dropping pleasure. "Fuck, you're huge."

"No, I'm just right for you," Mikael countered. Denton hummed his agreement and sucked him deeper. This was perfect, amazing, awesome, mind-blowing, and like coming home all at the same fucking time. Mikael thrust forward slightly, and Denton sucked harder, taking all of him.

The air flew from Mikael's lungs, and he grasped the bedding, his hands shifting to claws that sank into the fabric. He knew he should try to change them back, but damn, he was too overwhelmed to care.

Mikael spent much of his life being in control. But Denton pulled that away from him. Within a matter of minutes, Mikael's own body seemed out of his control, and that was an amazing feeling. He released the bedding and forced his hands to shift back. He wouldn't hurt his mate, and he needed to touch him the same way he needed air to breathe.

"Denton!" Mikael called as his head began to swim.

"Like that?"

"Hell yes," Mikael gasped. Denton closed his lips around his cock once again, sucking him like his life depended on it. Mikael wound his fingers into Denton's long, soft hair, loving the feel of it on his skin. Hell, Mikael loved everything about Denton—the way he touched him, his silky hair, the way his eyes shifted from wolf to human in the span of a few seconds as he looked up while Mikael's cock slid between Denton's amazing lips. At the thought Mikael nearly lost it. He had to close his eyes and think of something to cool him off, or he would fucking come right that very second. The main thing holding him back was that he wanted more.

Mikael growled loud and long, pulling Denton into his arms and then rolling them on the bed. He stared down into Denton's surprise-filled eyes. "One of the benefits of being bigger than you." He flashed a quick smile and wriggled his hips, sliding his cock along Denton's to soothe away the argument he could see forming. "It doesn't mean that I see you as less than me."

"You don't see me as a lesser alpha?" Denton asked. Instantly, Mikael realized how hard that must have been for Denton to ask.

"I will never see you as a lesser anything," Mikael answered and punctuated his point with a hip thrust that made Denton's eyes roll. "I always knew my mate would be special, but what I didn't know was that I'd need and want one as strong and formidable as I am." Mikael bared his teeth and nuzzled Denton's head to the side to get access to his neck.

"I'm not a pushover," Denton said as he fought back, meeting Mikael's gaze.

"I don't want you to be. But my wolf is pushing me to take you and make you his. The thought that you don't belong to him is pushing him and me over the edge."

"I know how you feel," Denton whispered as he cradled both sides of Mikael's head in his hands. "Mine wants me to claim you as well. But how in the fuck would that work? The dominant wolf claims the other. That's how it's always worked."

"Screw how it's worked in the past. When the time comes, we'll make our own rules, and I say we'll claim each other. If we are going to be mates, somehow, then we need to be equals. It's the only way things can work for us." Mikael worked a knee between Denton's, spreading his legs before using his strength to press his legs farther apart. "What happens when we're in bed is between us and no one else."

"You remember that all those around us are wolves. They will be able to hear most things even in the next cabin. They had better not talk about it, but they will hear at least part of what happens, especially if we do it right."

"So? I will tear anyone apart who says or does anything that disrespects you in any way, and I hope you'd do the same." Mikael added the last part in a hurry. It was hard for him to remember that if he was ever going to make things work with Denton, they had to be equals. Packs had one alpha, one leader, and generally an alpha mate who sometimes acted on the alpha's behalf.

"Of course I will." Denton tensed, and Mikael kissed him and then slid down his body, licking and sucking his way. He left a trail of small nips along the way that only inflamed Denton more, judging by the scent of arousal that increased with every passing second. He pressed Denton's legs apart, holding his thighs, and stared at his throbbing cock bouncing slowly up and down against Denton's belly.

"Fuck, you're beautiful," Mikael breathed as he raked his gaze up acres of golden pale skin that made Denton look like a god. Hell, as long as he was *his* god that was perfect. He licked up Denton's length, giving his wolf another taste of his mate. Mikael leaned forward and took him into his mouth. Denton tasted better the second time, primed with need and a good dose of want.

"So are you," Denton whispered. He might have tried to say more, but Mikael ran his tongue around the head of his cock, savoring him and at the same time reducing Denton to whimpers and groans. Those were the exact sounds he wanted to hear from his mate. Pleasure and nothing else. That's what Denton deserved, and Mikael intended to have him reduced to only the sounds of his wolf as often as possible.

Denton stiffened when Mikael let his cock slip from between his lips and licked down his shaft, nuzzling Denton's heavy balls and then to where his mate's scent was the strongest. Mikael licked toward his opening. Denton gasped and shivered when Mikael blew on his wet, sensitive skin. "I will never do anything that you aren't ready for, and it's too soon to claim each other." There were so many things still up in the air that going too far too fast would not be good, but that didn't mean Mikael had any intention of stopping. He wasn't a fool. He had every intention of making Denton wish they had gone further. He inhaled and then ran his tongue around Denton's opening, teasing the skin. Denton's high-pitched whine was almost too much, but Mikael went for it, probing Denton until he shook like a leaf in a summer breeze.

"Mikael," Denton gasped, shaking as he stroked himself. He raised his head, staring up Denton's body. His half-lidded eyes shone with passion. Damn, how long had Mikael waited for someone to look at him just that way? He couldn't remember, but that look went straight to his heart, and it would remain there for the rest of his life. Mikael had no doubt that the next time he was at home and alone in his own bed, that expression would be the one that would come to mind.

"Are you close?"

Denton nodded, and Mikael stilled Denton's hand, gently knocking it away before swallowing Denton's cock. He sucked and tightened his lips until Denton threw his legs over Mikael's shoulders.

Mikael saw the second Denton gave up the last of his control. He flopped back on the mattress, arms at his sides, and Mikael proceeded to suck Denton's brains out through his cock. The sort of trust that Denton had just displayed was rare in their world, and Mikael accepted it for the precious gift that it was. When Denton stiffened and his breathing became shallower, Mikael knew he was almost there. Mikael stroked up Denton's smooth belly to his nipples, tweaking each one until Denton cried out and sweet saltiness filled his mouth. Mikael swallowed greedily until Denton sighed and lay still on the mattress.

He let Denton slip from between his lips. Licking them, he grinned wickedly as he climbed Denton like a hill, bringing their lips together in a deep kiss that left him breathless. Denton was, without a doubt, an amazing kisser, and Mikael feasted on his lips. "Can you move?" Mikael asked proudly.

"Give me a minute," Denton responded. "You didn't wear me out that badly."

"Good to know. Next time I'll have to work a little harder." Mikael smoothed Denton's sweat-dampened locks away from his face so he could get a closer look at him.

"You really are trying to kill me."

"Oh no. I want you to remember this night for a very long time. And when I go home, I want you to spend every minute thinking about what we could be doing if we were together." Mikael pulled Denton into his arms and then rolled them on the bed. There was something comforting about having Denton on top of him, solidly weighing him down. "I'll protect and care for you, no matter what."

"How can you promise that?"

"My wolf knows, and he's an impeccable judge of character." Mikael pulled Denton down into a kiss. He knew enough not to push it. They were mates, and that meant if he was patient, things would work out. The Mother had told him so.

"If I said I wanted to claim you right now, would you let me?" Denton stroked lightly over Mikael's belly.

"Yes," he answered without hesitation, which seemed to catch Denton off guard.

"Have you ever... done that before?" Denton swallowed, and Mikael had his answer to the same question.

"No. But that doesn't matter. You're my mate, and that's all I need to know. Being with you like that would be an amazing experience because it's you. Coming together with you and having you claim me as yours would be a once-in-a-lifetime experience that I would never forget, so yeah, if you said you wanted me as your mate tonight, I'd let you claim me, and then I'd claim you. Then in the morning, you and I would figure out what we're going to do with two packs, two families, and all the responsibilities that go with that." Mikael gathered Denton into his arms, resting his chin on Denton's shoulder. "But I doubt either of us is that impetuous, and we're both good alphas who aren't willing to make our families pay in anxiety and upheaval for an impetuous act. Yes, I want you as my mate, but I also want you in my life for the long term, so I'm willing to take things slowly and make sure we understand how that could affect everyone in our lives."

"What if nothing ever comes of it?" Denton asked.

Mikael swallowed and rolled onto his side so Denton rested on the mattress. "If that's what you want, I'll have to learn to live with it." What a way to completely kill the mood. "Is that what you think you want?" The thought of rejection stung deep.

"I don't know." Denton moved closer, pressing to him. "Everything has changed very quickly, and I don't have all the answers. Right now I can say that yes, I want things to work out, but at what cost to my family?"

"Hey, I understand that. You know I do." Mikael sighed. Every time he got closer to Denton, it seemed there was another block added to the wall he needed to crawl over, and he'd hoped he'd torn some of those blocks down in the last hour.

"I know, and I'm not saying no. I'm saying we need to be careful and—" Denton kissed him, pressing Mikael back on the mattress. "I don't know what the future will bring. Can we be happy being together? Tonight I can guarantee to be with you all night long. After that we both need to go back to our lives and responsibilities." Denton straddled him, massaging Mikael's chest with his warm hands.

"Yes, we do, but even those can't rule our lives. My pack is important, as is yours, but our happiness is also important." Mikael pulled Denton down to him. "Why don't you show me some of that happiness." Mikael smiled and did his best to push aside the uncertainty that had crept into an otherwise remarkable night.

"Gladly," Denton told him with a sly grin and proceeded to make Mikael forget all about packs, family, worries, and everything else for quite a long time, and when Mikael fell asleep it was thanks to complete satiation and exhaustion.

HE WOKE in the morning with Denton pressed to him, a leg over his. Mikael hadn't slept this close to another person since he'd been a pup. It was comforting and felt dang good. "Are you awake?" Mikael asked, and Denton grumbled something before rolling over. "I'll take that as a no."

"Yes, I'm awake, but I don't want to be." Denton cracked his eyes open and sighed. "I was having the best dream, and now I think maybe it wasn't a dream."

"I'd like to think it wasn't." Mikael smiled and pressed Denton back on the mattress. "How about we see if I can refresh your memory."

"I'm all for that," Denton whispered as a knock sounded on the front door. Denton sighed once again, and Mikael moved away. It seemed the outside world had very different ideas.

"Mikael." Catherine's voice barely reached his ears. "I know you're in there. I followed your scent, and so can the rest of the pack. So I think the two of you...." She actually chuckled. "Forget it."

Mikael turned to Denton. He'd apparently heard part of what was said, but not all of it. "I think that was Catherine's way of warning us that if we don't want to be caught like this together, we'd better get up. Although if she followed my scent, then I think the rest of your pack will be able to as well."

"It doesn't matter. They're my pack, and we don't generally try to keep secrets from each other. They're definitely going to figure things out sooner rather than later." Denton shrugged and sat up, throwing his legs over the edge of the bed. "I think I'd better get up and see to things after last night's excitement."

Mikael was already getting out of bed as well. He gathered his clothes and began pulling them on. "Sometimes being the leader of a pack sucks. Just once I'd like to be able to sleep in." Denton leaned back, and Mikael caught him, holding him around the chest, gently stroking his skin. "This is so nice. I could really get used to this."

"That's the idea."

Denton nodded and said nothing. Mikael took that as progress. "Let's get started and see what Vadim can tell us." Denton stood, and Mikael found his gaze glued to Denton's back and, especially, that tight butt that bounced slightly with every step Denton took.

"You know, I really don't care about Vadim or other pack members, or frankly any fucking thing right now." Mikael got to his feet and forgot that he hadn't yet fastened his pants. They slid down his hips before he could grab them, and he nearly ended up flat on his face on the floor. Mikael caught himself and managed to latch his arms around Denton's waist.

"What got into you?" Denton asked, chuckling.

"You were waving this in front of my face, and I went for it." Mikael lightly patted Denton's butt.

"I know what kind of man you are."

"Damn right, and I'm proud of it, especially when the man in question has a rear end as statuesque as this one. You know, if I didn't know better, I swear you could have modeled for all those naked man statues in museums all over the world."

Denton glared at him for a few seconds and then broke into a grin. "Yeah, right."

"Come on. I'm a man who knows man butt, and I can tell you that yours is world-class." Mikael growled and pulled Denton closer, grabbing the butt in question and giving it a good squeeze. "Hard as a rock and... damn." He leaned his head against Denton's chest and inhaled deeply. "I love how you smell too, like the fresh outdoors mixed with wolf and man... all man."

"You're going to give me a big head."

Mikael doubted that was true, but a certain head was getting bigger, and Mikael took the opportunity to give it some very special attention that left them both breathless and made for a very good morning.

"WHAT'S THE plan?" Mikael asked as he and Denton strode toward the cabin where Catherine had spent the night watching over Vadim. He had instructed Catherine to contact their pack to let them know they were okay.

"I'm not sure, honestly. Let's see if Vadim can tell us anything, and we'll need to figure out what to do with him. I'm not sure it's a good idea for him to stay here."

"Probably not. Once we talk to him we can make some final decisions, but one of my pack members knows him, and he knows her, so maybe that would be a better fit." The truth was, he didn't have a much better answer than Denton. He wasn't interested in adding someone to his pack who might cause trouble, but it was also apparent that Vadim needed help, and so far Mikael was the only one who could get through to him. "Let's see what we can find out."

Denton nodded as they approached the cabin.

Catherine opened the door as they got close and stepped outside. "He's slept most of the night. I think he's been going and going for so long that he's completely worn out."

"Has he tried to return to his wolf form?" Denton asked.

"No. I think the longer he's in his human form, the more balanced he's getting. I'm sure the sleep is helping. I think his human was too exhausted to fight his wolf, if that makes any sense. I know we're one being and can change shapes, but…."

"I agree. It's like Vadim's human and wolf got partially split somehow." Mikael paused to think. "I know we need to spend time in both our forms in order to help maintain the balance in our lives, so it would make sense that if Vadim were somehow forced or coerced into maintaining his wolf form that his balance would get messed up. But the idea of one form being nearly lost is frightening."

"Let's talk to him," Denton suggested, and Catherine turned, leading them inside.

Vadim was curled up on the small bed, appearing even smaller than he had the night before. Under the blanket he seemed to be in a fetal position, his legs drawn toward his body, and other than the slow rise and fall with his breathing, he didn't move.

"I would have expected nightmares and some sort of internal struggle." Mikael stepped closer and sat in the chair near the bed. It was still warm from where Catherine had probably sat for the night. "Vadim," Mikael said as gently as he could. He didn't want to startle him awake. "I hope you've slept well."

Vadim moved and then sat straight up, staring blankly around him at first. He pulled the blanket up, using it as a shield. Mikael sat still and let the memories of what had happened come back to him.

"How are you feeling?' Denton asked from behind him. Mikael turned to glance at his mate and had to suppress the silly smile that threatened. "You're safe here."

"I g… guess I'm okay."

"Do you remember why you're here?"

"Last night. I was supposed to leave the deer and get away, but I got caught." Vadim's gaze shifted to each of them as though he wasn't sure who he should talk to. Then finally his gaze settled on Mikael.

"As you might imagine, we have a lot of questions. But I think the one we need an answer to is why did you come here?"

Vadim shrugged. "A group of us were supposed the leave the deer as far into your territory as we could. He didn't say why."

"Who?" Denton asked.

"Anton, my alpha, or...." Vadim lifted his gaze. "I'm not sure what he is. But he did this to me. I know that."

"What did he do to you?" Mikael asked.

"I don't know." Vadim held his head in his hands. "He did something and turned me into all wolf. It was like I wasn't there anymore." Vadim turned toward the wall. "The wolf was always in control, but it didn't even feel like my wolf. I mean, it was, but it wasn't. I know that doesn't make sense, because even I don't understand it, but that's how I felt. Then you knew my name and called to me, and I was able to make my wolf back down, and when I did that I got stronger and thought I could shift, and here I am."

Mikael shared a glance with Denton and then turned back to Vadim. "Has he done this to others?"

"I don't know. I wish I could help you, but I don't know. All I want is to go home. Can you call Gregor, my real alpha, and see if he'll let me come home?"

Mikael swallowed. "I'm sorry. Anton challenged him a few weeks ago and won."

"Oh. I was so out of it."

"Anna is a member of my pack now, and she's very concerned about you." Mikael glanced at Denton, who nodded. "Get some more rest, and once we figure a few things out, Catherine and I will take you back with us." Mikael stood. "Will you stay with him?" Mikael asked Catherine, who nodded, and then he and Denton stepped outside.

"What do you think?" Denton asked.

"It isn't likely Anton shared his plans with him. I suspect he knows more than he realizes, but after what he's been through, he needs a chance to settle and feel more like himself. Maybe then he'll be able to tell us more. But he did confirm my suspicion that Anton sees himself as the ruler of everything."

"He's delusional."

Mikael agreed with him there. "I'm wondering about the deer."

Kaiawa approached them. "We burned the deer last night as you suggested," He tilted his neck to Mikael, which Mikael found strange after the way Kaiawa had acted the day before. "It was infused with bad spirits, but they are gone now. When it cools, we'll spread the ashes like you said and give the deer's spirit back to the Mother."

"Good. Whatever Anton was trying to do doesn't seem to have worked." He wished to hell he could understand what was going on. "Do you have any insight?" Mikael asked Kaiawa, who shook his head.

"I appreciate your help. I think Catherine and I need to get back, but we'll keep an eye out, and you do the same. I'll share anything that happens. I'll also pass on any information that Vadim shares. I don't know how much that will be, but I'll communicate anything we find." Mikael knew it was time for them to leave, but he wasn't ready. He'd never be ready to leave his mate.

"Thanks," Denton said, and that was it. Mikael had hoped that he'd offer a chance for them to get together again, but Denton's expression seemed so closed. Kaiawa must have sensed the tension. There was no way he couldn't. He stepped away and then hurried across the compound. Mikael stared at Denton expectantly, crossing his arms over his chest.

"What do you want from me?" Denton whispered just above the breeze.

"I want…." Fuck, what did he want? Yeah, he wanted his mate to want him, but he'd be damned if he would beg Denton to accept him. When they had been together the night before, the connection had been undeniable. Mikael knew Denton felt it too. "Why does this have to be so hard?"

"I don't know. But it is, and there isn't anything either of us can do about it. Maybe we need some time to think and figure things out. I don't know, but I have to tell you I don't see a solution to this. You have your pack, and I have mine. Last night was…."

"Yes, it was, and this morning too."

Denton's cheeks reddened, and fuck if Mikael didn't grin like a satisfied teenager. "But it doesn't change anything."

"Maybe not. But there's also the fact that you're my mate, and we only get one," Mikael said. "So we both need to put our heads together—the big ones this time—and figure out what we can do." Mikael moved quickly until he was standing directly in front of Denton. He wound his arm around his waist and pulled him tight against him, their heat instantly mixing. "You can't tell me that the way you feel right now is anything other than amazing. All you have to do is touch me and I want you more than I've ever wanted anyone. You're strong, smart, purposeful, and the sexiest man I have ever seen. You are my mate, and I will have you in my life. So you figure out what it is I have to do so we can be together, and I'll do it. You are mine, and I am yours. The Mother said so, and I say so." Mikael stared deep into the oceanic blue of Denton's eyes. "From the way you're panting, you know what I'm saying is true." He challenged Denton to deny it. Denton quivered in his arms, and the hard bulge in his jeans spoke volumes.

"But...."

"You can argue and put up as many barriers as you like, but neither of us can fight this." Mikael closed his mouth over Denton's, and the energy he'd been talking about burst between them. Kissing Denton was like kissing an amazing live wire. There was no way he couldn't feel it. "That was just to give you something to think about while I'm gone." Mikael released him, and Denton took a step back. He stumbled slightly and caught his balance. Then, without a word, Mikael turned and went back to the small cabin.

"Are we ready to go?" Catherine asked, and Mikael nodded. "That was quite a display the two of you put on out there. You do realize that every one of Denton's pack members saw it. Not that there was much doubt about how the two of you spent the night. If you were staking your claim, you did a dang good job of it."

"I don't want to talk about that now," Mikael said. "We need to get back to the compound." Vadim stood up and stared at the two of them. Someone must have found clothes for him, because he now had on pants, a T-shirt, and a pair of sneakers. "Are you ready?" Mikael asked him. Vadim nodded shyly. "Then let's go."

"What about...." Catherine looked pointedly out past him. Mikael ignored her. He'd said his piece and showed Denton how he felt. There was nothing more he could do right now. The ball was in Denton's court, and Mikael understood that the only way he could possibly drive his point home was to leave. He leveled one of his hard alpha looks at her, and she grew quiet.

"Let's go." Mikael turned. He half expected to see Denton staring back at him. He'd felt him and was pretty sure that had been who Catherine had been looking at. Mikael left the cabin with Catherine and Vadim following behind. He walked toward the truck, thanking each person he met. If he were honest, he'd been looking for Denton, but he didn't see him until he approached the truck. Denton stood leaning against the bed, legs crossed.

"Were you not going to say good-bye?"

"Of course I was," Mikael answered with a smile.

"Look," Denton said as he came closer. "I don't know how anything is going to work, but I said before that I'd try, and I meant it. I really appreciate you coming."

"How about we take it one day at a time?" That was all Mikael could hope for, and he hoped like hell that Denton would miss him enough that something would change.

"Yeah." Denton smiled, and Mikael turned and got in the truck. He rolled down the window and waved as he pulled away from the compound and began the trip back to his own pack land.

"I know it's hard, but he'll come around," Catherine said over Vadim, who sat in the middle, after they'd nearly bounced their teeth loose driving out to the main road. "He's going to feel the same loss you do."

Mikael made the turn and let out a deep sigh. "How do you know?"

"I saw the way he looked at you." Catherine turned to look out the side window.

Mikael hoped she was right.

CHAPTER 6

"SO HOW is Vadim settling in?" Denton asked when he called a few days later. Mikael had spent much of that time up in his studio. It seemed to be the one place he could think and clear his mind. Karl and Catherine had told him more than once that he was grumpier than a bear in spring and pricklier than a porcupine. Even the pups were staying away from him.

"He's doing okay. He was able to shift into his 'real' wolf—the one he had been before Anton took control. Anna welcomed him and seems to spend almost as much time fussing over him as she does her boys. Apparently they think Vadim is pretty cool and have adopted him as a kind of big brother."

"Does he remember anything?"

"No. But I haven't pressed him. I think he needs time, and getting back to a normal life with people he knew as a human is probably best. At least I hope it is."

"Do you think he's still a threat?" Denton asked.

"I don't know. I've had everyone on the lookout for any gifts Anton might have sent our way, but we haven't seen anything."

"It's been quiet here too."

Mikael stepped off his stool and wandered over to the windows, instinctively looking toward Denton's pack land. He'd done that a lot lately, so much so that he knew every tree and contour of the land by heart, even better than he had before. "That's good. Catherine has the men walking patrols to keep our borders clearly marked."

"We're doing the same." Denton grew quiet. "I have to ask you something. Did anyone in your pack look at you differently when you got home?"

"Why, because I smelled like you?"

"Yeah."

"No. They know I prefer men, and they hoped I'd find my mate someday. My mother has been beating the bushes trying to get information, but Catherine will say nothing unless I allow her to, and right now I don't feel like talking."

"Why? Are you ashamed?"

Mikael coughed and nearly dropped the phone. "Fuck no. I don't talk about it because I don't want to try to explain what I don't fully understand. You are my mate, and I would call it from the highest peak if I could. But as you keep saying, it's complicated, so I just want fewer questions from my nosy and sometimes gossipy family. They smelled you on me, and I think Karl has an idea about us, but he too will keep quiet, or he knows I'll beat his ass into next week." Mikael stopped as a thought entered his mind. "Are you?"

"Sometimes. Of course the pack knows I was kissing you that morning, and they smelled you all over me. Kaiawa keeps looking like he wants to ask me something, but doesn't. The others act like everything is okay, but they won't say anything. I'm afraid they don't see me as much of a leader any longer."

"If you want them to see you as the leader, then take the bull by the horns. I'd call a pack meeting and find out what's wrong, if anything. They may just have questions." Mikael sighed. "You know you're allowed to have a life and a mate. You are the alpha, so be open with them, but let them know that who you spend your time with and allow to share your bed is your business. You want and promote their happiness, right?"

"Yeah."

"Then they should do the same thing for you," he said softly as hope sprang in his heart. If Denton was worried about his pack accepting him, then he had been thinking about Mikael as his mate. "That's what being part of a pack is all about."

"I know what a pack is," Denton retorted.

"I'm not saying you don't."

"You were only trying to help."

"Actually, what I'm saying is let them help you the same way you help them." It was a pretty simple concept to Mikael. His father had taught him that. One thing that was becoming clear to him was that

Denton had never had the example or the training that Mikael had been given. "They'll probably surprise you."

"Do you think so?"

"Of course. They're your family, and they love you as much as you love them. So tell them how you feel. You don't need to have all the answers."

"But you haven't told your family."

"I don't have to. I haven't talked to them about it, but they know from my scent and how growly I've been these past few days. And I'm sure my mother has been telling everyone that I'm in love and to give me time."

Denton gasped.

Mikael clamped his eyes shut and wanted to hit himself on the side of the head with his phone. This was not at all how he wanted to use the "L" word in front of Denton for the first time, but the words had just spilled out of his mouth. "I don't worry about what my mother says because no one can control her, not even me. But no matter what, I know everyone here has my back, and when I'm ready to tell them, they'll listen and be happy for me."

"Oh," Denton breathed. "So I shouldn't worry about it and just be honest with them."

"I think they already have half an idea about what is going on, so fill them in, and they'll be less likely to fill in the blanks on their own."

"All right, I'll think about it."

Mikael smiled. He knew that was as close to an agreement as he was going to get from Denton. Mikael wanted to help him, but he didn't want to undermine Denton's authority or his confidence. Being a pack alpha was a tough job, and being a good one was difficult as hell. Often the needs of the pack came before the needs of the alpha—it was just the nature of the job and something his father had made sure Mikael understood well.

"So how is work?"

"Not bad. We had all that rain, and now it seems the waterworks have turned off completely, just like we were all afraid of. So in a week or so everything is going to start to get very dry, especially if these hot temperatures continue."

"How do you handle that?"

"Most of us will go on fire patrol starting next week. The key is to try to catch any fire before it gets out of hand. That huge one in 1988 that burned large sections of the park taught us all a major lesson. The policy at the time was to let fires burn, but they also didn't let nature manage the forests, so they allowed a buildup of dead wood and then could do nothing when it caught fire. I hope our packs have learned from that experience."

"My dad told me about that fire. The pack managed to survive but lost just about everything. After the fire, the pack had to rebuild from scratch. Granted, there wasn't much because of the way we had to live at the time, but still…. Dad always said we were lucky to get away with our lives. I was just a baby at the time, so I don't remember it."

"The stories of that fire were why I became a ranger. The fire burned some areas and left others unaffected. My pack was lucky, and their homes, such as they were, were spared. But they had to hide even more because a lot of the wooded areas they used for cover were gone. So now I help protect the park and the forests."

"I have to say it fits you."

Denton chuckled softly. "I do love it. So how is your painting coming?"

"I finished the portrait of Gregor and started something new."

"I'd really like to see your work sometime," Denton said.

"Then why don't you come over here and pay us a visit? I know my mother is dying to meet you." Mikael figured he needed to explain. "You are welcome to visit anytime, and I would love to show you around. But once you do, my pack is going to know all about you and me. They won't be able to keep from asking questions."

"And you still want me to come?"

"Definitely. Catherine will be thrilled that the cat's out of the bag." And the rest of his pack would be thrilled for him, he knew. Denton would also see that they were happy for him.

"You're serious?"

"Of course. I can show you all the pieces I'm working on and give you a tour around our pack land. They're similar to yours, but there are some gorgeous places I'd like to take you." His mind was already making a list of the places that were particularly special for him. "When do you want to come?"

"Is next week okay? I have to work through the weekend."

"Sounds great." Mikael's excitement grew. At least there was a plan in place for seeing Denton again. He heard small but quick footsteps in the house. "I think I need to go, but I'll talk to you tomorrow. Have a great day at work." The footsteps got closer, hurrying up toward the studio steps.

"Alpha Mikael, are you up there?"

"Yeah. You better go." Denton was still laughing as he hung up.

"Yes, Alexi." Mikael put his phone in his pocket as the pup raced into the studio. "What can I do for you?"

"Mama said she needs you."

Mikael scooped him into his arms and headed for the stairs. "Did she say why?" He was about to put him on his shoulders and begin to play, but Alexi squirmed to get down.

"She said Vadim is trying not to change into a wolf. Why would that be bad? I change into a wolf all the time. Wanna see?"

"Not right now." He held Alexi tighter and ran down the stairs and out of the house. He made it across the compound to Anna's and opened the door.

"Thank goodness you're here," Anna said. "Vadim tried to change into a wolf. He changed back, but now he says something or someone is trying to pull him back into his wolf form." She pointed toward the back door. "He rushed outside when he felt it, I think to protect me and the boys." She pushed open the door. "Stay here with your brother and lock the door."

"But, Mama, I wanna see."

"No, Alexi. Stay with your brother," Mikael said in his alpha voice. He closed the door, and Anna led Mikael around the back of the cabin to where Vadim lay on the ground.

"What's happening?" Mikael asked Vadim.

"He's pulling me to shift into the wolf again. Not my wolf, but the one I was before. I can feel him."

"It's all right. You have the power to be who you want, and no one can make you do anything. So tell him no." Mikael placed his hand on Vadim's shoulder to help maintain a connection with him.

"He says he's my alpha, and I have to do what he says."

"Is he your alpha, or am I your alpha?" Mikael asked and stared into Vadim's eyes. "You need to choose once and for all where your loyalties lie. When you do, scream it in your head, and he'll get the message." Mikael squeezed lightly and pulled his hand away. He stepped back, pulled out his phone, and made a call. "Denton," he said quietly, when Denton answered. "There's been a development, and I think you and probably Kaiawa need to get over here. It's Vadim. Somehow Anton is trying to control him." Mikael watched Vadim writhe on the ground. "I'm going to give you Catherine's number. She can give you directions."

"Okay. I take it he's struggling."

"Yes, and I need to help him."

"Go," Denton said. Mikael rattled off Catherine's number and then hung up, returning his full attention to Vadim.

"You need to tell him."

"I have but he won't stop. The wolf is so close, and he wants out," Vadim said between gritted teeth.

"That wolf isn't you. The one you changed into for Alexi and Misha is you. Not this one. Your wolf is the one you remember as a pup. The one you explored the world with. He's part of you. This other wolf isn't yours." Mikael knelt and once again placed his hand on Vadim's shoulder. "I need you to call on your wolf so he can help you drive this one away."

"This is my wolf, Alpha," Vadim said and then groaned before lying still. Mikael wasn't sure if the danger was over or not. Then Vadim groaned again, the sound turning into a cry that echoed off the surrounding hills. "You are not my alpha!" The last word repeated over and over.

"I am your alpha, and you can fight this. You're strong enough to let your wolf live and be in control. This other wolf needs to go, and you can send him away."

"I know, Alpha," Vadim said and began to shift. Mikael backed away slightly, wondering just what kind of wolf he was going to encounter, the docile one he'd seen once Vadim began to emerge or the rabid one he'd encountered in the cage when they first met.

"What's going on?" Karl asked as he raced up. "I heard the cry. Was he yelling at you?" Karl's teeth had already elongated, and he was seconds from shifting.

"No. He was yelling at Anton, fighting to keep him from taking over." Mikael didn't take his eyes off Vadim as he finished shifting. The wolf was gray and small, but when he stood, he blinked at Mikael and approached slowly, tilting his head in respect. "I think he won, and we have a new pack member." Mikael stroked Vadim's back. "Anna, thank you."

"I didn't do anything."

"You stayed with him and sent for me." Mikael smiled at her, and she mustered a smile back, but her eyes showed no joy whatsoever. The back door of her cabin opened, and a few seconds later two pups raced out to her. They stopped next to her, sniffed, and then took off to Vadim, pouncing on him in playful abandon. Anna appeared concerned, but Vadim lay down and lightly played back.

"Do you think they're okay?" she asked, and Mikael saw how tired she was.

"Yes. He made his decision, and once Anton got the message, there was nothing he could do. He's lost control of him. Not that he really had any to begin with. He ruled Vadim through fear and guilt, and when he rejected those things, Anton's hold was gone."

"How did you know?"

"I didn't. I just hoped he was strong enough to fight him," Mikael admitted. "Now you," he began, "need to start sleeping and taking a little time for yourself."

Anna scoffed without heat. "I have two boys. When am I supposed to sleep?"

"When they do," Mikael told her. "I know it's damned hard, but you need to take care of yourself for them." He moved closer and took her hands. "Gregor would want that, and so do the rest of us. Stan and Catherine will watch your boys, and I bet that once Vadim gets stronger, he will too." Tiny growls caught his attention, and he turned to Alex and Misha facing off.

"That's enough, you two. Go back inside and shift. Your mother needs you to have some quiet time, and Vadim needs to rest too."

The pups looked at each other and then back at Mikael before slowly padding off into the house. "But I don't wanna take a nap. They're for babies," Misha said a few seconds later and then appeared naked in the doorway. "Mama, I don't want a nap."

"Get your clothes back on, and you can sit quietly and watch a video. Your mama needs a rest and so does Vadim. So you need to watch over them, okay?"

"Yes, Alpha," Misha said, mollified. Then he turned and went back inside.

Mikael rolled his eyes. "Go get some rest if you can."

"I'll try." Anna seemed skeptical.

"If they don't behave, then I'll send Catherine over in full enforcer mode. That's enough to scare anyone into behaving. Believe me." Mikael winked, and Anna smiled more broadly.

"What about Vadim?"

"He's going to spend some time with me this afternoon. He and his wolf need to reconnect, so he can stay in that form for a while. I have some things to do, and then it seems we are going to have company." Mikael released her hands and turned back to Vadim. "Come with me." He turned and headed toward his own place. He held the door for Vadim and motioned toward the great room. Vadim looked around and made his way toward one of the pillows Mikael kept near the fireplace. Often during the winter, they would build a fire, and many would come in wolf form to settle near the fire's warmth to nap.

Vadim settled on one of the thick pillows and curled up in a ball. He huffed a few times and looked at him until Mikael sat down in one of the chairs. Only then did Vadim close his eyes. Mikael figured he might as well rest too. He was going to need it.

He didn't actually sleep and heard the jeep coming down the drive long before it pulled to a stop. Mikael slowly stood and walked over to the door, opening it for Denton and Kaiawa as they got out. Mikael stepped out of the house to meet them.

"What's going on?" Kaiawa demanded.

Mikael grabbed him around the throat, his hand shifting as he moved. "You don't make demands here—not on my territory and certainly not in front of your alpha. You disrespect him and you disrespect me." Mikael moved closer. "I could rip your throat out before you take your next breath. Do you understand me?" Mikael released him, and Kaiawa leaned his head to the side. "That's better." Mikael hated that Kaiawa didn't seem to know his fucking place. What bothered him even more was Denton's either inability or reluctance to show it to him. But they were in his territory now, and Mikael didn't have to hold back. He turned and motioned for Denton to come inside. He didn't care where Kaiawa went at the moment. Mikael made sure he closed the door before the other wolf stepped inside.

"Vadim is in here," Mikael said, leading Denton to the great room.

"I wasn't expecting to come here so soon," Denton said, looking back toward the front windows.

"You don't need to worry about Kaiawa. Karl or Catherine will already have scented him, so he won't be alone for very long. They'll also scent where I touched him, and they're smart enough to figure out why." He said no more as they entered the great room. Vadim was on all fours, watching both of them.

"I think you better shift back to your human and then tell both of us what happened," Mikael told Vadim. He grabbed the blanket off the back of the sofa and placed it near him. When Vadim hesitated, Mikael stared at him. Soon Vadim's bones reconfigured, and he slowly transformed. He picked up the blanket and wrapped it around his shoulders. "You remember Denton, the alpha from the Evergreen pack."

Vadim nodded and showed the proper respect. "I don't know anything."

"You probably know more than you realize. But I think we need to start with what happened to you when you left Gregor's pack two years ago. Because this isn't the snarling beast we captured a week or so ago," Mikael prompted.

"I was stupid," Vadim said and slowly sat on the edge of the far sofa cushion. Mikael sat on the other side and offered Denton the leather chair he usually used. "I thought I knew how to do things better than Alpha Gregor. I was too small to challenge him, so I left. I figured I could do better on my own. I didn't. I was hungry all the time, and I had to stay off pack land, so I didn't know where the good hunting areas were."

"Is that when you met Anton?"

"Sort of. I met one of his men, Clyde. He's a beta, I guess. He took me in and made sure I got fed. He was really nice to me and seemed to watch out for me." Vadim turned away and color rose to his cheeks.

"There is nothing to be ashamed of with us. We need you to be honest."

"I thought he loved me."

Mikael turned to Denton for a second, sharing a knowing expression, and then he returned his attention to Vadim. "We aren't going to judge you for something like that. Secrets and guilt have a way of leading us to their brothers, desperation and recrimination. We've all met them at one point or another."

"Well, after a month or so, he introduced me to Anton, who liked me. He treated me well and included me in what he was doing. I felt important being in the alpha's circle. He even listened to me and gave me advice. He said I was a much fiercer wolf than I was a human and if I wanted to advance, I could do it that way. So I started shifting and staying shifted."

"How did he gain such a hold on you?"

"I don't know. He asked me to do things for him, and I did. Now I know they were bad things. I'd bring messages to people like the ones I brought to you. I never hurt anyone unless they threatened me, and I never killed. I know that."

"But you really don't remember much, do you?" Denton pressed.

"It's like it's in the shadows." Vadim drew the blanket more closely around him.

"Okay. Don't worry about it. That's all in the past, and you know to be responsible for your own actions now."

"I wish I'd stayed and listened to Gregor," Vadim whispered.

Denton shifted in his chair, leaning forward. "None of us can change the past. All we can do is learn from it and make the most of our future." Denton glanced at him, and Mikael wondered if Denton's words were meant for Vadim or him. They fit either way, but with very different meanings.

"Do you know anything about Anton's background?"

Vadim shook his head and then stopped, staring at them blankly. "I don't know if it's real or not. He told me a story when I first met him. He said that he and I were a lot alike. That he understood what it was like to be under an alpha who didn't value him, just like I thought Gregor didn't think much of me." A tear ran down Vadim's face. "I was a stupid kid. I left the one person who really did care for me, and I ended up in the lair of the devil because of it."

"That's over now. You're here, and you can help us. Anton has taken over pack after pack, and the message you were supposed to bring was the first salvo in gaining another one."

"I don't know anything about that."

Mikael wasn't surprised. Anton had thought Vadim was completely under his influence, so he wouldn't have shared plans with him. He would have simply told Vadim what he wanted and expected it to be carried out. What Anton had not counted on was Vadim being apprehended. "It's all right. Tell us what Anton told you about himself."

"He said he came from a pack where the alpha was this old guy who had been the leader for a long time. His mom and dad were members but nothing special. Anton apparently thought he should be one of the betas or even the alpha apparent. He said he was strong and capable, and the alpha was old. Anton thought the pack should be run by the strongest person and wanted the alpha to make changes. But he didn't, and the pack members backed the alpha and even said they'd stand in if he was challenged. Anton challenged him anyway. Anton said he took mercy on the guy and agreed to leave for the pack."

"I doubt that. My guess is that he got his clock cleaned and was forced to back down. At that point he was most likely told to leave as well."

"Anton said the alpha was weak, and when he was on his own, he grew stronger and founded his own pack." Vadim lifted his gaze from his feet. "He said that he took over that old pack as soon as he could and didn't stop until there was nothing left of the alpha. At the time, I remember thinking that they got what they deserved, but I don't know anymore."

"Did he say where the pack was?"

"Montana," Vadim answered.

"That has to have been Alpine," Denton said and glanced at Mikael, who nodded. It certainly sounded like them.

"It could be. I haven't had a lot of contact with other packs, but that fits what I know." If so, Anton's reach was quite large.

"That's all I can remember."

103

"It's all right. Go get dressed and get some rest. You've been through a lot."

"But what if Anton tries again?"

"You know how to get him to back off—you did it once, and you can do it again. All you need to do is remember who you are and that he can't have you. Your life is your own, and while he tried to suppress your free will, he didn't take it away. Now that you're aware of him and what he was doing, he's lost his hold."

Vadim didn't look convinced, but he stood and quietly left the room after acknowledging each of them.

"He seems like a scared sheep," Denton said.

"He is, and that's part of why Anton was able to get his hooks into him so deeply, but I keep wondering how. The story Anton told him was obviously highly embellished and altered to make Anton seem like the one in the right. There's a framework of truth there, but the lies are wrapped around it."

"Why do you think it's important?"

"Because Anton is a riddle, and if he's to be defeated, and I'm beginning to think he has to be in order for any of us to be safe, we need to figure out that riddle. I think his background is important."

"How?" Denton asked.

"I don't know. But there has to be a starting place, and this is all we have." Mikael paused and leaned closer to Denton, lowering his voice. "The last time the Mother spoke to me when she said that I was going to meet my mate soon, she said that only the two of us together could defeat him. When I asked her why she was taking my side against one of her children, she said Anton wasn't of the light. Then you brought up dark wolves, and I really think Anton is one. That deer on your lands wasn't just a message. It was some sort of sacrifice to the dark ones—it had to be."

"Where are you getting all this? You said those are just stories."

"I've changed my mind. You didn't see the way the Mother looked when she told me these things. She was concerned, and the Mother doesn't do anything lightly."

"So she made us mates to take out Anton?"

"No. We were born mates. I don't think even she has that much power. I was taught that the Mother is more like a caregiver. She makes sure all the forces of nature continue to work in harmony with each other, and she just chose to give us a push toward each other. Otherwise it wasn't likely we would ever really meet. It isn't as though packs have a great deal to do with each other."

"I keep wondering how you can be so sure of everything."

Mikael chuckled. "I was taught that a mate was the best thing we could hope for. That when I met my mate, I would know, and he would be what I needed, my other half. I tend to be rash and often react physically, but you think things through and go more slowly. Patience isn't something I have in great supply. When I see something I want, I go for it." He slowly got to his feet and took small steps toward where Denton sat. He worked his feet between Denton's feet, leaning slowly over him. Mikael put his hands on the back of the chair, and it reclined. Denton stiffened, and Mikael leaned closer. "I don't have to touch you to make your body react to me." He inhaled, and Denton's arousal came through loud and clear. "I knew how I was affecting you the minute I stepped outside the house, and I'm willing to bet Kaiawa smelled it too. I also think he knows you're my mate."

"How do you know?"

"Our scents will start to change as we get closer." To emphasize his point, he leaned in, bringing his lips to Denton's without actually touching them. "I think they already are."

"So what do we do about our packs?"

"I think as we spend time together and our families start to get used to us that something will present itself and make the decision obvious." Mikael knew what he wanted. If he had his way, he'd have Denton move here, and then he'd figure out how to meld the packs together, but he knew he shouldn't push. Packs merged through challenge, but rarely on their own, and he doubted there had ever been a pack merger because the two alphas turned out to be mates. "I think what's truly important is keeping our packs healthy and prosperous while we figure things out."

"So... what?"

"We see each other and date each other like any other couple." Mikael touched Denton's lips with his. He loved his taste. Denton slid his hand around the back of his neck, pulling him closer, deepening the kiss. When it came to being intimate, Mikael seemed to be the one initiating, but when Denton took the lead, it was awesome.

"Alpha Mikael," Alexi called. The back door closed and little footsteps ran through the house.

Mikael huffed and held his temper. "You need to learn to knock, pup," he told him when Alexi bounded into the room and skidded to a stop.

"Sorry, Alpha." Alexi looked down and shifted from foot to foot. "There's a strange man walking around in back. He's a wolf like us, I smelled him, but I don't know who he is, and Mama always said I should tell you if I see a stranger I don't know."

Mikael had already straightened up. "You did very well, and your mama is right." Mikael held out his hand. He wasn't going to dissuade anyone from raising the alarm when they found a stranger in the compound.

"He's a stranger too." Alexi looked at him. "Were you kissing a stranger?"

"This is Alpha Denton, and he isn't a stranger. I know him, and I think the other stranger is Beta Kaiawa. But let's go see."

"It isn't like Kaiawa to wander in someone else's territory," Denton said as they walked out of the great room and through the unusually quiet kitchen to the back door. Mikael stepped out.

"That's him," Alexi stage-whispered and pointed to where Kaiawa and Vadim sat on the steps of Anna's cabin, talking quietly.

"It's okay. I know him. He came along with Alpha Denton," Mikael told Alexi.

"He looks different," Alexi whispered again.

"Maybe, but we don't judge others by how they look." Mikael knelt down, releasing Alexi's hand. "I want you to go find your mama and brother."

"Are you mad?" Alexi asked, pushing out his lower lip.

"No. You did what your mom told you." He smiled and sent Alexi on his way. "And you should always listen to your mom. Now go find her." Mikael added the last part in a whisper, and Alexi then hurried away. After a few seconds, Alexi called for his mother, zooming past Vadim and Kaiawa as he raced indoors.

The two men ended their conversation, and Vadim wandered toward the edge of the compound while Kaiawa approached Mikael and Denton. He showed his neck to both of them before facing Mikael. "When we found him he had the taint of blackness about him, but he doesn't anymore. He told me what you did to help him."

Mikael nodded but said nothing, sensing that Kaiawa had more he wanted to say.

"He has a long way to go yet. The darkness took away a lot of what was in him. It will take a lot of time for him to find his way all the way back."

"What do you mean?" Mikael asked.

"Kaiawa sometimes talks in riddles," Denton explained.

"Those who are touched by the darkness... it gets into their soul. The darkness is gone, but its impression and effect can last for much longer. The darkness is gone, but it has left a stain on his spirit, and that he will need to work through. I was just telling him that he needs to be patient and relearn what it is that will make him happy. It won't be easy because the darkness took away part of him and then took its place. Now he seems empty because nothing has moved back in to fill the emptiness."

Mikael nodded. "I appreciate you trying to help him."

"This is something he needs to do for himself."

"Have you encountered this darkness before?"

"Besides what he brought with him? Yes. When I was a child I sensed it once, but then it went away. My grandmother used to tell me about the dark ones and how I should watch out for them, but thought they were just stories."

"We all did. But now I think we're learning that isn't the case," Denton said.

"Kaiawa," Karl said as he strode over to join them. They shook hands somewhat warily. "Is there something you needed from him?" Karl asked Mikael, who shook his head. "Then how about you and I have a beer?"

"Okay," Kaiawa agreed and followed Karl across the compound while Mikael turned, smiled at Denton, and took his hand.

"Come on. I have something I want to show you." Mikael led him to the edge of the compound. "We need to shift." Mikael pulled off his shirt, kicked off his shoes, and loosened his pants, letting them slide down his legs. He shifted immediately and then turned toward Denton, waiting for him to do the same. *What are you waiting for?*

"You know it's creepy when you talk to me without moving your lips. And you're in wolf form." Denton let his shirt drop to the ground, and Mikael trotted over to him. He sat and watched as the remainder of Denton's clothes fell to the ground. He blinked at how beautiful Denton was, a honey-gold god of a man. Mikael yipped when Denton stopped to stare at him.

"What?"

You said it was creepy when I talked to you, so I was telling to you hurry the hell up or I'm going to lunge for you. Mikael yipped again for emphasis, and Denton shifted into a white wolf. Mikael had never seen another wolf that color, as white as the snow. *Does everyone in your family have wolves like that?* Denton blinked at him and shook his head. *Okay, you can tell me later.*

Mikael took off and heard Denton behind him. He was laughing in his head, knowing Denton could hear him. He paused at the creek, which was low. He drank and waited for Denton to do the same before swimming across and bounding out onto the opposite shore. He took off as soon as Denton caught up, laughing again in the throes of wolfish joy and playfulness.

Denton nipped at his heel. *Is that your way of saying to go faster?* Mikael knew there would be no answer, but took off full speed with Denton falling a little ways behind. He slowed to jump over a fallen log, sailing through the air. Yeah, he was showing off, but what the hell. Denton was his mate, and he was damned happy. He skirted thickets and briars, taking a roundabout way. *We're going to the meadow. It's one of the Mother's sacred spots. I'll show you why when we get there.* Mikael continued and made a fast turn. Denton was just far enough back that he couldn't see him. When Denton caught up, Mikael pounced on him, tackling him playfully. They rolled together for a few seconds, and then Mikael took off again. *We're almost there.* He laughed and then came to a stop. Denton walked up, tongue lolling and stopped next to him. *This is it.*

He slowly entered the meadow, stepping out from the line of trees. The land stretched out flat and clear for a long way. The creek meandered through, splitting into two and creating an island before joining once again to go on its way. A single tree broke the sight line, growing in the center of the island—an oak as old as the land itself, gnarled and twisted with years of weather and life, but it stood strong and proud.

The sun beat down on them as soon as they stepped out of the protection of the shade, its warmth immediately soaking through his coat. Mikael followed the creek and then waded across to the island and the shade of the tree. *This is the Mother's representative for us.* Mikael sat down in the grass, the breeze rustling the leaves overhead. Denton sat next to him, and Mikael turned to him, licked his nose, and then rubbed against him. He loved his wolf and the senses it brought him. The scent of everything in the meadow mixed together in a heady bouquet that filled him with joy. And his mate was here with him, alone, just them.

Mikael pressed harder, pushing Denton onto his side. He stood over him, nuzzling his neck and belly. He wanted him so badly that it took his human restraint to keep his wolf from mounting Denton and taking what he wanted.

He stepped back and huffed, shaking his head and then his entire body before changing his train of thought. Within seconds, he stood in the shade of the tree as a man, looking down at Denton's wolf. He moved closer, carding his fingers through his coat. "You are the most beautiful thing I have ever seen, in wolf or human form." He leaned closer, running his cheek over Denton's coat before burying his nose in his fur. He smelled the same, maybe a little earthier than he did in human form, but he was most definitely Denton.

Energy surged through Denton, and Mikael released him. Denton shifted and stood in front of him in all his human, excited glory. Mikael grinned and pulled Denton to him, entwining his legs with his, bringing their hips together. "God, I want you," he whispered into Denton's ear before sucking the lobe between his lips. "Forever, you are mine. Can you feel it?"

"I feel something big and hard poking at my belly."

Mikael chuckled. "I mean can you feel the energy in this place? It's coursing through me right now." Mikael kissed Denton hard, guiding him down onto the carpet of soft grass.

"I can," Denton answered breathlessly before returning his kiss with increased passion.

Mikael continued kissing Denton until he quivered. Then he pulled away and slowly licked down his luscious body, taking in all of his mate. He nipped a few places, just hard enough to leave a mark. Mikael purposely avoided Denton's neck because if he started, he wouldn't be able to stop. When he reached Denton's belly, he moaned softly and then slowly sucked Denton's cock between his lips.

"Mikael!" Denton yelled, the cry filling the meadow in an instant.

"I know." He held Denton's ankles, taking him deep before releasing him and carefully lifting his legs. He pressed Denton's knees to his chest and buried his face between his perfect cheeks, probing deep at Denton's entrance. Denton moaned, and Mikael ran his hands over the smooth skin of Denton's ass. God, the man felt good everywhere. Mikael teased Denton's puckered entrance, laving at the skin until Denton swore and cursed between gritted teeth.

His moans quickly grew louder and more frantic while Mikael feasted on his trembling mate. Mikael loved everything about him and was determined to show him just how much.

"I want you, Mikael... now!"

"Are you sure?" Mikael rasped and then blew over Denton's wet skin.

"Fuck yes, I'm sure," Denton growled at him.

Mikael grinned and went back to driving his mate wild. He loved that Denton shook and even beat the ground as he seemed to lose part of himself. Mikael knew as an alpha that remaining in control was important to Denton, but Mikael wanted him to trust him and give his pleasure over to him. Mikael lifted his head, meeting Denton's gaze, seeing his eyes roll and darken. He continued rimming him until Denton gasped for breath. Then and only then did he back away and slowly get into position. He ran his fingers down Denton's cleft before breaching him. Denton's body gripped him like a vise, and Mikael prepared him as best he could before lubricating himself with spit and pressing his cock to his entrance.

He held still, cock throbbing, wolf pressing him forward, but Mikael held back. All instinct told him to enter his mate and claim him as his. Instead he remained still. "Is this what you really want?" Mikael whispered, leaning over Denton and kissing him ravenously before he could answer.

"Yes," Denton answered when Mikael released his mouth.

Mikael pressed forward, his gaze glued to Denton's, watching his eyes deepen and then shift as his cock breached Denton for the first time. It was Mikael's turn to be short of breath. The heat and pressure were nearly overwhelming. He slowly sank into Denton and then stilled, inhaling deeply, surrounding himself in Denton's aroused scent, which only added to the bubble of heat that seemed to cocoon them. He stroked up Denton's chest, smooth skin flowing under his hands. "You look so good right now." Mikael flicked his hips just slightly, and Denton groaned. Yeah, he'd found the right spot. Mikael did it again, and Denton arched his back.

"What the hell was that?" he demanded, hissing as he inhaled. "Am I supposed to feel this full?"

"Oh yeah." Mikael kissed him. "You're full of me, and it's perfect. You're perfect."

"You're just saying that because your dick is buried in my ass."

"No," Mikael countered, slowly withdrawing and holding still just inside. "I'm saying that because it's true." He slid home, filling Denton once again, his eyes shifting back to human and then once again to the amber eyes of his wolf. "You know it too."

"How can you fucking tell?"

"Because I can see your eyes shift, and I bet your teeth are elongating too. You're losing control." Mikael kept his movements slow, listening to and watching each of Denton's reactions. The warm breeze blew over them, but Mikael hardly noticed, his attention so fully on his mate. "I love it, and you can trust me, so let yourself go. Allow yourself to feel what it's like to be held in the hands of your mate without worry. There are no packs, no families to be concerned with, just you and me." He withdrew and kissed Denton hard as he slowly slid back into his searing heat. "God," he whispered against Denton's lips. "You amaze me."

"Me… amaze you?" Denton pulled him down into another kiss. "You blow me away." Mikael loved the sound of that. He wound his arms around Denton, thrusting deeper, loving on him with everything he had. Denton was his mate, and Mikael damn near let the last threads of control slip away. He licked and sucked at the base of Denton's neck, tasting the sweet skin and wanting to go further.

Mikael pulled away and arched his back, looking down at Denton, watching as sweat glistened on his golden skin. It shimmered in the changing light from the sun dappling through the leaves. There had never been anyone more enthralling or more dear to him, and he had to show him. Denton needed to know how much he wanted him, cared for him, and hell, loved him, even if Mikael was reluctant to say the words.

"I can't last much longer," Denton begged, stroking his long, perfect dick.

Mikael swallowed hard. "Then don't. Give me what you have. I want it all, everything. Come apart in my arms and let me cradle and hold you." Mikael thrust faster and harder, the need for release building faster than he'd ever thought possible. "Give it all to me!"

"I am. I will," Denton cried as his eyes shifted once again and his ears changed to his wolfen ones. Mikael never thought anything could be so sexy, and he nearly came at that moment, but he was determined to wait for Denton. That was more important, and within seconds, Denton gasped and stiffened before coming in white ropes on his smooth, pale skin. Mikael followed right behind, the pressure of Denton's body around him too much to bear.

He stilled and pulled air into his lungs before turning his head toward the sky, howling his unfettered joy for all to hear. When the sound tapered off, he gasped for breath and then did it again. Then he looked down at Denton, seeing his smile. "I'm glad I made you so happy." His eyes and ears were back to normal, and his eyes shone. Mikael knew it was for him, and he wanted to howl again, but instead he leaned close. He slipped from inside Denton's body as their lips touched. They both shivered. Mikael gathered Denton into his arms, holding him as tight as he could while they basked in the warm summer afterglow.

"Do you think it's okay that we did this here?" Denton asked as they still lay together. "If it's a sacred spot, then what if we did something wrong?"

"We didn't. Making love is never wrong, and I brought you here on purpose. The Mother is here, and making love, showing how much her gifts mean to us, is the best way to honor her." Mikael knew she'd been here in the breeze and rustle of the leaves, but he kept that part to himself. "Finding a mate is special. The only thing better would have been to make the bond permanent. But we'll know when the time is right."

"My pack members told me that I've been nearly impossible for the last few days. I was snappy and very short-tempered." Denton moved closer. "There were times when my stomach ached, and nothing ever makes us sick, you know that."

"I do. It's being away from your mate. The only time we feel really bad is when our human and wolf aren't in tune with each other. Your wolf has met his mate, and he wants him. Your wolf, just like mine, knows his mate, so he aches for him. I'm sure that Karl and Catherine would tell you that I've been a major pain in the ass these last few days. Even the pups have stayed away from me."

Denton nodded. "So what do we do? I don't want to be without you any longer. But I have responsibilities and so do you." Denton sighed. "I need to speak to my pack. They need to know what's going on and how I feel. I can't keep this from them."

"Is there anyone who can step up as alpha?" Mikael asked.

Denton stared at him, wide-eyed. "I should have known. I was going to ask you the same question. Why should I be the one to give up my pack? I worked hard, and I care about my family just as much as you care for yours. But I'm supposed to give up my pack and come live with you."

Mikael had tried to be sensitive to Denton's feelings, but there was no question in Mikael's mind. "Yes."

"Why?"

"Because I'm the stronger of the two of us," Mikael answered levelly, wondering why Denton didn't see it.

"So? Why should I give up everything because my mate is stronger than I am?" Denton sat up and then pulled away. "I should have known you had some ulterior motive in all of this. Let me guess, once I was part of your pack, you'd challenge the new alpha of Evergreen and take it over."

"Denton," Mikael said as reasonably as he could. "You know that's not true. If you listen to your heart, you know I'd never do that.

I'm being practical. Wolf society is still very primal, and you have to admit that I'm the stronger wolf. That doesn't mean you're less of a wolf or a man. I love your strength, but…." He didn't know how else to put it. "You know that if I were to leave my pack and join yours, all of the pack members would sense my strength, and eventually, whether we wished it or not, they would see me as the leader. It's how wolf society works, you know that."

Denton nodded and turned away. "I'm sorry. I know you would never do anything to hurt me or my family. But… I can't leave my family rudderless. They have already been through so much." Denton turned toward the tree, looking up to the leaves. "I like leading my pack. They mean the world to me, and unlike you, I didn't become alpha because my father died. I had to fight for my position, and I'll fight to keep it." Denton whirled back around.

"I won't fight you," Mikael said. "I don't want to take anything away from you." But dammit, he wanted Denton with him. The Mother had warned him that he'd need to persevere, but he hadn't expected things to be this difficult once he'd found his mate. They were ordained by the gods themselves. They were to meet and would be right for each other.

"But that's what you're doing. My pack and my family."

"You'd be an alpha of my pack. The alpha mate carries the status of their mate, you know that. There would be no reduction in status."

"Except that you'd be the alpha and I would be your mate. I'm an alpha in my own right. I lead and care for my pack. If I came to live with your pack, you'd do all that, and I'd just be the alpha's mate. I won't… I can't." Denton sat back down. "I wouldn't be happy, and you and I would fight because I'd want to make decisions that should be yours." Denton lifted his head to the tree. "If the Mother is watching us, then she'll need to help figure this out. If we're truly supposed to be together, then there has to be a solution that I don't see."

There was the possibility of merging the packs together. Mikael had thought about that, but the logistics would be even worse. There would be so much fighting and jostling for position. For a second, Mikael wondered how Anton did it, but then he figured he ruled with an iron fist, and everyone just did what he said. All the power was with him, so there was no need for jostling. Anton most likely pronounced what would be, and dissenters were taken care of quickly. Mikael pulled his mind back to the present as he realized that whatever the solution, Denton had to be the one to figure it out. As much as he wanted to have the answers and be the alpha, this was an area where in order for him to get what he wanted, he had to let Denton come to the realization and find the solution on his own. He couldn't do it for him.

"I think we should get back. I have to get home, and I'm sure you have things you need to do." Denton stood, but Mikael lunged for him, tackling Denton back to the ground.

"Just because the answer isn't easy, doesn't mean there isn't one." Mikael kissed Denton hard. "You are still my mate, and I will not give you up easily. My wolf wants you and so do I. I might not have said what you wanted to hear, but I don't lie or have ulterior motives." He pulled Denton to him. "I am who I am. I know I'm not perfect and never will be."

"But you know your place in the world. It was handed to you."

"I have to work every day to be the best leader I can for my pack, and very little in my life was handed to me. You know your place in the world too, but you're fighting it." Mikael released Denton and stepped behind him, then sat at Denton's back. He wound his arms around Denton's middle and rested his chest against Denton's back. "Close your eyes and lean back. I know you're a good alpha and you care about your pack. That isn't a question, so let that go. Just think about what makes you happy and what you really want. Not what you think you want or what your head tells you. Go deeper."

"Is this some kind of trick to get me to see things your way?"

Mikael chuckled. "No. It's a trick to get you to see the things you really want. Yes, I want you in my bed and in my life every day. I want to wake up next to you, take care of you, and if you want the truth, I want to fuck you every night so hard that you fall asleep from exhaustion and let me hold you till morning. I know what I want and it's strong and clear. I'm not poetic or full of romantic notions, but I'm honest and not afraid to say it." Mikael placed his hands on Denton's temples, making small, light circles on his skin. "Think about where you want to be in five years. Picture it. Not where you think you should be, but what you truly want. Where will you be safe and cared for? Where your opinion and wants will be valued and needed?" Mikael swallowed hard and pressed closer to Denton, his renewed cock nestling at the base of Denton's back. God, he felt good, and for a second his fingers paused as his mind took an intimate detour.

He leaned forward, kissing Denton's shoulder before licking up his clavicle to the base of his neck. Mikael tasted him, leaving a small mark. Denton was his, and all Mikael could think was how the two of them would make a great team. Neither would need to bear the burden of being alone. The other would understand and be there for support, have someone to trust and share the weight of leadership with.

"What do you see?" Mikael whispered.

Denton sighed and sat still, remaining otherwise quiet for quite a while. "I see... I mean, I want...." Denton pulled away and out of Mikael's arms. "I think we better go back now. I have to get back to my family in case they need me."

Mikael let his arms fall to his side and stood up. "All right." He wondered what Denton had thought of, but didn't ask. He could sense Denton's stubbornness and his conflict. Whatever it was, Mikael was not going to get him to change his mind. He could out-stubborn just about anyone if he needed to, but Mikael didn't want to goad his mate into being with him. He wanted, no, *needed* Denton to want him, to choose him. He stood naked in front of Denton, letting him see his arousal. Whatever Denton's feelings or misgivings, he was Mikael's mate, and just being around him sent Mikael's hormones racing. No words or show of reluctance would stand in his or his wolf's way.

Mikael smelled Denton's arousal. He didn't have to see it, even though he looked. There was no way he couldn't. Denton's cock stood straight and tall, trying to reach his belly button, balls pulled tight to his body. "You can't deny your feelings and what you want forever."

"I can if that's what's best for my family. It's what I'll have to do. I have no other choice."

Mikael watched as Denton shifted into his white wolf. Mikael blew his breath out through his nose and shifted as well before slowly walking to the edge of the island. He waded across the creek, the cold water doing nothing to dull his excitement or to numb his disappointment. He knew that nature and attraction were on his side, but Mikael had no idea how long he was going to have to wait or if

Denton would remain as stubborn as bloody hell forever. He did know that the rejection stung and that he needed to try to get past it.

He took his time leading the way back. Unlike the trip out there was no romping or play, just a somber walk back. There was no hurry, and he took little joy in his surroundings. Once they reached the edge of the pack compound, Mikael shifted and began dressing, keeping his back to Denton. He'd be damned if he'd let Denton see just how disappointed he was. "We should find Kaiawa and Karl." He strode off as soon as he was dressed and heard Denton hopping to pull on his pants the rest of the way. Normally he would have paid money to see Denton jumping to pull his jeans up over his pale, perfect butt. Not today. It would only be a reminder of what was denied to him.

The door to Anna's cabin burst open, and Alexi and Misha bounded out in pup form. They skidded to a stop when they saw him and then raced over and jumped around his legs. "Why don't you two go on to Catherine's and play with your friends." Normally he would be ready to play and teach the pups what they needed to know, but today he wasn't in the mood. Thankfully the two boys raced away after each other. Mikael watched them go, jealous of their youthful innocence. Sometimes it really sucked to be an adult.

Of course, it didn't take long to find Karl and Kaiawa—all Mikael needed to do was follow his nose. As soon as they approached, both men's attention turned to them, and Denton motioned with his head toward where he'd parked his car. "We need to go."

Kaiawa said good-bye, and he and Denton headed to their vehicle. Mikael and Karl shared a glance, and then Mikael turned away. "I'm going up to my studio." Mikael stomped away. He wasn't in the mood to speak with anyone, and that was the only place he knew that would guarantee him privacy and time to lick his wounds.

117

CHAPTER 7

DENTON HADN'T called in days, and Mikael's calls had been ignored. Last night he'd shifted and run the entire way to Denton's pack land. He'd stayed off the pack areas and found a location on high ground where he could see into the compound with his strong eyes. Mikael had spent hours watching and ended up howling his heartache and disappointment to the stars. He had little doubt that Denton and his pack members could hear him. When he was done, he stood proud on the rock outcrop and listened, hoping for a response.

Mikael heard nothing at all. The night remained quiet, too quiet. Not even natural wolves answered him, which was very strange. He scanned the horizon, his wolf sight cutting through the night, using the light from the stars to illuminate the world. But he saw nothing out of the ordinary. He strained his ears, listening to the night, but other than the quiet of the wolves, nothing sounded strange. And he'd been scenting the air continually without a clue.

A light shone under him, so Mikael shifted. In human form he shivered in the night. Mikael unhooked the cord around his neck and looked at the screen.

"I heard you," Denton said as soon as Mikael answered the phone. "What are you doing?"

"What do you think?" He'd spent days away from his mate, and his wolf demanded he do something. "I was going crazy and needed to make sure you were okay." Mikael smiled. At least he'd gotten Denton to speak to him. That was progress, and his wolf was more than happy to hear Denton's voice.

"You missed me?"

"Duh," Mikael retorted very quickly. "My pack is pretty frustrated with me right now, and my mother told me that if I didn't do something to fix what I'd messed up…. Her words were that she brought me into this world, and she was going to take me out of I didn't stop acting like an ass."

Denton laughed. "I have the same issue. My aunt told me that she'd rather take on a bear in winter than be around me for another two seconds."

"So what do we do?" Mikael asked as he looked down on Denton's pack compound and saw a light come on in the darkness.

"We keep coming back to this, but I don't have any more answers than I did before." Denton sounded tired. "I don't know how much more I can take. I don't have an appetite, and I'm not sleeping. I know that's not good, and I'm so tired I almost feel sick."

Mikael knew those feelings very well. He'd been working nonstop for days. That would be great, but what he produced was dark and complete crap that he could never sell and would probably destroy eventually. "Every time I stop to think, I see your face." *Smell your scent, hear those little moans, growls, and groans you make when we're together.* All Mikael had to do was think of Denton, and waves of want and loss would flow through him.

"I can't go on like this," Denton whispered. "But what I can do is beyond me. I know you're stronger and what you said makes sense, but I can't just walk away. I have told the pack about you and what I've been feeling. They support me, but they're afraid. During the last leadership change, there was so much upheaval—no one wants to go through that again." The pain in Denton's voice went right to Mikael's heart.

"I think we need to talk. Things can't continue the way they are, for either of us."

Denton sighed. "Okay. But there is another possibility, and we need to think about that as well."

"What's that?" Mikael asked warily.

"We haven't completed mating by trading bites, so we could find mates that are more… appropriate given our status and…."

Mikael growled, loud and long. The thought of someone else with his mate made his blood boil in an instant. "If anyone touches you but me, I'll rip them apart. Fuck, they'll wish they'd met Anton first by the time I'm through with them." Mikael growled again, and his wolf paced inside him, aching to run to Denton and mark him as his. "So you can fucking push that thought out of your head. If I shifted right now, my wolf would be at your door, and I'd take you right there." Mikael's cock throbbed, completely oblivious to the cool caress of the air, or anything else for that matter. "Am I making myself clear?"

"Don't use your alpha voice on me." Denton's voice had deepened. Mikael wasn't sure if Denton even realized it, but that told him a hell of a lot about how Denton really felt. "I know that trick."

"Stop acting like an ass and I will." He let the words rumble in his throat. "And you may have an alpha voice, but you know damn well I'll do what I say." He blinked as his eyes shifted, and his teeth ached as his canines lowered. Two could play that game. "How are you going to feel if I find someone else and mate with *him*? The bond between us would be severed, and the pull you feel would be gone."

"That would be a relief."

"Would it? Knowing I chose someone else over you and that I was mated to them for life and there was no chance for us? Not ever? What we had in the meadow could never be again. Even if we got together again, that intensity, passion, and energy would be gone forever." A soft growl came through the phone. "You would know that no matter how long you lived, you would never have that intensity with anyone else, no matter how you felt about them."

"Bastard!"

"No, I'm just telling you the truth, but you already know that. Deep inside, your wolf is telling you that anyone else will always be second best, just like my wolf is ready to jump out of his skin to get to you and claim you as his." Mikael grinned. "How about I see if Vadim is interested? He's always looking at me with those big doe eyes of his. And with his narrow hips and let's not forget those luscious lips, he's a looker, and if I were to ask…."

The growl through the phone filled the night. Mikael didn't need to have the phone anywhere near his ear to hear it. "Don't you fucking dare! A kid like that. You… you'd actually go for someone like him!"

Mikael laughed. "See? That suggestion isn't any more popular with your wolf than it is with mine. So I take it that particular suggestion has been filed with other brilliant ideas like snow cones at an Alaskan Christmas party."

The line was quiet. "Snow cones?" Denton said. "I don't know where you get this shit, but yeah. I think we can file it with faux fur bathing suits."

"Oh...." Mikael grinned, and the bowstring-taut tension eased a little. "Funny."

"I'll call you in the morning, and we can figure out where we can meet to talk. Now, for God's sake, go home and stay out of the night air. You've got half my pack wondering what the heck is going on with that mournful howling act you were doing. I wondered who'd died and had to call."

"How'd you know it was me?"

"You think you're the only one who knows his mate's scent or the way he sounds in the night?" Mikael's heart leaped. That was the first time Denton had ever referred to him as his mate. "You could howl from the moon and I'd know it was you." Denton lowered his voice. "I'm beginning to understand this whole mate thing. There have been half a dozen times over the past few days that I've wanted to call you but didn't. It seems now whenever I want to talk to someone, I used to look for Kaiawa, but now I expect to see you come around the corner. I know it's stupid since we haven't spent that much time together, but that's what's been happening."

"It's the same for me. So we'll talk and figure something out."

"Okay." Denton hung up, and Mikael hung his cell phone back around his neck. He shifted and stood on the edge of the outcropping looking over the valley below. With the additional light in Denton's compound, he could see it much better. After watching for a while, he turned and disappeared into the woods, making his way home.

THE FOLLOWING morning, Mikael woke and knew something wasn't right. He felt it deep inside. He lifted his head off the workbench in his studio and sniffed the air. Mostly he got the tang of drying paint. He worked the crick out of his neck and walked over to the windows. He opened one and stuck his head out, inhaling deeply. He got the clean scent of the earth and the forest, the carbon scent of cold, charred wood from the dead fire in the center of the compound, and, of course, the scent of his pack, which he knew well, but nothing else. He left the window open and walked to the other side of the room, to the opposite bank of windows.

The green carpet of treetops spread out beneath him, accentuated with occasional rock outcroppings, all familiar and as they should be. Whatever felt off wasn't coming from the environment, but inside him. "Catherine," Mikael called before turning and heading down the stairs.

"She's with the boys," his mother said as she met him at the bottom of the stairs. "And there's no need to shout. We're wolves—I bet everyone within a mile heard you. Now what were you bellowing about?" She turned and walked to the kitchen.

"Something is wrong, and I need her to help me figure out what."

"Everyone is fine. I saw most of the pack members this morning, except Anna and her boys, but Vadim said she took them to bathe in the creek. I heard them giggling down there a few minutes ago. Now, why do you think there's anything wrong?"

"Just a feeling."

His mother nodded and motioned toward the snack bar. "Go sit down. I'll get you some coffee and an aspirin for your stiff neck." She turned away without another word, and Mikael sat down, wondering how she knew. She poured him a cup of coffee and placed two aspirin in his hand. "Don't argue."

He popped the pills into his mouth and used the coffee to chase them down. "What do you want to say?"

"Your father used to get those same feelings. But he used to tell me that they never had anything to do with the pack. Pack members were vocal and would always let him know if something was wrong. Your father used to tell me he always knew when I was upset or afraid, because he could feel it." She leaned on the counter across from him.

"So you're saying Denton is the source of this?"

"Quite possibly. But it could be this whole nonsense about you being apart. It isn't healthy for either of you."

"He said he'd call me today so we could meet to talk things out." Mikael hoped like hell they could figure a way through this. "He's so stubborn, I doubt anything will come of it—anything real, that is."

His mother slapped his hand, and Mikael bared his teeth.

"Don't you dare talk back or growl at me. You were my pup before you became this big alpha, and he's not the only one who's

122

as stubborn as a mule. There are times when I actually expected you to shift into one."

"But I'm the stronger wolf...."

"So you just expected that he'd come here and give up everything in his life and all he's worked for. I bet that boy works just as hard for his pack as you do for yours. Big only goes so far." She poured herself a mug of coffee before turning back to him. "Try to find some middle ground that will make you both happy. That's the key to a long-term, happy relationship. I know that's what you want." She walked around the bar and sat down next to him. "Your father was an amazing pack alpha, but he was also a wonderful husband, mate, and father. Those roles weren't always in sync with each other. But your father always did his best for all of us, no matter how hard things got, and...." She touched his hand. "There were many times when he put himself and what he wanted last."

"Yeah, but...."

"You see, every time he put himself last, more came back to him than he ever expected. That's how things work. So my advice is to worry less about pack structure and who's the biggest wolf. What matters is who has the biggest heart." She patted him lightly, then stood up and carried her mug out of the room.

Damn, when she was right, she was right. Catherine could step up as pack alpha, and his family would be just as strong and just as stable. Yeah, it would be hard to be the alpha mate instead of pack alpha, but he would support Denton, his mate, to help make him successful.

Mikael pulled his phone out of his pocket and dialed Denton's number. After a few rings, the call went to voice mail. Mikael left a message and hung up. Then he walked out the back door and across the pack compound.

"Mikael," Karl called as he raced up to him. "You need to come see this." He turned and ran away. Mikael followed, wondering what was going on. Karl led him into the woods and up a hill.

"What's going on?" Mikael called, and Karl pointed as they reached a lookout spot.

"I just noticed it a few minutes ago. There's smoke over there, just on the horizon."

Mikael looked where Karl was pointing. Wisps of black smoke rose from the trees. "What the hell…."

"That's what I was wondering about. Wood smoke is white, so if that's a forest fire, why is it black and getting thicker by the moment? Of course, that means it's growing, but it's still black. That isn't natural."

"No." A chill ran through him, even in the growing heat. "There's something about it that's… menacing. People don't come to this area." Mikael continued watching as the smoke grew thicker and heavier. "There are no trails or roads into that area. It's remote and next to pack land. Denton's pack land." He sniffed the wind. Thank goodness it wasn't strong, but Mikael wished he scented some water in the air. Unfortunately, it seemed bone dry. Just perfect for a section of the forest to go up in flames.

Then, as if on cue, the breeze picked up, and Mikael swore under his breath. As the heat of the day built, so would the wind, driven by the warmth. "Fuck."

"The fire is moving," Karl said.

"Yeah. It's being driven by the breeze, which is going to build as the day goes on."

"True, but we aren't in any danger. It may grow, but as long as it doesn't change direction, the wind will carry it away from our land." The smoke lightened to a normal white and gray, but a black core still remained in the center.

"True, but get word back to the pack that they are to gather supplies and anything essential. If we have to, we'll head to the cave to wait this out." Mikael never took his eyes off the horizon. The smoke died down and then flared once again, this time wider and definitely stronger. "We need to get back. The wind is making the fire grow and strengthen. We should be safe enough, but there's another big problem. That fire is heading for Evergreen lands, and their compound, if I'm not mistaken, is right over there." *In direct line with the fire.* When Mikael shifted his gaze back to it, the amount of smoke had doubled. "We need to go now. They're going to need help."

Mikael raced down the path.

"What are we doing?" Karl asked

"If I'm right," Mikael began without looking around, "that fire is heading straight for the Evergreen pack compound. If it stays on its current course, it's going to sweep over them, and we need to help."

"Why? They aren't our pack."

"No. But they could be." Mikael stopped. "Their alpha is my mate."

Karl stopped and turned toward him, an unreadable expression on his face. Mikael wondered if this was the beginning of a blowup. "I know you two have been together—I smelled him on you, but there was no mark on him when he was here or when he left." Karl didn't sound upset, just a little surprised, which was a relief.

"He's my fated mate," Mikael corrected, and Karl stared openly. "We're still working things out, but he's mine, and like I said, we need to help." He tried to stop the growl, but it came out anyway.

Karl ran right past him. "What are you waiting for?" he called just before disappearing around into the foliage. Mikael took off, overtaking Karl and then leaving him behind. "You can't stand not to be in front, can you?" Karl called, and Mikael heard him trying to catch up, but it was like his feet had wings. If he had been willing to stop long enough to shed his clothes, he would have shifted, but he didn't want to stop even for a second. He reached the compound and saw everyone milling around.

"We're going to need every vehicle we have," he said to the gathered pack members. "There's a fire heading for the Evergreen compound. We need to get over there and help them get out of its path. Karl, I want you to stay here to organize supplies and space. They're going to need a place to stay." Mikael lifted his gaze to the entire group. "I know these people aren't our pack, but they are wolves, and they're our brothers and sisters. It looks as though they are about to lose their homes, so be welcoming and help as best you can."

"Is it true that their alpha is your mate?" Stan asked rather quietly. It surprised Mikael that he spoke up; he usually didn't.

"Yes. He is. So I'm asking all of you to put aside the unease this is going to cause. We are going to help our brothers and sisters. We'd hope they would do the same if the situation were reversed." He let his gaze fall on each worried face, trying to reassure them. He wished he had time to talk to each of them individually, but he couldn't take the time. Even the pups were nervous, keying off their parents and the rest of the pack. They stared up at him with huge eyes, moving closer. Catherine's pups crowded around her, and Stan looked at them and then at him as Mikael tried to think of what he could do to reassure them. "No one is going to hurt anyone, and as nervous as you are, they are probably even more scared and upset, so be the best of who we are. As a pack we are strong together. Evergreen is going to need to borrow some of our strength for a while. Okay?"

"You go and do what you need to," his mother told him. "We'll take care of things here. Don't you worry about anything." She turned to the others and took charge with a list of tasks that would have made any drill sergeant proud. Mikael stepped back.

"Karl, I appreciate you staying and helping. Catherine, get in the truck and get going. I'll be right behind you." He scanned the crowd, and his gaze fell on Vadim, who stood away from the others. He caught his attention. "You're with me." Mikael left the hive of activity that the compound had become and headed for the vehicles. Catherine got in the truck and headed out with Mikael and Vadim right behind her.

The drive took too damn long. Mikael grew more and more agitated the longer it took. By the time they got close, wisps of smoke drifted over the treetops and the scent grew stronger and stronger.

"Are you okay, Alpha?" Vadim asked at one point.

"Yes." He'd lied; he was not okay. There was more to this than just a fire. His left leg jittered and shook, and that never happened. He gripped the steering wheel until his knuckles were white. More than once he was in such a hurry he nearly rear-ended Catherine to get her to go faster, even though the roads were rough. Finally they reached the entrance to the Evergreen compound. Catherine pulled off and Mikael did the same.

"How do we approach this?" Catherine asked. "If we march in there, it could cause trouble."

Mikael listened. "It's chaos. They need help." He sniffed and was able to discern the wolves and their near panic over the smoke. "Something is very wrong. You stay here." Mikael took off down the dirt road and after a few minutes emerged into the pack compound, which was filled with people yelling and running from building to building.

"Stop," Mikael roared at the top of his lungs. Everyone skidded to a halt. "Kaiawa, where is Denton?" he asked, turning to Denton's beta. He kept his gaze hard, brooking no test of his authority.

"We don't know," Kaiawa finally answered.

"I saw two men take him that way," a boy who looked about eight said, pointing toward the back of the compound. "I never saw them before."

Jesus Christ. Every instinct Mikael had told him to race after him, but he breathed to calm himself. "Okay. The fire is heading this way. Pack a bag apiece. We have an extra vehicle at the end of the drive. Everyone will get out. No running. Everything will be fine as long as we keep our heads."

People slowed down, scattering across the compound to cabins.

"What's your name?" Mikael asked the boy who'd seen where Denton had been taken.

"Connor, sir," he answered meekly.

"Well, Connor, I need you to tell me everything about what you saw and then go help your mom and dad pack."

He nodded. "Two wolves in people form. They had the alpha between them. He seemed asleep, and they were pulling him along. They left just before everyone started running around. Maybe ten minutes ago."

"Thank you. I need you to show me which way they went." The boy nodded, and Mikael followed him to the back of the compound, where Connor pointed toward a path. "Great. Now go gather your things."

Mikael raced back to where Catherine and Vadim were waiting. "I need you to take charge here and get everyone out of here and over to our compound. Load everything you can. They have a few vehicles, so use them as well. Do not wait for me. Leave one vehicle with the keys in it and take the rest." Mikael turned to Kaiawa. "You're with me. We're going to get Denton." Kaiawa nodded. Mikael was sure he'd know the land and all the paths in the area.

"I've got it here," Catherine said. "Go find your mate."

Mikael nodded and turned to Kaiawa, already beginning to remove his clothes. As soon as the last stitch was off, he shifted and stared at the other wolf. Kaiawa took longer, but soon a gray and black wolf raced past him and down the trail. Mikael followed.

I have his scent, but it's faint, he sent to Kaiawa, and the other wolf came to an instant halt. *No time to explain, just lead on.*

Kaiawa yipped and took off once again. If what Connor said was still true, then Denton's captors couldn't be moving at too fast a pace. Which also meant they either had an escape route or were planning to kill Denton. But if that were the case, why take him at all? No. They wanted him alive, and he'd be weighing them down.

Is there a road back here? A way they could get Denton to a vehicle?

Kaiawa yipped and left the trail, picking up speed as they raced cross-country. Mikael lost track of Denton's scent, but after about five minutes, he caught it again, even through the thickening smoke. They had to be getting closer.

"Get him the hell inside so we can get the fuck out of here," Mikael heard at the edge of his auditory senses. Kaiawa must have heard something as well. They shifted direction, and Mikael poured all his energy into going as fast as his legs would carry him.

The smoke thickened, and in the distance, Mikael heard the roar of what had to be the leading edge of the fire. Denton was close and so were two other men.

Circle around them and cut off any escape. Kaiawa made no sound but headed off while Mikael continued getting closer. He reached a break in the woods and blinked. Through the smoke, he saw two men shoving Denton into the back of a jeep. One closed the door, and they both hurried to get in the front. He had just seconds. Mikael raced toward them, making no sound until he was on the first one. He leaped, catching the man's arm.

A scream went up as Mikael tore into him. He ripped open flesh, blood spurting everywhere. Mikael released his grip, landed, and then leaped again, this time catching the wolf midshift. He went right for the throat, and when the half-shifted wolf tried to cry out this time, nothing but gurgles came out before the abomination fell to the ground. Mikael didn't take a second to howl his victory. He turned and started at a huge dark wolf.

You pile of shit, Mikael sent to him. Then the dark wolf growled and leaped. Kaiawa barreled into the dark wolf in midair, slamming him against the side of the jeep, leaving a massive dent in the door. The wolf fell to the ground. He recovered, but Kaiawa was too fast for him and already had him by the throat.

Hold him, Mikael sent to Kaiawa and shifted. "I will gut you and leave you tied to a tree in the fire's path unless you shift and talk to me." Mikael stormed toward the wolf. "Shift now!"

He did. Kaiawa continued holding him as the wolf shifted into a large man.

"Who's behind this?" Mikael said.

"Not going to say," the man croaked.

"Fine." Mikael shifted his hand and swiped it down the man's leg in one movement, then shifted his hand back instantly. "You're messing with the wrong wolf."

The man screamed, and the scent of urine reached Mikael's nose. "Anton sent us to bring back the fag alpha. He has plans for him." The man shifted back into a wolf, and Kaiawa set his teeth against the wolf's throat again.

"Well, this fag alpha has plans for you." Mikael turned to Kaiawa. "Just hold him. You can kill him if he so much as moves, and if he bleeds out beforehand, so be it." Mikael walked around to the back of the jeep and yanked the door open. Denton's eyes were closed, but he was breathing. Thank the Mother. He placed his hand on Denton's chest and felt his heart beating. Mikael was tempted to crawl in the back with him for a closer inspection, but there was no time for that now. He had to take care of the wolf they'd captured and get the hell out of there. Denton's hands were tied, so Mikael freed them, holding the rope.

A cloud of smoke passed over, making Mikael cough. He made sure Denton was as comfortable as possible before closing the door once again and walking back to where Kaiawa held the man. "I'm going to tie him up, and then we'll toss him in the jeep and get the hell out of here."

His bleeding had already slowed, so Mikael used the rope to tie his hands and then ran it down to his feet. By the time Mikael was done, the guy looked like a trussed hog. Kaiawa shifted and helped Mikael get the asshole into the back. Kaiawa found a rag on the floor and shoved it into the guy's mouth.

"Keep him quiet."

Mikael got in the jeep. The keys were in the ignition. He pulled the door closed and started the engine. "Find one of these men's phones." He put the jeep in gear and floored it. The smoke was thick as hell, and in the rearview mirror Mikael saw flames and heard small pops as trees burst from the heat.

"No signal," Kaiawa said.

"Where does this road lead?"

"To another path just ahead. Turn left and we'll go toward the main road that leads to your compound." An explosion sent flames and sparks showering down on them. The fire was getting closer by the second. Heat built inside the cab, and Mikael went as fast as he dared in the smoke, hoping the road didn't make any fast curves. He reached the other road, turned, and sped onward. He hoped they were moving away from the fire. The smoke lessened, but they were still in its path until they reached the main road and could get the hell out of there.

"Check for a signal."

"Got one, barely."

Mikael rattled off Catherine's number. Kaiawa dialed and put the call on speaker.

"Mikael?"

"We have him, but we're racing the fire. Get everyone out of there. This thing is hotter than hell, and trees are exploding ahead of it." He coughed and was thankful he'd turned off the air intake, not that it did much good.

"We're loading the last few people. Do we need to leave the vehicle for you?"

"No."

"Great. Load those people in that truck. You… can you drive? Good. Follow me. We leave in two minutes. Vadim, get going. We'll be right behind you. You, follow him." Catherine sounded breathless. "Mikael, I put your clothes and Kaiawa's things in my truck and will take them back to the compound."

"Be safe."

"You—" The call ended, and Kaiawa put the phone aside.

"Leave it on, just in case, but I think we're on our own." Mikael accelerated and they took off as fast as possible. He took curves as fast as he could, checking his rearview mirror every few seconds. Visibility got bad again when they changed directions, and that gave the fire a chance to catch up. Then they changed once again and started heading out of it. For almost half an hour, they wound around, with the fire seemingly on their tail.

Finally they reached the main road, and Mikael turned toward his compound. He went as fast as possible. A few times he heard Denton groan, which eased some of his worry. The wolf on the backseat grunted and groaned almost steadily, but Mikael couldn't have cared less about him. If he was bruised by the time they were out of this mess, so what? The bastard had tried to hurt his mate.

The smoke began to clear, and Denton rolled down a window for fresh air. He wondered where the others were, but if they were driving, it was best he let them get back safely.

"What's happening?" Denton mumbled from the back.

"Just relax. Kaiawa and I will have you safe just as soon as we can. Did you call in the fire to the forest service before all this started?"

"Yes. They were going to send teams to fight it," Denton answered groggily. Mikael hoped they arrived soon, or what little hope existed for Denton's pack compound would be gone.

He drove the last of the way home, thankful for fresh air. The drive was choked with vehicles as he pulled in. Mikael parked where he could as Catherine hurried over.

"Everyone is here. Your clothes are in the truck over there."

Kaiawa walked over to the truck and pulled some clothes out of a backpack.

"There's nothing left of the Evergreen compound. When we made one of the turns, I saw it go up," Catherine said softly. "That fire is hot and fast. We've heard helicopters and planes overhead, so it's being fought now, but it's too late for them."

"It's all right. We captured one of the men responsible. He's in the backseat of the jeep we liberated. Take charge of him and use whatever you need to in order to get him to talk." Mikael was so angry he was beyond caring.

Catherine smiled one of those smiles that made Mikael glad she was his sister and had his back, because he would not want to be the wolf trussed in that backseat. No way in hell.

"Is Denton okay?" she asked.

"Yes. I'm going to go get him inside."

131

"Put on pants first. I'll sit with him until you get back." Catherine hurried off, and Mikael located his clothes. He pulled them on. By the time he was done, Kaiawa approached, buttoning his shirt.

"What do you want me to do?" Kaiawa asked quietly.

"Please help make sure your pack is getting settled. This is a lot of upheaval for them, and they should feel as comfortable as possible. We have tents for those who would rather be outdoors, and there are extra rooms in the main house."

"I moved Anna and the boys to the main house," Catherine called to him. "She volunteered, and the two boys wanted to be closer to you, so that freed up their cabin."

Mikael nodded, and Catherine turned back to the jeep. "Okay. Well, please help soothe frazzled nerves. The most important thing is to keep everyone calm," Mikael said.

"They will want to know what is going to happen," Kaiawa said.

"We don't know. For now, this will be your home." Mikael reminded himself that they would need to make a run for supplies as soon as possible. They had many more mouths to feed.

Kaiawa nodded and headed around the main building as Mikael went to help his mate. When he approached the jeep, he found Denton sitting on the back with the tailgate open, holding his head. "They must have shot me with elephant tranquilizers, because I feel like I've been hit by a truck."

"You'll be all right. I'm going to get you inside and settled. Then I need to make sure your pack members have what they need."

"Is there anything left?"

"I'm told the compound is gone," Mikael said as he helped Denton to his feet. "But as far as I know, we got everyone out, and they're all here. You were the one who gave us a real scare." Mikael cradled Denton's chin in his hand. "At least you gave me the scare of my life." He locked his gaze with Denton's before kissing him lightly. God, the thought of losing him still had him shaking in his shoes. Mikael backed away and looked Denton over, sniffing and scrutinizing. If he thought he could get away with it, he'd have stripped him down and licked him all over just to be damned sure. Once he was certain his mate was okay, he helped him toward the house.

Anna, Alexi, and Misha were in the great room on the sofa, Anna holding her pups. The normally active pups were quiet and subdued.

"Alpha Mikael, is we going to be okay?" Alexi asked. "The fire isn't coming here too, is it?"

"No. I'm sure Mr. Karl has someone watching, just in case. Now let me get Alpha Denton upstairs, and I'll be back." Mikael helped Denton up the stairs, and Alexi followed quietly behind. Mikael opened the door to his room and then helped Denton undress and get in to bed. "Will you stay with him and make sure he's okay?" Mikael asked Alexi, who nodded.

"Is he your boyfriend?" Alexi asked.

"He's my mate. So watching over him is very important. Can you do that?" Mikael asked. Alexi nodded, then ran to the bed and propelled himself up onto it.

"I watch him real good for you." Alexi sat on the edge of the bed, staring at Denton. That wasn't exactly what Mikael had in mind. But Denton closed his eyes and instantly fell asleep. Whatever they'd given him didn't seem to be out of his system yet.

"Just stay here and be quiet. He's been hurt and needs to get better. Come get me if anything happens, okay?" Mikael smiled when Alexi nodded. "That's a good pup." He leaned over the bed and lightly kissed Denton. He smelled heavily like smoke, but his scent was still the same under all that, and the brief touch sent a shiver through him. He'd come so close to losing him. "I'll be right downstairs."

Mikael left the room and went downstairs. He didn't think Denton was in any danger, and he needed to sleep off whatever he'd been given. His heart was beating strong; Mikael had heard it loud and clear. But Alexi needed something to do that would make him feel important. Anna met his gaze, still holding Misha. "You didn't need to give up your cabin."

"The boys are going to feel better being closer to you, and all those wolves were going to need the space. I hope you don't mind. Your mother got us settled, and she's out back shepherding everyone where they need to be. I thought I'd stay out of the way."

"You're just fine. Take charge of the house and get anyone whatever they need." He peeked around the corner to where Stan had his pups sitting around the table

"Where's Mama?" William asked.

"She's outside handling a bad guy for me. You stay here with your daddy."

"There's lots of strangers out there," William added.

"It's okay. They're Denton's pack, so they're friendly. But if you want to stay here with your daddy, that's fine. Misha is in the other room with his mom, so you can play in here as long as you're quiet."

William nodded and slid off his chair. Stan got up as well, and the two of them went into the great room. Others filtered in from the family room, got some drinks, and then returned.

Mikael went out back. There was plenty of activity, but not the chaos he expected. A lot of wolves—some he knew from his visit and others he didn't—all sat around the central fire. His mother sat with them, talking quietly. He should have known she'd make everyone as comfortable as possible.

"I have everyone settled, but there's no room for the beta who just arrived."

"He can stay in the house with us. The attic room hasn't been used in a while. There's a bed, but it needs to be cleaned up and gotten ready."

"I'll take care of that. Where's your sister?"

"Having the time of her life," Mikael answered. His mother nodded. Catherine had always taken pleasure in getting people to tell her what they didn't want to. When they were kids, she'd known everything about everyone, except him. Mikael had always been stronger than she was. "I'm sure she'll be done soon, and then we'll know a lot more about what happened." Mikael looked around the fire, meeting the gaze of each of Denton's pack members, sharing a quick smile of reassurance. "If you need anything, my mother is the one to help you." He patted his mother lightly on the shoulder. "She's the best."

"Thank you for taking us in," one of the men said, tilting his head to the side.

"There was no question. It was the right thing to do. What's really important is that no one was injured. Kaiawa and I were able to rescue your alpha. He's tired, but okay. You're all safe, and we'll figure out what we need to do once some of the shock wears off. Until then, take care of each other and relax." A plane flew overhead, followed by another. "Once the fire is out, we'll figure out how this started and make those responsible pay." Mikael already knew who that was, and he had every intention of making that asshole pay. But he needed to be sure. This had to be a grab for more land and power, but a scorched-earth policy wouldn't help anyone. No, this had to stop and fast. Anton was going to pay for this.

A scream split the air, and everyone jumped.

"It's all right," Mikael's mother said soothingly and then turned to him. "I think you better find out what your sister is up to."

Mikael nodded and trotted off to see exactly what Catherine was doing. He followed the sound into the woods and came upon Catherine sitting on a log, with the man they'd captured hanging by his feet from a tree, swinging like a pendulum.

"He started squirming and hit the tree. It wasn't my fault," Catherine told him with a shrug without taking her eyes off the man. "He's all yours."

A slight rustling sounded behind him, and Mikael turned as a pup bounded up to him and then changed into a naked Alexi. "He's up and went down the stairs, so I hurried to tell you." Alexi looked at the man. "Can I swing next?"

"Go on back inside and find your mother. But shift first."

"But I want to swing."

"Later." Mikael knelt down. "You did very well. Now go find your mama and tell her I said you could have some ice cream." Alexi jumped in excitement and then shifted and ran in pup form back toward the house.

As expected, Denton found him a few minutes later.

"What's all this?" Denton asked.

"One of the men who nabbed you," Catherine answered. "He and I have been having a little fun, but I think he's going to pass out soon."

Denton sat down, and Mikael ignored the hanging man and sat next to him. "You should be resting."

"I heard that you'd captured him, and I wanted to hear what he has to say."

"Are you ready to talk?" Catherine asked the man, giving him a good, hard push.

"What"—*swing*—"do you"—*swing*—"want to know?"

Catherine stilled him but didn't cut him down. "What's your name?"

"Vince," he answered.

"Well, Vince, why did you start the fire?" Catherine asked. She was clearly in her element, and Mikael knew interrupting her would change the dynamic she'd worked to build. Vince had finally realized that Catherine had all the power, and that meant the power of pain or comfort.

"I didn't."

"Who did?" Catherine pressed and gave him a hard push. When he swung back, she stopped him none too gently.

"Anton. He used some power he has to start it. We had nothing to do with that. All we were supposed to do was get in and take the alpha when the smoke got thick enough for cover. Then we were supposed to bring him to Anton."

Catherine looked over at Denton and Mikael and then back at the hanging wolf. "What does he want with him?"

"I don't know," Vince answered.

Catherine gave him another hard shove. "Wrong answer," she growled.

"But I don't know," Vince said. "All Anton said was to bring the alpha. He wants his territory. Hell, he wants it all."

"Why did you do what he wanted?" Catherine asked, slowing him down.

"No one says no to Anton. Hell, he'd kill me if he knew I was talking to you."

"Then why are you?"

"Because you scare me more than him," Vince answered.

Catherine chuckled evilly. "It took you long enough to figure that out." She walked over to the rope and untied it from the tree, lowering Vince to the ground. Vince breathed a sigh of relief. He was looking green around the gills, and Mikael figured he was about ready to puke. "You are going to tell us everything you know, because these games are getting tiring, and if I get tired of talking, I'll gut you from neck to balls, you got that?"

Vince nodded. "Yeah."

"What is Anton playing at?"

"He ain't playing. His soul is as black as the ace of spades. There's no light at all in him. He has my family, and if I don't go back, he'll kill them, painfully. I saw him do it to someone else. The whole pack did." Vince turned away, leaned against the tree, and lost his lunch. "He killed Gregor in front of the whole pack as a warning. I got a mate and two pups, I can't... you gotta let me go."

"If you tell us what we need to know, we'll let you go," Mikael said.

"I don't know much. It isn't like he tells anyone what his plans are. No one knows, and none of us knows how he does it, but he has this control over people. He can get anyone to do what he wants, and if they don't, he makes them pay." Vince shivered.

"You do realize that the person you tried to take would probably have been killed or worse. You were taking him to his death."

"If I didn't, then my family.... He keeps everyone under his thumb."

"Why don't you take your family and leave?" Catherine asked.

"It's not like I have control over them. Anton keeps a close eye on wives and pups. He knows where they are all the time. That's how he keeps everyone in line." Vince swallowed hard. "I gotta go back, or who knows what he'll do to them."

"What else can you tell us?" Mikael asked. "Where is he headquartered? I'm going to show you a map, and I want you to show us exactly where he is. Then you can take your phone and the jeep and go. Tell him you had Denton but lost him in the smoke. You were jumped and your partner was captured. You escaped and made it back to the pack. I know you'll say nothing about talking to us." Mikael walked over to him. "I will know if you betray where we are or anything about us."

"How?"

"The Mother will make sure I know what I need to know." Mikael met his gaze, and Vince stared at the ground.

"I won't say anything." Then he lifted his gaze. "I know I'm not good, and you shouldn't trust me, but if I can get my family away from him, could they come here? I know I would never be welcome, but if I could get them away, they would need a place."

"Your family would be welcome," Mikael found himself saying before he could think about it.

Catherine hurried away and returned with a map from one of the cars. Then she untied Vince, and he got shakily to his feet. She showed the map to Vince, and he pointed out what Mikael needed to know. Mikael tossed him the keys to the jeep.

"You need to go now." Mikael kept his gaze as hard as stone while Vince half limped to the jeep. He got in and maneuvered the jeep down the drive and out to the road.

"Mikael, do you really think that was a good idea?" Catherine asked without any condemnation in her voice.

"We aren't a prison, and we don't have the facilities for keeping prisoners. What were we going to do, hold him indefinitely? Kill him? We aren't Anton. Besides, I think he was telling the truth when he told us about his family. There was genuine fear coming off him, and the sour scent that comes from lying wasn't there either. He's petrified and told us what we needed to know." Mikael turned to Denton, who nodded. "I should have asked your opinion before I went ahead. It was your pack who was displaced and lost their homes."

"You did what was right." Denton stood, and Mikael did the same, offering his help, but Denton shook his head. "I need to see my pack and make sure they're calm and then find them a place to stay."

"My mother and Karl already have everyone settled. Some of my pack members have moved into the main house, which freed up a cabin. We also have a room for Kaiawa."

"What about me?"

Mikael winked. "I have a very special room for you. There's already a large wolf who uses it, but he's more than willing to share." Mikael smiled.

"We can't impose…."

"Your pack, your family, is welcome to stay here for as long as it takes for us to figure this out."

"Yeah," Denton said heavily, like the weight of the world rested on his shoulders. "We're going to have to figure out where and how to rebuild. We don't have a lot of money."

"Don't worry about that now. Your pack needs you." Mikael took Denton's hand. "There are a lot of people who are going to be overjoyed that you're okay." Not least Mikael himself. Mikael squeezed Denton's hand and led him around to the center of the compound, where scared and dejected pack members brightened when they saw Denton.

"We thought you were gone," a man said.

"This is Jerry. His mate, Carol, is my cousin." A pretty, very pregnant woman with long black hair stood behind Jerry.

"Alpha Mikael was able to get me out of the hands of the wolves who took me," Denton said. "They tranq'd me, but I'm doing better."

"Are you all getting settled?" Mikael asked.

"Yes, thank you," Carol said quietly.

"Yeah. We all owe you a real debt," Jerry said. "No one knew where to go, and your people made sure everyone got out." Jerry smiled slightly as Catherine came around the main house, heading toward her family cabin. "She's something else."

Carol slapped Jerry lightly on the shoulder.

"Well, she is." He smiled indulgently at his mate. "She organized everything and everyone. Helped us get the important stuff and then into cars and away before anyone was hurt. We were all worried about you, though and...."

"Waiting for me would have put others in danger. Kaiawa and Alpha Mikael got me."

"I wasn't going to let you go without one hell of a fight," Mikael told Denton quietly.

"So you really are mates," Jerry stated and looked Mikael over. "You know, you could do worse."

"Jerry," Carol scolded. "Mates are sacred, you know that. And if Denton is Alpha Mikael's mate, then I think he's pretty lucky." She leaned close to Jerry, and he stroked her cheek. "After all, you were lucky enough to find me."

"If you need anything, just let any of us know," Mikael said to the couple and turned to Denton. "I know there are usually pack rivalries and that there could be issues. We're all wolves, and we tend to stay close to our pack mates and avoid strangers." Denton nodded his agreement, and Mikael turned back to the others. "So if there are any problems, bring them to Denton or me, and we'll handle them."

"I guess the biggest question is what are we going to do? The compound is gone and so is the area around it. If we want to rebuild in time for winter, we'll need to start now."

"Do any of the members of your pack have construction skills?" Mikael asked.

"Yes," Denton answered. "We do a lot of the building maintenance work inside the park. Jerry supervises a lot of it. He's very handy and understands building with local materials." Denton was clearly proud of his cousin-in-law.

"If there's something I can do to help while I'm here, just ask. I have to go to the park most days of the week, but I'm willing to help pull my weight," Jerry said.

"Thank you. Right now, just make sure your pack mates are talking and working through their loss. Everyone has had a real shock." Mikael smiled, and then he and Denton moved on to a group of pups curled together. They lifted their heads and sniffed at Denton before bounding over, coming to a stop when they got close Mikael.

"It's all right. This is Alpha Mikael. He's the one helping to take care of us. So you all need to be good. Where's your pop?" One of the pups turned and looked at the guest cabin, tail wagging slowly back and forth. "Okay. You three stay together and don't wander off." Denton stroked each of them lightly and then walked over to the guest cabin. "Those boys would stay outside all day and all night. They hate being cooped up indoors. I swear in the dead of winter they'd rather stay in a snowbank than come inside." Denton knocked softly on the cabin door.

It was opened by a man in his early thirties, by the look of him, although age was hard to tell from appearances with lycans. He broke into a wide smile when he saw Denton. "We heard you were all right, but it's good to see for myself." The man pulled Denton into a hug, and Mikael growled softly.

"This is Jerry's brother, Jack. Yeah, his mother had a thing for J names. Those are Jack's pups." No one mentioned the pups' mother. Mikael figured she had died, and the loss still hurt. "Are you and the boys getting settled?"

"Yeah. Jerry and Carol are staying here as well. It's going to be just like when we were all pups together." Jack smiled, but there was definite sadness around his eyes—not recent, but still present. "Is everyone else okay?"

"They seem to be," Denton answered and glanced at Mikael.

"Alpha Mikael and his pack have been good to us." Jack deferred to Mikael with a respectful nod of his head. "All your help is so very much appreciated. I know my pups would stay outdoors all they could, but living in the forest wasn't something any of us were prepared for."

"I want to make sure everyone knows that they are welcome, and I want them to be as comfortable as possible. We all know that things are very unsettled right now and that decisions need to be made," Mikael said, and then he went on to repeat the part about coming to them if there were any questions or issues. They said good-bye and moved on through the rest of the compound. He and Denton reassured everyone as best they could from both packs. His mother began carrying out plates of food, which also soothed shattered nerves.

After both he and Denton took the first plate of food, as was expected, they stepped back together and watched as the others ate. Mikael wound his arm around Denton's waist and pulled him closer. He nuzzled Denton's neck and licked the skin at the side of his throat.

"Aren't you hungry?" Denton asked.

"Not for food," Mikael responded deeply. His wolf desperately wanted to inspect his mate more closely. Yes, he knew Denton was all right, but his wolf needed to see, and Mikael wanted some time alone with him. He sucked a mark on Denton's neck. "You taste better than any food ever."

"I bet your mother wouldn't be too pleased to hear that," Denton retorted and stretched his neck, giving Mikael better access. "Mikael...."

"What?" he asked, moving his lips to Denton's ear.

"They're going to think...."

"What? That I care about you?"

"That I'm...." Denton's voice trailed off, but Mikael got the idea.

"You're a strong wolf and a good alpha. They know that. But there's no way you can resist my charms." Mikael grinned, and Denton turned to him, mid eye-roll. "Come on, then." Mikael stood and tugged Denton after him. The others were mostly engaged in either eating or talking, and Mikael didn't plan to waste this chance. He led Denton into the house and up to his room. As soon as they were inside, he kicked the door closed with a bang and prowled toward Denton.

Mikael tried to be gentle and get Denton's buttons opened, but he'd had enough and shifted his hand. The shirt fell away in tatters.

Mikael couldn't have cared less. He wanted access to Denton's skin, and he was going to fucking have it. "God, you're beautiful," Mikael growled as he pressed Denton back onto the mattress. "You have five seconds to get those damned pants off or they're going to be toast." His wolf would not be stopped.

"Mikael," Denton protested, panting even as he opened his pants.

"You are mine!" Mikael growled deep and low. "I think it's time we both come to realize that we need each other."

"So what are you proposing?" Denton asked as he kicked his pants to the floor. He still had on his boxers, and Mikael made short work of the flimsy fabric. Then he held Denton tightly around the waist and pressed his face to Denton's skin, inhaling deeply. Denton still smelled of smoke, but under that was what Mikael needed: the rich, sweet scent of his mate.

"I am saying that I'm not going to let you go. I've spent enough miserable time apart from you. I know what I want. So I say we work to merge our packs together. We can build additional cabins here. We incorporate your pack land with ours and rename the pack."

"With you as alpha," Denton said, sliding away.

"With us as a mated pair of alphas. The pack is going to need both of us. They are our family, and we need to care for them and lead them. Not you. Not me. Us." Mikael lifted his head. "Yes, I'm probably going to take over and make decisions. It's what I do. But you know as well as I do that being the leader all the time is not the picnic everyone thinks it is. You know what it's like." Mikael lightly stroked up Denton's leg, the muscles quivering under his light touch.

"But you need…."

Mikael lifted his face away from Denton's belly and kissed him hard, taking everything he wanted, loving that Denton gave as good as he got, and soon the heat in the room reached scorching levels. "I love Stan, but if my mate had been like him, I think I'd scream. He's perfect for Catherine, but I want more. What I need is someone strong, like you."

Now it was Denton's turn to growl, and he sat up, pushing against Mikael. "That's what you're going to get. I'm not a wilting flower or someone who will remain quiet and submissive."

"I never thought you were," Mikael retorted, tugging Denton to him. He expected more resistance and kissed him hard. For a few seconds he tasted blood, his and Denton's. Didn't matter. Their lips, tongues, and teeth battled in the best way possible. Mikael loved that Denton gave as well as received.

The two of them rolled on the bed, first right and then left. Mikael was on top, and then he had Denton pressing down onto him. Both positions felt incredible. Denton's skin was soft and smooth, sliding easily under his hands. With a loud growl, Mikael used his larger size to roll Denton onto his back. He held his hands, and the two of them nipped and growled at each other. Mikael's clothes were in tatters. He managed to get them off and pressed his chest to Denton's, grinding his hips and cock against Denton.

Instead of a growl, he got a whimper. Fuck, he loved that sound too. "You even sound good." Mikael licked a nipple, sucking and nipping as Denton writhed under him. "I need you so bad." Mikael kissed Denton hard and then flipped him over. He licked down Denton's back and over the curves of his ass before parting his cheeks. The intensity of his mate's scent slammed into him. Mikael licked down his crevice to Denton's opening. He needed more and pressed his tongue deep.

Fuck, Denton was tight, his muskiness filling Mikael's mouth. Even more amazing was the whine that reached his ears and zinged through his body, setting his heart and groin on fire.

"Mikael," Denton cried.

Mikael stopped and crawled up Denton's body, rubbing against him the entire time. He needed to be in constant contact with him. "You're mine forever." The kiss was sloppy at best, but Mikael could have cared less. Denton was here now, and they were together. He lifted his weight enough that Denton could roll onto his back. "I won't wait any longer. So you better stop me now."

"Not going to. I want you too." Denton pulled him into a kiss as Mikael spread Denton's legs, his cock sliding along Denton's cleft. "Fuck me, Mikael. Make me yours and give yourself to me." That was all the invitation he needed.

He reached to the nightstand, yanking the drawer so hard it fell to the floor in a crash. Mikael snatched up the small bottle of lube and clumsily coated himself and lubed Denton as quickly as he could before pressing his cock to his opening and entering Denton's body.

143

His wolf would not be denied another second, and it took all his control to keep from surging into Denton.

"Holy hell!" Denton growled.

"You can say that again," Mikael whispered throatily and paused. He had to give Denton a chance to breathe. "You feel amazing. I love your body and the way it feels around me, but I love you more. You are my mate and my heart, the other half of my soul, and I will hold you close to me for the rest of my life." Mikael pressed deep into Denton's body, his heat surrounding him. Mikael felt a loss of control coming on, and he used all his strength to keep his wolf from taking over. "Your family will be my family and mine will be yours."

Denton's gaze bored into Mikael's. "Mikael," he whispered. "Are you sure this is what you want?"

Mikael brought his mouth to Denton's, possessing it within seconds, then said, "I have wanted you since I first walked into that restaurant. You are all I have been able to think about for weeks. We are mates—you are mine and I am yours. Nothing will change that. You are everything I have ever needed, and I will strive to be that for you." Mikael withdrew and slowly sank back into Denton's heat and pressure. "Fuck!"

"Yeah!" Denton growled.

Mikael took that as a challenge. He moved faster, taking Denton, marking his mate with his scent, filling him. Denton was his, and when he leaned forward, licking and rubbing his neck, Mikael felt his heart beating.

"Take me," Denton said.

"I'm going to mark you as mine, outside and in. When I'm done no one will doubt that you're mine." Mikael couldn't hold back any longer. His wolf was taking over. His teeth elongated and his eyes shifted. The scent of Denton filled his nose, and all he could look at or think about was his amazing mate. He had been given a gift beyond measure. "You'll carry my scent, and I will wear yours like a badge of honor."

"Did anyone ever tell you that you talk too much?" Denton countered. "Just fuck me. Show me how you feel." He pulled Mikael down, kissing him hard. "Fill me and make me yours."

Those words were nearly his undoing. Mikael drove deep and fast, locking onto Denton's gaze, and when Denton leaned his head to the side, offering his neck, Mikael struck, sinking his teeth into the juncture of neck and shoulder, biting and marking him as his. Denton's blood filled Mikael's mouth, and he came in a rush of heat and passion, filling Denton, marking him inside as well as out. He pulled away so he didn't really hurt him. Denton would carry this one mark, this scar, with him for the rest of his life. Wolves mated for life, and now Denton was his.

Mikael raised his head, tilting his face to the ceiling, and let his wolf free, howling at the top of his lungs. Denton joined him after a few seconds, and Mikael's wolf rejoiced, crying his pleasure until the walls shook.

Once he was breathless, he leaned over Denton and held him tight. "You are special, you know that?"

"I'm glad you think so," Denton said. "But I've seen you in action, and I realize that I haven't been the best alpha." Mikael didn't know what to say. "I fought for the position because they needed me and I wanted to do right by my family. I thought being the strongest meant I was the best leader."

"You gave them what they needed because you cared. That goes a long way toward being a good alpha," Michael whispered.

"No. It went a long way to creating a huge ego, and I let that get in my way. I was a beta wolf growing up, and I always will be. I know that, and I should have been content with that. Instead, I let my pack get into trouble, and now they're homeless."

Mikael shivered when their bodies disconnected. He smoothed his hand down Denton's belly. "Your pack is not homeless. They have a place here. They will always have a place."

"Do you really think we should merge the packs? You know there will be problems."

"There probably will be, but I think we're stronger together. And yes, it will take some work, but it will be worth it."

Denton closed his eyes, and Mikael held him tight. "I love the feel of you next to me." He petted Denton's flat belly. "I don't see you as a beta wolf. You're an alpha, and you always will be an alpha to me."

"I don't have the abilities that you do. I know now that I was in over my head. I did my best, but they need someone stronger, and a better leader." Denton stroked his cheek. "They need you. I need you."

"Well, I need you too. I knew that the first time I saw you." Mikael chuckled softly. "You know this has to be the strangest pillow talk ever."

"Yeah, it probably is," Denton whispered.

Dammit. Mikael could see in Denton's eyes how hurt he was. Mikael tried to imagine how he'd feel if the situation were reversed. He was a proud alpha, and he knew he was a good leader. He hated that he'd brought on this crisis of identity he saw in Denton's eyes. He was the alpha of the Evergreen pack, and Mikael had somehow managed to pull his legs out from under his mate. *What should I do?* he asked himself.

"I can hear you thinking," Denton said. "There are some things that you can't fix and you can't change. Things happen that are outside of our control."

"Yeah, but...." Mikael thought being mated would make things perfect. Instead, it seemed to have brought more problems. "I want you to be happy. You're my mate." Mikael lightly soothed Denton's back. "I always thought I would be whatever my mate needed and that you'd be what I needed. But I can't seem to do what you need most."

Denton shook his head. "Sometimes what we think we need isn't what we really need. And just because you're my mate, that doesn't mean you need to be able to read my mind or provide every little thing for me. Yeah, I'm sort of lost right now because so much of who I am is wrapped up in leading my pack."

"But you're so much more than that," Mikael said. "Just like I'm more than an alpha." Mikael leaped off the bed and held out his hand. "Come with me. I want to show you who I really am."

Denton took his hand, and Mikael pulled him to his feet and then out of the room and up the stairs to the third floor. "Shouldn't we put on some clothes?" Denton asked.

"No," Mikael answered as they reached the top of the stairs. He pushed open the door and stepped into his studio. "This room has the second-best view of anywhere on our land." He walked up to the windows and maneuvered Denton in front of him. He scanned the land outside the windows and cringed at the huge blackened scar on the land and the smoke that still rose. Maybe this hadn't been such a good idea after all.

"If this is the second-best view, then where's the best view?"

Mikael kissed Denton's shoulder right over the fresh mating mark, his mark, and rubbed circles on his belly. "Well...." Mikael shifted closer, his cock taking a renewed interest with Denton so close to him. "I think the best view I've ever seen is right in front of me."

"Mikael," Denton moaned. "Did you bring me up here for round two?"

"No. But that's not a bad idea." Mikael moved Denton toward the windows and pressed him against the glass. He turned him around and then knelt, sucking his perfect cock hard. He pulled off and said, "Fuck, you taste good."

Denton strangled a moan as Mikael took him in again, sucking him even deeper. "Fuck me!"

"God yes," Mikael mumbled and continued sucking, swirling his tongue around the fat head of Denton's heavy cock. This man was incredible. His own cock bobbed between his legs. He ignored it, determined to give everything he had to his mate. Within seconds, Denton was panting hard. Mikael knew he was close; he could feel it.

"I'm not gonna last," Denton groaned.

Mikael pulled away. "I want to taste you." He sucked him deeply once again. Denton banged his hand back against the glass, one leg shaking slightly. Mikael loved that he could make Denton lose control.

Denton groaned resonant and long before thrusting forward and filling Mikael's mouth with salty sweetness. Mikael swallowed hard, relishing the taste of his mate.

Mikael let Denton's cock slip from between his lips and licked his way up Denton's belly and chest. Fucking hell, he loved the way Denton's muscles rippled under his tongue. When he reached the mark, which was already closed and healing, Mikael kissed it and then captured Denton's lips.

"I love you, Mikael," Denton whispered.

Mikael wanted to howl again but consoled his wolf with another kiss on his mate's swollen lips. "The Mother knows I love you too."

"How are we going to merge the packs?"

Mikael shrugged. His mind was already forming a plan, but he didn't want to talk about that now. "Let me think on it, and then we can discuss it." Mikael took Denton's hands. "We'll figure it out together."

Damn, that sounded almost gracious. Mikael knew he was many things, but no one would say he was gracious. Still, that was how he felt about his mate. He was special, and his opinion mattered above all others. "But for now, I have something to show you."

"Ummm," Denton began as he turned to peer out the windows. "I didn't know I'd been mooning the compound while we were…." He grinned.

"Like proper wolves, I'm sure they heard something, but they know to look away and ignore what they hear. I'm sure your family does the same, and as for mooning everyone…." Mikael growled. "You are mine, and they know better than to mention anything. At least they will soon." They were high enough up that most people wouldn't bother to look, but the thought brought out his possessiveness in a big way. He needed to be more careful in the future so no one got any ideas.

"I'm feeling pretty possessive about you too," Denton told him.

Mikael found he liked that. "Good. Because tonight, after we see to everyone, you and I are going up to my room, and this time it's your turn."

"For what?"

"To mark me," Mikael said.

"But one mark is enough, you know that." Denton touched his shoulder. "The stronger wolf marks the weaker one as his mate."

"We're both alphas, and you're my mate. I would be proud and honored to carry your mark with me for the rest of my life." Mikael crushed Denton to him and silenced him with a searing kiss. All his emotions were in such turmoil. He'd mated with Denton, and that was incredible, but he'd also come close to losing him forever, and the thought of that scared the piss out of him. He needed Denton the way he needed air. His wolf was happy and content, and to Mikael's surprise, he didn't rebel at the idea of having Denton mark him.

Denton pulled away. "You're mine." The words rumbled, husky and deep.

"And you're mine. Forever and always." Mikael cradled Denton's head in his arms, holding him close once again. That fear from earlier kept surfacing. "Come, I have things to show you before I need to take you back downstairs and claim you again." Mikael released him and motioned toward his work area, where half a dozen canvasses rested against the wall. Mikael picked one up and turned it around.

"That's stunning," Denton said breathlessly as he stepped forward. "Is that the one of Gregor you told me about?"

"Yes. You met one of his pups earlier, little Alexi. He watched over you for me."

Denton laughed. "He sat on the foot of the bed, staring at me. I thought I was being guarded. When I pushed the covers back, he jumped down and raced away as fast as he could."

"Yeah. He came to tell me you were up. His brother Misha is just as energetic, and they have Gregor's ability to make just about anything fun. Those boys are going to be alphas, no doubt about it. I can feel it. And I know it's my duty to teach them the way my dad taught me." Mikael set the painting aside and picked up another.

"My God. The pups at play."

"These are Catherine's William and Maria last year. Maria is so unlike her mother. Catherine is as strong as they come, but Maria is more like her father. She's quiet and likes her dolls and books. She is a wolf, but her human side is more dominant right now. That may change. This is completely from my imagination."

"That's impressive."

"Well, I have a powerful imagination." Mikael put the painting back and turned over the last one.

Denton stared. "You painted me?" he asked, swallowing hard.

"I had to. I kept seeing you in my mind, and the only way I could get any relief was to paint what I saw."

"When did you do this?"

"I started it right after I finished the one of Gregor. I don't usually do human portraits. It's not what I'm known for, but I had to paint you, and I think it came out very well."

"What's behind me?"

"That's the view of the mountains and trees outside the window in the restaurant where I first met you. That was the moment I wanted to capture. You were so serious and portrayed power and confidence. I loved that and wanted to remember that look. So I painted it."

"Oh. Will you paint more of me?"

Mikael grinned. "I thought about painting that expression of open-mouthed joy you get when you come, but I never will. That look is just for me, and I don't want to share it with anyone. Actually, my next portrait will be of you as a wolf."

"What do you do with all these?"

"I sell most of them. I have to. A few of our pack members don't do well in the outside world. They don't have the control required to deal with humans. They work well together, but on their own, they sometimes get lost. So they sit for me, and I paint and make a very good living that helps support us. Karl works and so does Catherine. I'm sure you faced the same challenges."

"Yes."

"I'm lucky my work is appreciated. It makes it easier to do what we need to." Mikael put the portrait aside. "So this is a lot of what I am. I like to think of myself as an artist first. That's what I truly love to do. Yes, I'm the pack alpha, but that's not...."

"You don't have your identity wrapped up in it," Denton supplied. "Have you ever thought maybe that's what makes you a good alpha? You lead your pack and do what's best for them, but your ego isn't involved all the time."

"I never thought about it that way, but I think you're right." Mikael pulled Denton close just because he loved the feel of his body next to his. "We should go back downstairs."

"I know what you're thinking." Denton smiled and reached down between them, wrapping his fingers around Mikael's shaft. Mikael closed his eyes and hissed at his mate's touch. "Because it's damned obvious, but we need to dress and get everyone settled for the night."

Mikael wished he could argue with him, but he couldn't. There was too much uncertainty surrounding everyone for them to hole up in the bedroom. They needed to be seen as strong. "Should we talk to everyone?"

"Soon," Denton suggested. "Today isn't the day for mating announcements. They're going to want to be happy for us, but right now they're too nervous and unsettled. That's only going to create more uncertainty. Let's give everyone a little time, and then we can give them all some real answers."

"Okay," Mikael agreed. They left the studio and went back to his room. After they took quick showers, Mikael got some clothes for Denton to wear and then dressed as well. Together they went outside and sat with the gathering in the compound. Mikael built up the fire for warmth, light, and a sense of comfort. At first everyone seemed to keep to themselves, but slowly as the night wore on, the members of the two packs began to talk to one another, sharing stories and even laughter. The pups all played together until parents took them to bed.

Small groups filtered away as the night wore on, and others shifted and curled together in makeshift beds under the stars. There was no fighting or arguments. Instead, Mikael wanted to think that the healing process was beginning. It had been a rough day on everyone, but as the evening drew to a close, he and Denton got up and headed to the main house together under the watchful eyes of members of both packs. Nothing had been said about their mating or the mark visible on Denton's shoulder. But that didn't mean they hadn't noticed it, and their silence could mean many things.

CHAPTER 8

MIKAEL ROLLED over and curled next to Denton, holding him close. The past few days had been remarkably calm after all the activity with the fire. He and Denton's mating seemed to have been accepted by everyone with little fuss or comment other than a few words of congratulations. A few seemed surprised that Denton had claimed Mikael as well, but both packs were happy for them, if still a little confused.

"I love waking up next to you."

"I do too," Denton said.

Mikael pressed against Denton. He needed him. After sleeping next to him all night, surrounded by his scent, Mikael's body was on overdrive, and within seconds his cock throbbed. "Are you sore from last night?"

"No," Denton told him, and Mikael rolled Denton onto his back, parted Denton's legs, and slid into his still slick passage. "Fuck yeah!" Denton cried. He had taken to being quite vocal when they came together. Mikael loved it. Of course, they had a tendency to wake the entire house, but even when they were quiet, with a house full of wolves, they were going to be heard.

Mikael snapped his hips. "You like that?"

Denton groaned. "Hell, yes. Fuck me with that fat cock. Make me yours again."

"You're already mine, and I'm yours forever," Mikael gritted through clenched teeth as he withdrew and slid quick and hard back into his mate. Every time he entered Denton's body, it took his breath away. Denton had fucked him a few times, but this position was Mikael's absolute favorite. He loved watching as Denton's eyes darkened, his mouth hanging open ever so slightly, and the way his ears and cheeks flushed as Mikael filled him. That was a glorious sight, and the color grew deeper as Mikael thrust harder and faster. His wolf was in control. Mikael didn't shift, but he nipped and licked at Denton's shoulder, especially over his bite mark. He drove harder as his passion and cock swelled. Denton moaned harder.

Mikael lost control. He clamped his teeth on his mating mark. Desire surged through him, and he came in a rush as Denton screamed his release, filling the room with his howl of uncontrolled desire. Mikael backed away, licking the small wound to soothe it, his cock still buried in his mate's incredible heat. There was nowhere he would rather be than right here, right now. Denton's eyes shone up at him, his golden skin covered in a sheen of sweat. "I love you," Mikael said as he nuzzled Denton's cheek. "You make me as happy as I can ever remember being."

"I love you too, but I keep wondering how all this could happen so fast. I know part of it is the whole mate thing."

Mikael snickered. "Sometimes you just have to take what you're given and be happy with it. Because sometimes the happiness only lasts for so long."

"That's a strange thing to say, even if I know you're right."

"I almost lost you, and I don't intend to let that happen again." Mikael withdrew from Denton, shivering a little, and then settled on the bed next to him.

"We might have awakened half the pack." Denton said.

Mikael laughed really hard. "You know, if we did, I bet there's plenty of baby making going on right now. That was hot. You make the best sounds, and I bet half the women in the pack are challenging their mates to get them to scream like that."

Denton smacked him playfully on the shoulder. "Stop that or your head is going to get too big to fit through the door."

"Well, when it's true, it's true." He couldn't help puffing out his chest a little. He was proud of the sounds Denton made for him, and he wouldn't apologize for giving Denton pleasure.

Denton shook his head and pushed down the covers. "I'm going to go to the bathroom, and then I think we need to go for a run." He glared at Mikael. "You need to work off some energy, and I don't think I can take any more of your chosen method of release."

"We need to check and re-mark our borders... and yours."

Denton looked at him quizzically.

153

"Just because the compound burned doesn't mean we're giving up your pack land. That's Evergreen territory, and we need to keep it marked. Anton will take it just to be spiteful. Territory, pack members—it's all power and prestige to him. Which means it will be fun to stick it to him and not let the asshole have it."

"Okay. So we can drive over today and run there. I know some of the Evergreen men have been anxious to see if anything is left."

"Sounds good." Mikael rolled onto his side and watched as Denton's bare, firm ass bounced a little before he disappeared into the bathroom.

"Have you thought about making an announcement about merging the packs?" Denton asked through the open door. Water ran, and Mikael figured he needed to get up as well. He should work, but he wasn't in the mood, and a run would do him some good and allow him to think.

"What I'm hoping," Denton began as he climbed off the bed, "is that things would work out on their own."

"How?"

Mikael joined Denton at the sink, encircling his strong mate in his arms. "Like give them a project to do together. We need more living space, so I was wondering if your cousin would like to head up constructing another building. We would make it a duplex for two families. I had intended to build another after Anna joined the pack anyway, and this would give everyone a chance to work together at something."

Denton caught his gaze in the mirror. "You're thinking if they do things together, they'll start to feel like one pack."

"Exactly. I thought we'd ask Jerry and Karl together. Maybe Kaiawa would like to pitch in as well. If they start working together, then they can lead the pack members, sort of show the way."

"What about Catherine?" Denton asked.

"She has other talents. Maybe we can take all of them with us on the run. Catherine will hold down the fort here. We'll need to scout out good trees that can be used for the walls. That could give them something to do on the run."

Denton shook his head. "My God. If you ever decide to take up matchmaking, you could have every single wolf paired up within days." He smiled, and Mikael stroked up his chest, lifting Denton's arms over his head.

"God, I like you like this." Mikael leaned close, licking his shoulder.

Denton groaned. "If you keep that up, we'll never get anything done, and there's plenty we need to get started." Denton stepped away. "So keep your magic hands to yourself for the rest of the morning. Lord knows my ass is going to ache all morning, and no one is ever going to mistake who we belong to."

"I can't get enough of you," Mikael whispered and then sucked on Denton's ear.

"I feel the same way, and I have the dozen or so hickeys to prove it. But the pack needs us to lead, and we can't do that from the bedroom... as much as I'd like to."

Mikael stepped away and left the bathroom. He had to get away from Denton or he was going to take him on the bathroom floor. Now that his wolf had had him and they had made love, he wanted Denton over and over... to make up for lost time, most likely. He pulled open one of his drawers and got out some clothes for Denton and then for himself. One of the benefits since the fire was that Denton wore his clothes and ended up bathed in his scent on a constant basis. It made his wolf very happy.

Mikael used the bathroom when Denton was done, and then they went downstairs together. Anna was already in the kitchen making breakfast. "The boys are still asleep, although how anyone could sleep through the noise you two make is beyond me." She smiled and winked. "Actually, I'm jealous, because it makes me miss Gregor and the closeness he and I had." She turned away, and Mikael thought about comforting her but stayed where he was. He was finding that when it came to her grief, she wanted privacy.

"You know you'll have that again, when you're ready, and your boys are something else," Denton said gently. "Mikael says they remind him of their father, so you'll always have a piece of him with you."

Anna turned around. "You know, you're right. I do." She took Denton's hand and squeezed it before pouring a cup of coffee and returning to the stove.

"Mama," Misha said as he came into the kitchen in his Superman pajamas with feet.

"Hi, Misha," Denton said, and the pup rubbed his eyes. Anna was busy, so Denton walked over and lifted the little boy into his arms. Misha stared at him for a second as though he was wondering if he liked it or not. Mikael thought he was about to let loose with a whopping scream, but instead he put his head down on Denton's shoulder and closed his eyes. Denton rubbed his back and walked him around the kitchen. It was an adorable sight. Pups could always tell good people, no matter what. Alexi came out in his Teenage Mutant Ninja Turtle pajamas shortly afterward, and Mikael lifted him into his arms. The boys half dozed while Anna finished breakfast. Other pack members wandered in, including some of Denton's, and everyone took seats around the table. The women helped Anna in the kitchen, and soon the house was a hive of activity.

Mikael sat at the table next to Karl and across from Kaiawa, still holding Alexi. "We're going for a run, and we thought we'd go over to Evergreen territory and see if anything can be salvaged. We'll also make sure the territory is still marked."

"We should look into rebuilding," Kaiawa said.

"We were thinking about adding another building to the compound here. We could do it before winter with the resources of the two packs, and that would ensure that everyone was safe and that we all make it through winter," Denton said. Kaiawa nodded, which surprised Mikael. He had expected resistance from the Evergreen beta. "Jerry would be in charge of the actual construction." Denton looked at Jerry, who nodded his agreement.

"Yes," Mikael told Karl. "We were hoping that you and Kaiawa could help Jerry. We thought we'd build using logs, so we're going to need to identify trees and get them felled and transported. This is a big job since we are thinking a two-family dwelling with at least two bedrooms each and a loft on both sides for extra sleeping space. We can research basic plans on the Internet and then begin building. Between both packs we should have all the skills we need."

Anna, Carol, and Mikael's mother brought food to the table. Mikael shifted Alexi around so he could sit on his lap at the table and then fixed him a plate. "Is that good?" Mikael asked the pup.

"Yes. Thank you, Alpha Mikael." He grabbed a fork and tucked in ravenously. Anna took pity on Mikael and brought him a plate.

"I can take him, Alpha," she said.

"He's fine. You cooked, so it's the least I can do." The truth was he liked pups. Catherine and Stan's always made him happy, and by the time Misha and Alexi had eaten, William and Maria came in. The boys slipped off his and Denton's laps and went in the other room to play. The room filled with conversation, the men talking about the new building and the women adding requirements to the list. It seemed the idea was a hit.

Mikael finished eating a huge breakfast and then praised Anna and the other women before stepping away from the table to organize the pack members into groups. Catherine would stay behind and make sure the compound remained secure. One group of men was to patrol and mark the territory around the compound, and the group with Denton and Mikael were going to head to Evergreen. Pack members pretty much split along old pack lines, with Karl going along with him. "Keep your phones with you and turned on, and make sure they are charged. If anything happens, call right away. We all know where the dead spots are, so try to avoid them if possible. No one wanders off alone."

"Why the security?" Jerry asked.

Denton stepped forward. "We believe that the fire was intentionally set by another alpha. He also sent the men to kidnap me. He wants to take over all the packs in the area, including Evergreen and Yellowstone."

"We don't know if he has people near our territories right now or not, but we need to be watchful. Report anything suspicious and don't take any chances. If you see anything, report it and get back to safety. Watch for animals with strange behavior. Use your skills, and if something doesn't seem right, assume it isn't," Mikael added. "Any other questions? If not, let's move out."

Mikael and Denton headed to one of the trucks, with Karl and Kaiawa taking the other. Others went along, and they convoyed over to the neighboring pack land. Denton got noticeably edgier and more nervous the closer they got to his old compound. Near the compound, the green of the forest suddenly gave way to blackened earth, the remains of trees, and the strong smell of charred wood and burned vegetation. It was so strong it burned his nose. In a few places smoke still rose in tiny wisps. Hotspots like that could last for days or even weeks if there was no rain.

Denton directed him because the landmarks Mikael had seen the last time he was here were gone. It was like driving through an alien, barren landscape. "That's the drive," Denton said softly, his voice filled with pain. It was obvious there would be very little left of what had been Denton and his family's home.

Mikael made the turn and got just a little way before fallen trees blocked the path. The main road had had a few, but they'd been able to go around. No such luck here. Thick, century-old trees had been reduced to fallen, smoldering remnants of their former majestic selves. Mikael heard a few sniffs from behind him but didn't turn around. Denton's pack members were allowed to grieve their loss without shame of any kind. "We're not going to salvage anything, are we?"

"It doesn't look like it," Mikael said as they got out of the trucks and started to walk toward what was left of the buildings.

They didn't find much. In movies, when rustic buildings burned, the fireplace was left standing, but this fire had been so hot that the mortar holding the stones in place expanded and cracked, leaving the chimneys piles of charred stone.

"There's nothing," Kaiawa said, kicking a burned timber that sent up a cloud of ash. "We have nothing left."

Denton stared at the wreckage, stunned into silence. The only sound was the wind as it swirled around them and then died away.

"You have plenty left," Mikael said. "You have each other. A pack is the people you love and care for. That's what being pack means. You help and stand by each other. It isn't a set of buildings—it's the way you treat each other." Every head turned toward him. "No one was hurt in all this, which is a miracle."

"Only because you came to the rescue of your mate. What would have happened if you hadn't?" Kaiawa asked.

"If Denton hadn't been my mate, I still would have been here to help. That wouldn't have made a difference." Mikael stood straight and tall. "You need to stop seeing me as a threat, because I'm not one to your position or to your pack."

"All this started after you came into our lives."

"No, it didn't," Denton said. "This was all in motion, every bit of it, before Mikael ever contacted us. And if he hadn't, I wouldn't be here, and what was left of the pack would be scattered or dead. Anton would have claimed the territory, and that would have been the end of all of us. You know that, and so do I. So stop blaming someone other than the one person responsible—Anton. We know he set the fire. This is his fault and no one else's. So let's search through this and see if we can find anything that escaped the inferno, and then we'll run. We'll make noise and let whoever is listening know that we are still here and aren't going anywhere. This is our pack land, and we are keeping it. The burned areas will regrow and became strong and lush once again."

Mikael smiled and nodded. "Can I ask something? Did any of the buildings have basements?"

"The main one did," Denton said, pointing.

"Then we need to clear off the debris, because that part of the building may have survived. I don't see a hole, so maybe the floor joists didn't give way." Mikael walked over and carefully nudged the pile of charred wood and ash. "Be careful. There is a floor, but we don't know how stable it is."

They worked to pull off the remains. Denton led them to the basement. A door and other parts of the building had fallen in over the entrance. It took them a few minutes to clear the stairs, but it looked as though the basement had survived.

"What was down here?" Kaiawa asked.

"Just some storage. I didn't use it for much." He didn't sound hopeful.

"There's a flashlight in the glove compartment," Mikael told Karl, and Karl hurried back to get it. He turned it on and handed it to Denton, letting him lead the way.

The space was tomb-like, the acrid smell of burned timber all around. The stone walls seemed to have held, and the fire hadn't made it to the basement, but the heat had. Some plastic items had melted over shelves. There were a few boxes, which he and Karl carried out and set aside. Mostly it was a lot of empty space. Denton found a few more boxes, and the men carried them out into the light, setting them with the others.

"What do we do now?" Denton asked as he looked over what little there was left.

"We'll put these in the truck and go for a run. Stuff isn't as important as the rest. It can all be replaced, but you can't be, and neither can your family." He placed his arm around Denton's waist.

"It's hard to believe it's all gone. Just like that—poof, everything we built is gone," Denton whispered. "I knew there wasn't likely to be anything left, but seeing it…. I guess I'd hoped something would still be here."

"I'm sorry," Mikael said softly. "I wish I could have saved this for you." He squeezed Denton a little closer. "But I saved you, and I'd do it again if I had to."

"Come on," Karl said to Kaiawa. "Let's leave these two alone with their mushiness. I'm ready to run."

"Me too," Kaiawa agreed.

Mikael rolled his eyes and then growled at Karl. His mate was hurting, and he'd be damned if he was going to discount it. The devastation of the compound and the whole area around it was hard enough to look at, but he couldn't bear to see Denton this morose and in pain. "Let's go," he whispered. "I think some green and growing things might help. There's nothing more we can do here."

"If I get my hands on Anton, I'm going to rip his nuts off," Denton growled.

Mikael smiled. "Now that sounds like my mate." He took Denton's hand, and they turned, heading back to the trucks. "I thought we'd head for the origin of the fire first, see if there's anything we can learn there. Then we can head for the borders of the land to check for encroachment and re-mark territory." Mikael began to undress and without thinking stepped between the others and Denton, shielding him from view. Denton stripped down and shifted, with Mikael right behind him. Karl and Kaiawa took care of securing the trucks, and then they shifted, along with the other men who'd joined them. They took off toward the west, following the edge of the burn line.

The fire had been hot—very hot. Mikael tried to see if he could smell anything strange, but the burned wood overwhelmed his senses. The fire had spread out, but not as much as it could have. He stopped and scented the air; the others did as well. Denton growled deep in his throat. Mikael smelled it too. Someone else was here. They were too far away for him to be specific, but the scent was there. Mikael moved closer to Denton, and they took off, running silently through the underbrush. They had the advantage in that they were upwind. As the scent got stronger, Mikael recognized it and stopped the group.

One of them is Anton himself, and I smell Vince as well. There's at least one other. Stay together and approach as silently as possible. The others signaled that they had received the message, and they made their way toward the source of the scent.

Mikael had to stop from sneezing as he got closer. Anton's scent was bitter and as acrid as the burn area. He hadn't noticed it so much before, but now it was plain and unpleasant. How could any wolf stand to be around him?

"Now that we've driven the pack away, I want this territory folded into ours," Anton was saying, the wind carrying his voice toward them. "Their alpha is dead, according to Vince here, and they are leaderless and scattered. It will be easy to round up any small bands and either bring them into the fold or do away with them."

Mikael felt Denton tense and silently nuzzled his side to soothe him. *We need to be calm and get as much information as we can.*

"Are you sure? We found Miles's body, or what was left of it, but not the alpha's. At least not where Vince said it was. If he hadn't been so quick to save his own skin…."

"I was captured and managed to get away," Vince said, sticking to the story, which was good. Mikael heard the fear in his voice; it was so clear he could almost taste it on the air.

"Enough," Anton said. "I believe Vince, because if he ever lied to me, he knows what would happen." Anton's voice had shifted to a deep growl. God, what Vince had said was the truth. Part of Mikael had hoped it wasn't true or at least that Vince had been exaggerating. The idea sent a chill through him.

We need to let them know that they are not welcome here. Kaiawa and Karl, circle around them. Let them catch your scent, but only for a second. Hopefully Anton will send his men to investigate. The two wolves took off together, and Mikael settled on his belly, going to ground. Denton did the same as they listened.

"Smell that?" Anton asked. "Harper, that must be one of our strays. See if you can round him up."

"Are you sure? I don't smell anything."

"The scent is faint, but it's definitely another wolf." Anton didn't sound happy at all about having his order questioned, and Mikael suspected Harper didn't waste time doing as Anton asked.

He and Denton waited a few minutes and then made their way closer. Anton and Vince stood next to a jeep at the edge of the burn line. Anton had his hands on his hips, bent over the hood, looking at a map.

Mikael shifted and stepped from the trees. "I think you better get out of territory that isn't yours."

Anton whipped around just as Denton stepped from the trees to join Mikael.

"My pack is just fine, and as you can see, reports of my death are greatly exaggerated. Your Vince here left me to die, but I was able to get away." Anton's surprise lasted only a few seconds. "You didn't waste time encroaching on my territory."

Anton seethed and stepped toward Denton, puffing himself up to appear as large as possible.

Don't you dare.

Anton came to a complete stop.

Mikael knew his ability to communicate directly with others was rare, but he'd half expected Anton to be able to do it as well. He obviously couldn't.

I know what you are, and I know what you can do. The thing is, you don't know what I can do.

"So you can talk to my mind," Anton said.

"Yeah. But what else can I do?" Mikael said out loud. Anton's stared at him, his black gaze searching. Mikael stared right back, meeting his gaze until Anton turned away. "Your dark tricks won't work on me. I'm of the light, and the darkness is scattered and banished by the light." He figured Anton needed a demonstration. He walked forward and swiped his hand. During the motion, his arm shifted, sliced one of the tires on the jeep, and shifted back. Air whooshed from the tire, and the jeep settled at an odd angle.

"That's some trick," Anton said.

"It's more than a trick," Denton said from behind him. "I suggest you and your lackeys get off my pack land, now. You have no business here. Your other man will be joining you in a few seconds." Denton smiled and pointed. "That direction is the quickest way back to your own territory. I suggest you start walking and don't think about shifting until you are out of my territory."

"You have no power over me," Anton countered, puffing his chest again.

"Well, we came up on you without any of you having a clue. Do you think we came alone? There's an entire pack waiting to descend on you." Denton sounded so powerful and strong, Mikael had to remember that now was not the time to get excited. "Get going."

"Not without Harper," Anton said.

"You're in no position to make any demands. Not now or ever," Denton said. Mikael inhaled and caught the scent of blood on the air, followed by a grunt and then silence. Denton must have caught the scent as well. "It looks like he wasn't smart enough to back away, and somehow I don't think he's coming back." Mikael did his best to keep the smile off his face. "Now go." Denton pointed, and Anton seethed as he and Vince stepped into the trees. "You're not welcome here."

Anton glared at both of them. "You'll pay for this."

Denton scoffed. "Please. You've been watching too many movies."

They watched them leave. Mikael followed them by their scent until it became less potent. He could also smell Karl and Kaiawa following them. Soon the acrid scent dissipated enough that his near-constant urge to sneeze faded away.

"God, he smells nasty," Denton said.

"Yeah. Whatever has a hold on him is rotting the guy from the inside. His eyes were dark when I saw him last, but now they look hollow, like he isn't really there any longer." He sighed and watched the area around them, staying alert. After a while, he smelled Karl and Kaiawa getting closer, and then they broke onto the road, shifted, and walked over to them.

"They're gone. They shifted as soon as they were off our territory, just like you said. Then they took off like the devil was after them."

"What happened to the other one?" Denton asked

"He came after Kaiawa, and he took care of him. The guy was huge but as dumb as they come."

"You know the type. They're used to their size carrying the day, and that's all they have. He was strong but slow. I opened him up

163

quick. His pack did this to us." Kaiawa's gaze was as cold as the dead of winter. "They'll think twice before messing with us again."

"Let's hope so," Mikael said without believing it. Whatever was driving Anton would not let this go easily. They'd given him a sting to his ego and sent him packing, but Mikael had little doubt that he'd be back. "I think we've done enough for today. It's going to take Anton time to recover and decide what he wants to do next."

"Is it possible he'll turn his attention somewhere else?" Denton asked.

"Yeah, I suppose. But we need to put an end to this. We'll never be safe as long as he's around. He burned out the Evergreen compound, and he did it on purpose to scatter your pack and make you vulnerable. You heard him. It was part of his plan. That part backfired, but if he decides to try burning out Yellowstone, we will be scattered. That can't happen."

"What should we do with the jeep?" Kaiawa asked.

"Let's change the tire and get it off our land. After that it's Anton's problem."

"Okay. Once we get back to the trucks, Kaiawa and I will take care of it, if you like. We can bring the truck out here and drive it off our territory. Then we can return."

"Good idea," Mikael said.

"What are we going to do about Anton?" Karl asked, his gaze shifting to both of them.

"I'm not really sure," Mikael answered honestly. "Let's head back." He turned to Denton. "We need to give this some thought."

Karl and Kaiawa shifted and headed off at a fast run. Denton shifted as well, and Mikael took the chance to admire Denton's wolf before he too shifted, and the two of them raced back toward the burned-out compound. Normally Mikael would nip at Denton's heels and play, but he wasn't in the mood. He loved the look of Denton's wolf, strong and powerful, but being in this place with everything around them burned to a crisp, it just didn't feel right. So instead he set his mind to figuring out a course of action, but nothing came. The pack was already on edge, and he didn't want to add to it. They needed stability, and the members of Denton's pack needed some peace in order to heal. Somehow he had to help them get that. They deserved it.

"Did you come up with anything?" Denton asked once they had shifted back at the truck and were beginning to dress.

"No. Every scenario I ran in my head doesn't get us any closer to where we need to be. The best I can come up with is closer monitoring of our borders and even setting some traps. But those plans are all predicated on us letting go of the Evergreen territory. That sort of defense requires a smaller perimeter, and that isn't acceptable." Mikael pulled on his shoes and yanked open the truck door. "I need some advice, and there's only one person I can go to with this."

"Who is that?"

"I need to ask the Mother for her guidance," Mikael replied.

"Can you do that?"

"I can ask. It doesn't mean she's going to answer. I can't tell you how many times I asked her for things when I was a kid. Stupid stuff that didn't really matter but seemed so important at the time. Of course, she didn't answer. But I know she listened and then let me puzzle things out for myself. She may do that this time, or she may feel she can help. I won't know unless I ask." Mikael climbed into the cab, and Denton went around to the passenger side. The boxes from the basement had been secured in the bed of the truck. Mikael carefully turned the truck around and started the drive home.

"How do we contact the Mother?" Denton asked. "Do we go back to the tree in the meadow?"

Mikael squeezed Denton's leg. "No. We have to go to a more sacred place, but first there are things we'll need to do."

"When do you want to do this?"

"Tonight. It would be better if it were a full moon because that's when our wolves are the strongest, so that's when we're closest to her, but I don't want to wait."

"Okay. Tell me what we have to do."

MIKAEL SPENT the rest of the afternoon working with Jerry on his plans for the new building. He needed to think about something other than Anton and the threat to the pack for a while. More than once he wondered if they'd handled the situation with Anton correctly but kept coming back to the fact that anything other than a show of strength would only encourage him. Anything else would be perceived as weakness that he'd try to exploit. They might have taken him as a group, but that wasn't their way, and while Anton would have done it, Mikael was a child of the light and would never resort to dark-wolf tactics.

As sundown approached, Mikael found Denton in the kitchen. "It's time." He squeezed Denton's shoulder, and he stood. "I'll show you the way."

"Where are you going?" Mikael's mother asked. Sometimes she still treated him like he was a pup.

"We need some guidance. Catherine will watch over things here. If anything happens, she's in charge." Mikael kissed his mother on the cheek and then led Denton outside. He could make this trek in the dark, blindfolded. It got darker and darker, and they reached the stream as the last light of day disappeared from the sky. Mikael stripped off his clothes and piled them on a rock, then waited for Denton to do the same. "We need to wash and make sure we're clean. This water is cold as heck, but it comes straight from the mountains. It's clean and clear."

Denton cried out in shock when he stepped into the water. Mikael did the same. Goosebumps raised on his skin, but he continued until he'd washed completely. Then he got out of the water, shifted to his wolf, and shook himself dry. Denton followed suit, and then Mikael led him to the cave entrance and inside. He shifted back to human form and handed Denton a robe. He lit a candle and set it on one of the rock ledges. "This is where my pack hid during the dark times, when we couldn't be ourselves. The Mother protected us while she worked to make the world safer for us again. This is where the pack makes important decisions and where I always felt we were closest to the Mother."

"So what do we do?"

"There's nothing mystical about it. No spells or incantations to make her appear. We sit together and ask her to join us. We tell her our problem and hope she'll lead us to an answer."

"How will we know when we've gotten one?"

"No matter how she chooses to answer, if she does, we'll know. The Mother knows how to make her wishes known in her own way. Twice she's come to me in dreams, and a few other times I swear she's put ideas into my head, little pieces of understanding. Most of the time I'm not sure if it's her or if I'm hit with a flash of insight. Either way, I always thank her, because everything we have comes from the Mother."

"What about the fire?" Denton asked.

"The Mother can't shield us from the bad things in life. She doesn't shield us, but she does see to it that we receive our share of life's benefits." Mikael spread two rugs on the stone floor and took Denton's hands. "Think of the day in the meadow, making love under the tree, caressed by the breeze. That was the Mother—she was there with us as we showed our love for each other. That's what we need to remember and hold in our hearts. The bad things are hard to let go of, but we have to, otherwise they eat at us."

"If you say so."

"I mean it, Denton. Close your eyes and remember the happiest parts of your life. The Mother was there with you. She was with your parents when you took your first steps, and when you shifted for the first time and played with your friends as a pup." Mikael ran his thumbs lightly over the back of Denton's hands. "She's always there when we take a run, and when we howl our happiness and joy at the moon, she listens. That's the music we sing to her, that we all give her. The music of life is hers. So just remember and listen." Denton closed his eyes, and Mikael did the same.

That was beautiful, Mikael heard in a gentle female voice from behind him. *But I'm also in the spring rain and the summer sunshine.*

Mikael lifted his head and opened his mouth to speak, but the Mother said, *I don't have much time. I know your quandary.*

Can you help us? Mikael asked, slowly opening his eyes. The cave was filled with light, and birds and butterflies filled the space.

I can guide you, but that's all. I'm forbidden from direct interference. But sometimes the best defense is a good offense. However, you cannot challenge Anton directly. Any challenge with a chance of truly defeating him must be issued by Anton, and you must stand together. Only the light can defeat the darkness.

So should we—

I can't do any more for you, she said.

Mikael felt the breeze caress his cheek, and Denton started.

167

But know I'm with you and will do my best to keep those you love safe. The light faded, and the birds became silent and faded away.

"Was she here?" Denton asked.

"Yes, of course. Didn't you hear her?"

"No. But I felt her touch me." Denton released one of Mikael's hands and touched his cheek. "It was like the way my mother used to caress my cheek when she held me." Denton squeezed Mikael's hand. "I get it now. She was always there, even in the way my own mother touched me."

"She's the mother of us all," Mikael said and then gently drew Denton to him. They shared a kiss and moved closer together. "She's there in the way a mother holds her child, and she's there when we show our love for each other." Mikael drew Denton closer, caressing his chest.

"So it's okay to do this here?" Denton asked as he tugged at Mikael's robe and then slid it down his shoulders.

"Yes. Our pack has made love and conceived pups in this cave for generations. The stones are imbued with the Mother's blessings." Mikael met his lips and pressed Denton back onto the rug. He opened Denton's robe and let the fabric part to either side of Denton's magnificent body. He licked Denton's chin and over their mating mark, then down his chest before sucking on a nipple. "Here you can make as much noise as you want. We are truly alone. There's no one to hear, even with wolf ears."

"That must be a first for us." Denton snickered.

Mikael went about making his mate happy, and judging by the fact that his words trailed off in a deep moan as Mikael sucked and nipped at the now-hard bud, he was doing just that.

"I love how sensitive you are," Mikael whispered.

"Only for you. I never was before."

Mikael stilled, hoping for an explanation.

"I always thought there was something wrong with me. You aren't my first," Denton explained, and Mikael growled at the thought of anyone else touching his wolf. "I'm sure I wasn't yours either, so stop being so... alpha." Denton smiled. "It's just that I thought I didn't feel things the way others did. I didn't have places that could be touched to make me feel special. But I now know that I was waiting for you, because everywhere you touch feels special."

Mikael lightly pinched Denton's nipple, and he shivered, proving his point. Mikael grinned and lightly ran his fingers down Denton's ridged belly, the muscles fluttering under his touch. "Like this?"

"You're being mean," Denton protested without heat, and Mikael tested the theory by licking a spot on Denton's side just above his hip. Denton went wild, squirming and pressing for more. Now the hunt was on. Mikael was determined to find all those great spots, and he laved up and down Denton's chest and sides, even his arms, finding a particularly great area at the base of his neck.

"Roll over," Mikael growled. All of Denton's moans and cries had sent him on a passionate trajectory that left Mikael throbbing for his mate. But he wasn't going to rush. They had all the time in the world, and he intended to take it. When Denton turned over, Mikael straddled his legs and kissed his shoulders before nipping and soothing the skin down Denton's spine.

"Fuck, Mikael, you know I'm humping the stone floor here."

"Yeah." Mikael sucked at the base of Denton's back, lifting his mate's hips. Denton's cheeks parted, and Mikael dove in, sucking at his tight entrance while Denton filled the cave with a symphony of love growls, moans, and whimpers. Damned if his mate wasn't something else. Mikael had always been taught that when he found his mate, he would be what he needed, and he'd know what his mate wanted. But he never dreamed two people could be like this. When Mikael nipped at Denton's puckered skin, Denton whimpered like a needy pup, and when Mikael thrust deep with his tongue, Denton growled like the wolf that he was.

"Mikael, I need...."

"I know." Mikael blew on Denton's wet skin and felt him shiver. Reaching between Denton's legs, Mikael stroked his cock and brought it back, sucking on the head.

"For fuck's sake...." Denton growled, and Mikael chuckled.

"The sounds you make." He dove between Denton's cheeks again, probing deep as he stroked Denton's cock. His mate's entire body quivered, excitement and energy filling the entire cave.

"Just fuck me and make me yours!"

Mikael growled. "You are already mine, and you always will be." He pulled back and spit into his hand. He coated his cock and lined it up with Denton's spit-slicked entrance before surging forward. He heard the air whoosh from Denton's lungs, but his wolf would not be denied. Denton's yell filled the room, filling it with even more passionate energy.

"Yes, hell yes!" Denton slammed back against Mikael. "Don't you fucking dare stop."

Mikael withdrew and snapped his hips forward, taking Denton, needing him. The sharp slap of skin on skin filled the cave. His wolf came to the surface, determined to possess his mate. Mikael growled. "Losing control."

"The hell you are," Denton said and scrambled forward. He rolled over and pulled Mikael to him, gaze to gaze. "You are mine and I'm yours." Denton guided him until Mikael was once again buried deep inside. "I love you, but I'm making love to the man. You are who I want and need."

Mikael's wolf settled back, and he regained control. "I'm better."

"I'm your mate, and I'll always be able to soothe you, just like you calm me." Denton tightened his muscles, gripping Mikael tightly. "Now, unless you're some kind of quitter, I suggest you fuck me through this stone floor!"

That Mikael could do and did. He wrapped Denton in his arms and thrust hard while kissing him. Mikael needed it all, and fuck if Denton didn't lock his legs around his waist, driving him crazy. "You're a pushy bottom, you know that."

"And you love it." Denton tightened his legs, pressing Mikael closer and keeping him from moving. Mikael's cock jumped and throbbed in the tight, hot confines of Denton's passage. "Never forget that you're mine too. You may be stronger, but you're still my mate, and I'm not some shrinking violet."

"Thank the Mother," Mikael said and moved back, then drove into Denton. They both shook with the force. Mikael had been prepared to lift Denton off the ground, but it hadn't been necessary. Mikael realized that the two of them weren't in sync, and he took a deep breath and backed off. Denton was his mate, and he needed to pay closer attention to him. His mate was incredible, and they moved together after that, passion building within seconds. There were times when he loved being a wolf, and being able to see Denton's eyes and watch the way his lips parted, even in the darkness, listening to his gasps, was the greatest thing in the world. "Fuck, you're hot as hell."

"So are you." Denton placed a hand on Mikael's chest, sending tingles through him. Maybe it was Denton or maybe this place, but everything seemed heightened and more alive. Mikael possessed Denton's mouth, devouring him while he thrust deep inside. He didn't stop until Denton pulled away and gasped for air. Mikael did the same and then took possession of his mate once more. Yeah, he knew he was being intense, but he was part wolf, dammit, and his wolf would not be denied, not in this place.

"Mikael...."

He paused, forcing his mind to work. "Am I hurting you?"

"No. Love you," Denton whispered.

The last threads on Mikael's control snapped, and he thrust deep, feeling Denton come unglued around him. His mate's climax triggered his own, and he spilled himself in his mate, marking his territory and his love forever. No matter what happened, Denton was his mate and his love. Mikael quivered and shook as he collapsed into Denton's arms, unaware of anything else. He'd used up everything, given all he had.

"Man...," Denton breathed into his ear.

"I need to breathe," Mikael gasped, pulling air into his lungs and trying not to cough. He'd been on the edge, fighting for control for long enough that his energy was gone.

"It's all right." Denton closed his arms around Mikael's back. "You know I like holding you too. You don't let me do it all that often. Have you noticed that?"

"Yeah. My wolf is quickly developing this need to be in charge, at least as far as you are concerned. I don't think I've been that way in the past, not with my few other lovers, but with you it seems to come naturally. Protect, care for, hold, love—all these things I want to do for you at the same time."

"You've always been that way. I know you live to protect your pack and now me."

"I'll protect your pack too, because they're part of you."

171

Denton inhaled deeply and then released the breath slowly. "I think you'll have to, because I'm not giving you up either. The full moon starts in a few days, and I think we need to consider merging the packs. Something that important has to be done at that time. You'll need to ask each pack member to join your pack."

"No." Mikael slid off Denton, resting next to him. "I think what we need to do is dissolve both packs and form a new one, at least in name. Evergreen and Yellowstone will cease to exist, with a new, combined pack in its place. I was thinking naming it the Old Faithful Pack, since the landmark will be close to our territory. What do you think?"

Denton climbed on top of him, and Mikael wrapped him in his arms. "You'd do that?"

"Sure. A pack isn't a name but the people who make it up. And this way, everyone is on an equal footing. We would be the alpha pair, mates joined together. We'd lead the pack with our betas and enforcer. That would settle the doubts and uncertainties for both packs."

"So when should we tell them?"

"Tomorrow we'll call a meeting and let everyone ask questions. Then, at the full moon, we'll all gather here and create our new pack and ask the Mother's blessing. After that, united, we'll see what we can do about this Anton problem."

"What if something else happens?"

"It won't. The full moon is the time of the month when the Mother is at the height of her strength. Even the night is at its brightest. If what I believe is true and Anton is a dark wolf, then his powers, and the ones he follows, will be strongest at new moon when the world is at its darkest. Think about when he made his advances—it was right around the new moon." Mikael stroked Denton's cheek. "Regardless, we can't allow Anton or anyone to keep us from doing what's right for our pack."

Mikael closed his eyes, resting with Denton. A breeze, probably a puff of air from outside, blew over their sweaty skin.

"Did you feel that?" Denton asked.

"Yeah. I think she approves," Mikael whispered.

"I do too," Denton said and then kissed away further words.

They stayed where they were for a long while. Mikael might even have dozed; he wasn't sure. But eventually he and Denton got up, and after putting everything away, they left the cave and dressed by the edge of the stream. They walked back to the compound. As they approached, conversations, laughter, and even the unmistakable sounds of soft lovemaking reached Mikael's ears. He smiled and walked into the center of the compound, listening to the sounds of peace and tranquility. Conversations ceased when the pack members saw them. Mikael simply nodded and whispered good night to them before moving along with Denton.

Mikael approached the main house, sniffing and then breaking into a smile. He opened the door and embraced the young wolf inside in a nearly bone-breaking hug. Denton growled from behind him. "This is my brother, Christopher," Mikael said, releasing him. "He's home from college. Chris, this is my mate, Denton." The two shook hands. "When did you get in?"

"Half an hour ago." Christopher smiled his usual carefree smile. As the youngest, Christopher had always seemed to go his own way and make his own happiness. He followed the beat of his own drum and his own call. In some ways, Mikael was jealous because responsibility always landed on his shoulders, and Chris was free to follow his dreams. He had incredible eyes, with a light that shone from within, and a face that always turned heads. "So you found a mate?" Christopher said.

"Don't tell me Mom didn't tell you," Mikael said knowingly.

"Well, she might have mentioned it. But I figured she must have gotten her facts confused."

"It's hard to explain, but the short version is that Denton is the alpha of the Evergreen pack. But believe me, you've missed a lot. In the end, due to circumstances beyond anyone's control—"

"Don't worry, Mom told me about the fire and what was happening. It's still a surprise when you actually see everything. So who turned out to be the alpha?' Chris winked, and Mikael growled. "That answers my question." He laughed. "Come on, big brother, have a sense of humor."

Mikael wasn't sure how to take that. This wasn't a joking matter as far as he was concerned. "We've all been through a lot in the past few weeks. Change on top of change, and yet things are going very well."

"So will Evergreen be going back now that the fire is out?"

"Not unless individual members wish to leave. We'll be talking to the entire pack tomorrow," Denton said. "We're working through details of what we want to do."

"Wow," Christopher said.

"What is that for?" Mikael asked, sliding an arm around Denton's waist. He glanced at him, and Denton put an arm around his waist and slowly rubbed Mikael's back. Instantly he felt better and much less like taking his little brother's head off. One of Christopher's other talents was pushing Mikael's buttons.

"Nothing. It's just that I've never seen you with such a ready smile. You've always been so serious. It's nice." Christopher leaned back against the counter. "So how did you two decide to get together? I would have loved to see those fireworks."

"He's my mate," Denton said, as though that said it all. Mikael knew it didn't, but the rest was none of Christopher's business. "The Mother made us for each other."

"Do you really believe that? I know Mom and Dad always talked about being made for each other, but I thought that was their way of saying how much they cared about each other."

Mikael nodded, but it was Denton who answered. "Well, when you've had the Mother herself touch you and give you her blessing, I think you need to accept it. Now, if you'll excuse me, we're going to get something to eat, and then we need to discuss some plans we need to make." Denton released him and went into the kitchen.

"Is he serious?" Christopher asked.

"Yes. A lot has happened, like I said. Not the least of which is that when Denton talks about being blessed by the Mother, you better believe it." Mikael kept the part about actually speaking to her to himself. His conversations and dreams with her were between him and the Mother. They were sacred. "He's my fated mate, and it's taken a lot for us to get where we are. And I'm afraid it's not over." Mikael decided it was best not to get into all that. "Go on and get some dinner, meet people. And for the record, it's good to have you home."

"It's good to be back."

"How long are you here?"

Christopher looked around. "With all these wolves, it's hard to keep a secret, but I don't know. I finished my coursework and have my degree. I didn't take part in the graduation ceremony because I wasn't really interested. At first I figured I would stay in Cheyenne. But I've been missing my family, and something kept pulling me back."

"That's because you're pack, and you've been away too long."

"I know and I forgot the reason I went away in the first place. I went to study so I could help the pack, so I packed my things and came home."

"What kind of job are you looking for," Mikael said.

"The state is interested in hiring me. With my degree in forestry, they have opportunities."

"Well, we have opportunities here too. Denton works for the forest service, and we have a ton of land now that's going to need to be managed and looked after. So we can definitely keep you busy." Mikael moved closer and pulled Christopher into a hug. "I'm proud of you and glad you came home."

Christopher patted him on the back. "Thanks. I thought I'd see about working in the park," he said. "I can't decide."

"You have time, and when you decide, if you still want to work in the park, you can talk to Denton and ask him about it." Mikael was interested in what role his brother wanted in the pack, but that could wait. Maybe it would sort itself out. There was no need to borrow trouble. "Have you eaten?"

"Yeah. Mom fed me as soon as I walked in the door. I think she figured I hadn't eaten since I left." Christopher laughed. "Go on and join your mate. We'll have a chance to talk later, and from what he said, you have important things to discuss."

"You know where your room is...." It was the only one in the entire compound that hadn't been filled. Mikael had been hoping Christopher would come home sometime soon. "And if not before, I'll see you at breakfast." Mikael shared a smile with his brother and then went to join Denton in the kitchen, where a plate of leftovers had been heated and sat at his place at the table.

"He's interesting," Denton said once Mikael had sat down.

"You don't like him," Mikael observed.

"I don't know him."

Mikael heard the way Denton bent the truth. "Christopher is my pain-in-the-ass little brother. He hasn't had much responsibility in his life, so he hasn't had to grow up. He'll do that soon. And he isn't a bad guy, just young and a little full of himself. He'll settle down. Wolves don't like change, you know that. We settle in packs because we want the familiar around us, but there's been a lot of change, and he wasn't here to see any of it."

"Don't make excuses for him. He was rude, and if he wasn't your brother I would have knocked him down a peg or two."

Mikael hardened his gaze. "You treat everyone the same. And my brother isn't any different from anyone else. If he's rude, call him on it."

"You'll back me?" Denton asked.

"Of course I will. You're my mate, and no one is going to be rude to you and get away with it. Besides, if he wants to work with the forest service in the park, then he's going to need to be nice to you."

Denton leaned closer. "You goaded him on purpose."

"Of course I did. Christopher is most likely trying to figure out how he can change the not so good impression he made with you right now. He's smart but brash. Just don't let him off the hook too quickly and you'll be fine. Christopher needs to learn respect."

"What he needs is to find his place," Denton said. "He's always been the son of the alpha or the brother of the alpha. You told me yourself that he wasn't sure what role he wanted to play in the pack. That sort of place he has to earn. It isn't given, not if he wants to have the respect of the rest of the pack. The thing is, after being away, he doesn't know where he fits in."

"I'll...."

"No, Mikael. Stop trying to fix everything for everyone. He needs to figure things out for himself. And he will, if you just let him." Denton went back to eating.

"I don't try to fix everything," Mikael argued.

"Yes, you do," Denton countered quickly. "It's part of what makes you an excellent leader and a great alpha. But sometimes you have to let things unfold on their own, and that's hard for you. See, the whole 'fixing things' thing is also part of you being in control. You like to have everything in its nice neat box with everyone knowing their place. And that's okay most of the time. But your brother is a handful—I can see that, and you know it too. He's also young and needs to find his way. And you need to let him."

"Okay." Mikael put his hands up in surrender. "I'll do my best."

"That's all I can ask for." Denton smiled at him, and Mikael forgot about everything else.

"Let's finish eating." Mikael leered. Other appetites were beginning to rise. Denton brought out the animal in him.

"Okay, but we have to meet with Jerry and the other men about the new building, and then we need to go over what we want to talk about at tomorrow's meeting."

"You're such a slave driver," Mikael said with a wink.

"And you're turning into a hound dog," Denton teased, his smile bright. "Not that I'm complaining." Denton's eyes danced a little.

"I should hope not." Mikael returned Denton's smile and sat at the table looking at him. Fuck, he'd turned into a lovesick fool. But who the hell cared? He certainly didn't.

"Finish your dinner," Denton said, chuckling.

God, Mikael loved to see that smile, and he would move mountains to see him happy. Yes, he was in love: big, gooey, wet, sappy love. The Mother had told him he'd have a mate, and she'd even pushed them together. But what he felt for Denton was more than just matehood. He loved him. His wolf had found his mate, but his human had found love. Mikael was supremely lucky.

He looked down at his plate and went back to eating. Even after all the excitement and drama of the past few weeks, Mikael was happier than he could ever remember. Denton made him happy, and the weight of responsibility for his pack didn't seem so heavy, even if it seemed that his pack was going to more than double in size. The pack hadn't ever been particularly large, but it seemed very likely that after the meeting and the ceremony at the full moon, his pack was going to grow significantly and that he was going to be the one responsible for them. Mikael watched Denton eat and realized that wasn't true. He wasn't going to be responsible for them all—he *and* Denton were. He now had a partner, someone to share both the joy and the burden of leadership with.

"You keep looking at me like I'm your dessert," Denton commented as they finished their food. Mikael left his dishes where they were and walked around to where Denton sat, wrapping him in his arms and resting his chin on Denton's shoulder. He said nothing because there was nothing to say. Words couldn't describe how happy he was, so he simply let things be, at least for the moment. Denton leaned his head slightly, and they touched, cheek to cheek, a gentle touch that Mikael wished would never end.

Heavy footsteps raced inside, and Mikael looked up as Christopher came to a stop in the kitchen. Mikael turned and lightly kissed Denton's ear before straightening up. "We'll be right there," Mikael said firmly. Christopher opened his mouth, most likely to argue about something, then closed it again. Mikael met his little brother's gaze with a hard stare. Once Christopher broke the gaze, Mikael gently patted Denton's shoulder and took the last of the dishes to the sink. Then he waited for his mate to join him before following Christopher outside to see what was up.

Jerry had set up a light on one of the porches, and pack members were gathered around asking questions. Their voices quieted as Mikael and Christopher approached and joined the group. "What do you think?" Jerry asked.

Mikael looked over the plans and smiled. It looked great to him. "You're the expert. The size looks good—simple, and there's a good use of space on both sides." Mikael turned to everyone else to see their reactions.

"Your thoughts?" Mikael asked Denton.

"I like it. Where were you going to build?"

Jerry rushed off to the far end of the compound. "I thought in this area here. It seems a solid place with good ground. It would provide both privacy and access to the communal areas without crowding any of the other buildings. If more are built, they could run this way." Jerry motioned, and Mikael nodded.

"Sounds like a good idea to me. Is everyone in agreement?" Mikael asked and shared a smile with Denton. "Great. We'll start gathering the materials we need right after the meeting tomorrow morning at eleven. We'll meet here in the center of the compound, and everyone, young and old, is welcome to attend."

"What are we going to talk about?" Christopher asked.

"The future of our packs," Denton answered, and Mikael moved closer to him.

"Decisions need to be made that will affect all of us, so Denton and I thought we would lay them out for you."

"But you're the alpha," Vadim said.

"Yes, and many alphas would make these decisions alone, but we feel that this is too big and too important for us to make alone." Mikael took a step forward. "You are all members of our family, and as such, it's important that you have a say in your future. Denton and I have mated—you know that. So that mating will bring changes for us." Mikael met the various gazes with what he hoped was a gentle and reassuring smile.

Pack members began to talk quietly among themselves, some about the meeting and others about the building and what would be needed to construct it. Kaiawa approached Denton and asked to speak with him. Mikael watched them go. He stepped away, and Catherine came up beside him.

"You know everyone would have accepted it if you and Denton had just announced that you planned to merge the packs. We all see what's happening with the two of you, and we're all pleased. Both packs seem to be." Catherine bumped his shoulder with hers. "That being said, I'm impressed that you're doing it this way. You're a good leader."

"I like to think we both are," Mikael told her.

"That's definitely true." Catherine smiled, and Karl joined their small group.

"I love the plans for the new building. I think it's going to be perfect."

"It will get us through the winter more comfortably. We can make plans and preparations while it's cold and then build more in the spring," Mikael said.

"We could make it through winter as it is if we had to," Catherine commented and turned to him. "You're giving everyone a project, something to do together."

"That was my original idea, and it seems to be working." Mikael was very pleased that his plan seemed to be bearing fruit. He'd have to see how it worked once they started construction, but the initial signs were good.

"Look at them," Denton said as he approached from behind. Mikael held out his hand, and Denton took it, the touch welcome and warm. "They're working together, laughing, and mixing easily."

"What did Kaiawa want?" Mikael asked. Catherine and Karl excused themselves and joined the others.

"He was concerned about his place in the pack. He's always been supportive, and he's a good beta. I told him he would be one of ours. That we need him."

"Of course." Mikael squeezed Denton's hand. "There are going to be difficulties and issues. The best way to deal with them is to communicate." He got a chill up his spine, and he stilled as a cloud, dark and ominous seemed to float across his thoughts. He pushed it away and looked around.

"Is everything all right?"

"Yes, I'm fine." He took a deep breath and pulled Denton closer. They stood together watching their pack. "Let's go inside and talk about what we want to say tomorrow." He led Denton to the house and up the stairs to their bedroom.

"I thought you wanted to talk," Denton teased.

Mikael closed the bedroom door. "We can talk in here."

Denton scoffed and tugged his shirt off over his head. "I think you have a very different kind of conversation in mind." He dropped his shirt to the floor, and Mikael stalked forward the way his wolf would hunt prey. Fuck, Denton was gorgeous. Mikael lunged, pulling Denton to him, sucking on one of his perfect nipples, hard and taut on his magnificent chest. "What's gotten into you?"

"I intend to be getting into you," Mikael whispered huskily. "There's no way I can get enough of you. I'm happy. Our packs are largely content, and things have worked out better than I ever hoped. I have you in my life. There isn't much more I could ask for." Mikael rested his head against Denton's chest, listening to his mate's heart beating in his ear. "I probably shouldn't have said that."

"Why?"

"Because as soon as I have nearly everything I could want, something happens to try to take it all away." Lord knew that had happened to him before. "I was happy before I lost my father. Not like this, not like I am with you, but I was happy."

Denton wrapped his arms around him. "You know when we're together, you don't have to be in charge all the time. You can act who you are... even be vulnerable."

Mikael wasn't so sure about that. "I've seen what happens to alphas who are vulnerable. I watched Gregor get torn apart in front of his mate and pups."

"Do you really think Gregor was vulnerable?"

Mikael shrugged. "I don't know why Anton went after him, but I will not allow him to come for my pack—our pack," he corrected quickly. "Sorry, I really meant our pack."

Denton released him, looking up, eyes blazing. "You say that I'm your mate and that you love me, but you don't trust me." He stepped away and walked toward the door.

"I do trust you."

"Trust is being able to show who you are. It's you being able to tell me what you're feeling even if you're not comfortable with it. Do you understand?" Denton put a hand on the doorknob. Mikael's heart skipped a beat. He didn't want Denton to leave, but he wasn't sure what to say to make him stay. "You don't." Denton pulled his hand back. "Sometimes you can be the densest man on earth, you know that?" Denton's expression softened. "You can also be the sweetest when you want to be."

"You're going to have to help me here, because I'm lost."

Denton smiled. "See? Was that so fucking hard? You don't have to have all the answers, and you don't need to be the one in charge all the damn time. Maybe out there, yes, you need to be strong, because it's what they expect and need from you. It's what makes you the leader you are. But in here, when it's just the two of us, you get to be as scared, nervous, and yes, vulnerable as anyone else. That's trusting someone."

"I don't get it."

Denton sighed. "Do you trust me?"

"Of course I do."

"Then come here."

Mikael walked to where a still shirtless Denton waited for him.

Denton took his hands and held them tight. "Close your eyes."

Mikael hesitated and then slowly slid his eyes closed. Instantly his sense of hearing and scent kicked into overdrive.

"Stop that. You're trying to smell me now. Well, it won't work, and don't you dare cheat, or I'll blindfold you." Denton chuckled.

"Maybe I'll do that anyway," He whispered in Mikael's ear. Mikael's wolf bared his teeth. "Don't you growl at me that way. I'm your mate, it's shameful."

"You sound like an old matron," Mikael teased.

He felt Denton move behind him and stood still. "Do I feel like an old matron?" Denton slid his hands around Mikael's side and over his belly, then down to the clasp of his pants. Instantly Mikael's cock went hard as a rock.

"Fucking pants are too tight."

"I can take care of that, but only if you stand still, right there, and don't move."

"Why are you doing this?"

"You, dear heart, need a lesson in trust. So I'm giving you one. Mikael, you can't always be in charge. It's exhausting. You need to trust others—well, me. You trust Karl and Catherine."

"Yes. They're my brother and sister."

"And I'm your mate," he countered firmly, which stung.

"Touché," Mikael said. "I just find it hard, I guess."

"Was that so hard to admit?" Denton snuggled closer, pressing his chest against Mikael's back, sliding his hands down his sides.

Mikael sighed contentedly and then held his breath when Denton's warm hand teased at the top of his pants. He wanted to growl. Hell, what he really wanted to do was drop his pants, grab Denton, carry him to the bed, and proceed to fuck his mate until he couldn't form a single coherent syllable. But he also got the idea that this was a lesson in patience as well as trust. He didn't want to fail, because he wanted Denton to be happy.

"I do trust you," Mikael whispered and leaned back a little. Denton was there, strong, holding him up, allowing Mikael to let go.

"See what happens when you trust the one you love?" Denton opened his pants and slid them down just enough that the cool air of the room kissed the skin above his cock. Denton didn't push them low enough to free his dick, and Mikael wanted to growl once again. "I can feel your frustration, and I know exactly what you want. But you're in my hands now, and you need to trust that I'm going to take care of you." Denton teased his fingers over the base of his cock and then took pity on him, freed Mikael's dick from its confines, and, thank the Mother, started stroking him gently.

"God, your hands…." He loved the way Denton touched him.

"See? When your eyes are closed and you let go, you can really feel me. Sometimes when we're together it's so intense…."

"Is that bad?"

"God, no," Denton whispered in his ear. "But it also means that we miss the little things. Like the simple touch of the person who loves you." Denton stroked him faster and harder. "I want you to think of how you feel right now. How your legs shake and the way you want me to touch you." Denton ran a hand up his chest and lightly pinched a nipple. Mikael quivered and kept his eyes closed, reveling in the sensation of Denton's magic hands. "You want me so bad you can barely stand it."

"Pretty sure of yourself," Mikael chided, and Denton stroked harder. Fuck talking. He inhaled deeply, filling his nose with Denton's scent. God, he loved that. Hell, there was very little about his mate that he didn't love.

"Sure enough that I can make you come right here, right now."

"Oh yeah…." Mikael groaned, not really putting up an argument.

"Yeah," Denton countered breathily pressing his cock to Mikael's ass and sucking his ear. "You're going to come for me right now because there's nothing you want more in the entire world."

As much as he wanted to be contrary, Denton's touch felt too damned good, and he gave in and let Denton take charge of his pleasure. Mikael's breath hitched, and the tingles of impending pleasure and release started at the base of his balls. He tried to control it, but Denton gripped him tight. Mikael gasped and came with so much force he nearly lost his balance.

"Maybe there's something to this trust thing," Mikael said with a smile.

"You better believe it. I have your back and you have mine. Always remember that." Denton held him tight as Mikael attempted to catch his breath.

"How could I possibly forget?" It was etched indelibly on his brain.

CHAPTER 9

THREE DAYS later, after a very successful pack meeting to lay the groundwork for the formation of the Old Faithful pack, as well as numerous discussions with members of both packs, Mikael led everyone through the woods. He carried Alexi in his arms and walked next to Denton, with Karl, Catherine, and Kaiawa around them. The rest of the pack followed. At the creek outside the cave, he stopped.

"This spot is sacred for all of us. It's where the Mother sheltered some of her children through the years of hiding. Now it is the spot where we are closest to her. We wash before entering, so please scrub your hands," Mikael said. He figured the Mother would forgive him for not having the entire pack strip down to bathe. He set Alexi down, and the pup rubbed his hands in the cold water while Mikael kept him from falling in. He helped his niece as well, and Maria grinned excitedly at him before washing.

"What do we do now?" Maria asked, making a big deal of not touching anything with her clean hands.

"We undress and shift. Everyone enters as a wolf, and then we shift inside," Mikael instructed. "Leave your clothes in neat piles. There are clean robes inside for everyone once you shift back." Mikael stripped off his clothes and waited for Denton to do the same before shifting and entering the cave. Once he and Denton were inside, he put on his robe and handed out others as one by one, their pack members entered the cave and shifted back. He stood next to Denton on the rock ledge at the back of the cave.

"Where do we go, Mama?" William asked Catherine once she had shifted back and put on her robe.

"Please be comfortable. There are no assigned spots for this," Denton said with a smile and then looked over at Mikael, excitement clear in his expression.

"Is anyone still outside?"

"No," Karl said, standing next to his wife. "I was the last one."

"Good. Tonight is the full moon, and normally we would run and hunt, but tonight is special," Mikael said. "Tonight we form a new pack. When we were outside, each of us were members of either the Evergreen or Yellowstone pack. But now, gathered here, we are all members of the new Old Faithful pack." Mikael took Denton's hand in his and held it up. "This is as we decided in our pack meeting."

Denton stepped forward. "Tonight we are here to formally become one pack, one family. Usually, packs join after a challenge, and those unions are born of bloodshed and violence. Ours is a joining out of love. When I took Mikael as my mate, I took his family as my own." He looked over everyone gathered.

"When I took Denton as my mate, I took his family as my own," Mikael said. "You have all seen our mating marks—he is mine and I am his. He is my mate, and you are our family." Mikael paused to let the echo that ricocheted off the walls die down. "In joining our packs, we are unique in that we have a mated male pair leading our pack. So rather than an alpha and alpha mate to lead the pack, we will have a mated alpha pair. We ask the Mother to shine her light on our new pack." Mikael turned and took a candle from the rock ledge right behind him. He struck a match and lit it. "This light symbolizes the Mother's light that shines on each and every one of us."

A breeze blew into the cave from the opening, making the flame flicker and waver. It remained lit, and the light intensified, getting brighter and brighter before fading once again to a normal candle flame. A buzz of whispers went up from the assembled group as Mikael handed the candle to Denton.

"Did the Mother do that?" William asked in a stage whisper that made all the adults smile.

"Yes. We take that as a sign of the Mother's blessing on our new pack." Mikael stepped to the edge of the rock ledge. "I, Mikael Volokov...."

"And I, Denton Arguson...."

They continued together. "Do promise to lead the Old Faithful pack to the best of my ability. I promise to love and honor my mate, cherish and nurture each pack member, and build and strengthen our pack to the best of my ability." The light that Denton held flickered

185

once again, and Mikael felt a soft, gentle caress on his cheek. He glanced at Denton, and from his expression, he knew he'd been touched as well.

"Do you former members of the Yellowstone pack promise to be loyal and true to all your brothers and sisters of the Old Faithful pack?" Mikael asked in a loud voice.

"We do" resounded through the cave, with even the little ones joining in.

A lump formed in Mikael's throat.

Mikael stepped back, and Denton stepped forward, handing him the candle. "Do you the former members of the Evergreen pack promise to be loyal and true to all your brothers and sisters of the Old Faithful pack?"

"We do" filled the cavern, and the lump in Mikael's throat grew larger.

"There is one item of business left," Mikael said and stepped next to Denton. "Will Anna, Alexi, Misha, and Vadim please step forward?" He waited while they filtered up. "Due to timing, you four were never inducted into either pack, so the four of you are officially the first new members of the Old Faithful pack. Do you promise to be loyal and true to your brothers and sisters of the Old Faithful pack?" He looked at Anna.

"I do, Alpha," she said and bared her neck. Mikael stepped forward and lightly touched her skin with his hand, shifted one finger, and made a tiny scratch to draw a drop of blood.

"Do you, Alexi and Misha, promise—" He didn't get a chance to finish.

"I do," Misha said loudly.

"I do too," Alexi said right behind him, and the adults chuckled. Both boys held their heads to the side dramatically, and Mikael lightly ran a claw over their necks, careful not to scratch them. Then he ruffled their hair and stood in front of Vadim. Denton stepped down and joined him.

"Do you promise to be loyal and true to your brothers and sisters of the Old Faithful pack?" Denton asked. Vadim exposed his neck, and Denton used his human finger and scratched and drew a drop of blood. Then he stood back.

"Do you accept these new members into our pack and family?" Mikael asked the gathered in a booming voice.

"We do," they said in unison.

Mikael held Denton's hand in the air once again. "Then we are the Old Faithful pack, and we are family." He turned his head toward the ceiling ten feet overhead and howled as deeply as he could. Denton joined him, and then so did the rest of the pack, including the pups. It was glorious and nearly deafening. After, Mikael faced his pack and his mate with a huge smile.

"What do we do now?" Denton asked.

"Can we eat?" William asked. "Grandma has been cooking all day and I'm hungry."

Mikael lifted his nephew into the air. He squealed with joy that increased when he passed him to Denton and lifted Maria. "If you're Uncle Mikael, is he Uncle Denton?"

"Yes. That's exactly who he is," Mikael answered, sharing a smile with Denton. "There's food back at the compound. You are welcome to come back with us or to run if you like. I do ask that if you decide to run, you don't go alone. There is still the threat from Anton, and I want everyone to stay safe."

"What are we going to do about him?" Jerry asked a little timidly.

"I'm not sure, but we're working on it. For now, we need to be cautious. But whatever you decide to do, enjoy the full moon and remember that this is a celebration." Mikael placed Maria back down, and she ran to her dad. "We are now one big family, so take the time to get to know someone new."

He and Denton watched as pack members slowly left the cave after putting their robes away and shifting so they could leave.

"It went so well," Denton said.

"That's because we'd already laid the groundwork a few days ago."

Denton leaned closer. "So what would you have done if there had been resistance?"

"Delayed and worked to change minds. If there had been a lot of issues, we would have had to develop a different plan. But things worked out, and they have been working together. Both groups have gotten to know each other and have worked together pretty well, so I was sure this would work."

"So what are we going to do tonight?" Denton asked as the cave emptied of the other members. "And I know where your mind is, and while I'm definitely up for some alone time, I have no intention of repeating what happened the last time we were here."

"You didn't like it?" Mikael asked, rather surprised.

"I did, but my back was sore for days. If you want a repeat, then I suggest a proper bed." Denton leaned closer. "You've done an amazing thing here, you know that."

"How?" Mikael wondered out loud.

"You took us all in and provided my entire pack with a home without being asked, and then you extended your hospitality and opened your heart to us. You could have used your strength to force that on us and there would have been nothing we could have done about it."

"What good would that have done except sow the seeds of resentment and the need for more force to keep the pack together? That's what Anton does, I'm sure. He takes over a pack by force and then has to use more force and intimidation to keep everyone in line. I don't want that in my life. Neither did my dad. That's why our pack was relatively small."

"Then I guess my pack and I were both pretty lucky."

Mikael shook his head. "You think any of this was luck?" He smiled. "I think this was by design. Maybe not the details, but the big things… yeah."

Denton walked across the cavern and took off his robe, beautifully naked in the ultralow lighting. Mikael watched as Denton shifted into his gorgeous wolf. He picked up the candle, carried it with him, and set it down after kneeling next to Denton. "You are beautiful as a wolf." Mikael stroked Denton's soft fur. It felt just like when Mikael stroked Denton's hair. He carded his fingers in Denton's fur and drew him close, petting and caressing him. Denton woofed softly. "I'll shift in a minute. I'm enjoying this."

Mikael blew out the candle and then took off his robe, placing it with the others before shifting. Then he followed Denton out into the night, stars blanketing the sky overhead. He lifted his head and howled, his cry echoing off the hills. The call was picked up by pack members from all around, and they filled the night with a cry of joy. Denton joined in as well, and once the cries died away, he nuzzled up against Mikael's side, and they stood together listening to the night as other calls went up from all around.

There were still a number of piles of clothing near the cave entrance from pack members who had decided to run. Mikael was tempted too, but he had other priorities. He shifted and began to dress.

"I thought you wanted to run," Denton said once he had returned to his human form.

Mikael paused and took in the sight of his mate. "I can look at you all day, every day, for the rest of my life." Mikael fastened his pants but didn't move to pick up his shirt. "I'm so unbelievably lucky."

"You're not the only one," Denton told him as he reached for his pants but held them without putting them on. "But there's so much more to you than just a sexy body. You have a good heart, and that's what I think I love most." Denton moved closer and then stopped. "You know if we start something now, we'll end up in the grass, and...."

"There are worse things than the grass, you know. It's soft here." Mikael smiled and looked up at the crystal-clear sky. The moon had risen, round and bright, and he closed his eyes. Its call was almost too much to resist, but he pulled on his shirt. "Come on." He waited for Denton to dress and then took his hand, leading him back to the compound.

When he reached the edge of the clearing, he skirted the buildings and entered the main house as quietly as he could. Once inside, he and Denton climbed the stairs to the top of the house. He didn't enter the studio or Kaiawa's room, thankful he was out running, but opened another door that led outside to a small balcony. "I love to come out here and look at the stars. It's a great view of the sky."

"Why don't you come out here more often?"

"This was built by my dad, and he and my mom used to use this on special nights. It was their spot, and I've never felt right using it." Mikael puled Denton closer.

"So why tonight?"

"I guess I understand why it was special now. It was their way of being close to the moon and stars. I always thought of it as their special nooky spot, and maybe it was, but the moon and stars feel so much closer up here. Everything is so clear I swear I can reach out and touch them."

Instead of making some useless gesture toward the moon, he pulled Denton to him. "I can't touch the stars, so I'll do something better—I'll grab you." Mikael closed his mouth over Denton's, kissing him powerfully, letting everything he felt flow into that single point of contact.

"Mikael," Denton breathed when their lips parted. He moved out of Mikael's embrace and took his hand. "You realize this isn't any more comfortable than the rock ledge, and there's a perfectly comfortable bed one flight of steps down." Denton chuckled and dragged him back into the house. He closed the door and then tugged Mikael down the stairs into the bedroom.

Inside the room, Denton released his hand and walked to the windows, pushing open the curtains. "See? There's a great view from here." He turned around and toed off his shoes. Then he tugged his shirt over his head and threw it over the back of the chair. Denton's pants followed. Mikael stared, unable to move as he watched the incredible show Denton was putting on. Once he was naked, cock sticking upward like a flagpole, Denton stalked to where Mikael stood.

"That's one hell of a view," Mikael whispered, then swallowed hard, mesmerized. He inhaled deeply, and his mate's rich, sweet, earthy scent pulled him out of his reverie. He stepped forward. His wolf urged him to lunge, grab his mate, and make him his. Instead, he sat on the edge of the bed, and Denton moved between his legs.

"How is this?"

"Don't tease, please. Not tonight," Mikael ground out. His skin felt as though it were crawling. "It's been a long time since I've felt the pull of the moon like this, and it's affecting my control." He breathed deeply. "My wolf is pounding to get hold of you."

Denton pressed to him, pushing Mikael back on the bed. "Then take what's yours."

"I won't hurt you."

"I'm a wolf too, and I can take care of myself," Denton growled. "Besides, you're my mate—you would never hurt me. I know that."

Mikael grabbed Denton, rolling them on the bed. Once he had his mate under him, Mikael tugged at his clothes. He had to get them off. His hands shifted, and the fabric tore, coming off him in shreds.

"What is it?" Denton whispered, cradling Mikael's head. "What's wrong? You never...."

"I know," Mikael breathed. "I need you. That's all I know. I need you more than I can say." He quivered as waves of desire washed through him. "I'm out of control."

"Then let me have control. Take what you need. I'm here." Denton stroked Mikael's cock hard and fast. Mikael gasped for air and stared at Denton through a fog he didn't understand.

He pressed Denton back on the bed and used spit for lube. Something in the back of his mind said that wasn't enough, and he tore into the nightstand until he came up with a tube of slick. His hands shook as he applied it to himself and Denton. Unable to hold off any longer, he entered Denton fast and hard, crying out as Denton's body gripped his. "Denton!" Mikael shook uncontrollably even as he needed his mate more than he could have ever imagined.

"It's all right," Denton told him softly, stroking Mikael's cheek. "You're always amazing. You feel incredible." Mikael's heart rate slowed from the pounding it had been seconds earlier. "Breathe, honey."

Denton's touch was like a balm, and Mikael came back to himself and slowly began to move. Denton always felt amazing, but today he was incredible—he kept his hand over Mikael's heart and locked their gazes together.

"I'm...." Michael gasped

"Just stay with me," Denton soothed, and Mikael changed angles. Denton gasped, and his eyes rolled back into his head. "Fuck yeah, Mikael. You always make me feel special. My wolf can feel yours and he's happy. They're both happy."

Mikael felt as though he hung balanced on a knife edge of control. His mind and body seemed separate. He knew what he wanted and how he wanted to love Denton, but his body had other ideas. Finally, after slow movements and steady breathing, his mind and body melded once again. He felt in control and knew that was due to Denton. "I love you," Mikael whispered, and instantly his heart filled with warmth. He stroked Denton's chest, bumping a hard nipple with his fingers.

"I love you too," Denton whispered, his words morphing into a delicious hiss when Mikael got the angle just right.

Mikael loved that he could make Denton feel so good... in a good way. "We have it all—a strong pack, great family, and each other. We can do anything." He stilled and clenched his muscles, letting his cock jump inside Denton. He felt Denton shiver and knew he loved it. "You are everything I could ever have hoped for."

Denton stretched out on the bed, his arms over his head, giving himself totally. Mikael's heart skipped a beat, and his wolf did a silent howl. For now, in this place, everything was perfect. And as they moved together, each picking up the rhythm of the other, the rest of the world, pack territory, politics, dark wolves—all of it became background noise. There was nothing but Denton, his golden skin, his eyes as deep as the sea, that little divot that no one else would notice on the end of his nose, the way he smelled as sweat broke out all over—all of it was perfect and his.

Denton reached for Mikael's legs and pulled in time to his thrusts. "Don't you dare stop!"

"Won't... can't... love you...," Mikael breathed as passion welled inside him. He held it off, thinking unsexy thoughts as he tried like hell to wait for Denton.

Denton quivered under him, stroking his perfect cock so fast Mikael could hardly see his hands. "Wait for me... almost there...."

"Yeah, right there...," Mikael gasped and clamped his eyes closed. He didn't want to close Denton out, but every expression drove him closer to release.

"Open your eyes!" Denton demanded, and Mikael slid them open. "And don't stop." Denton shook like a leaf and gasped hard for air. Mikael knew he was close. He himself teetered on the very brink of euphoria, and when Denton tightened around him, Mikael tumbled off into the abyss and came in a rush of heat that seared all the way to his soul.

Mikael stilled, afraid to move in case he broke the spell that surrounded them. Denton lay on the bed, the only movement the rise and fall of his chest. Otherwise, he glistened in the moonlight. Mikael finally regained control of his muscles and lightly stroked his mate's side. "I don't know what happened."

"It's okay. It's our first full moon as mates. Things were bound to be a little... weird." Mikael knew Denton was trying to be reassuring, but he wasn't buying it.

"I rarely have issues with control, and the moon hasn't affected me for a long time. Not since I was a pup."

Denton slowly sat up, lightly cupping his cheeks. "You didn't lose control. It may have felt like it, but you were always there, and I felt your love and care the entire time. There's nothing for you to be concerned about."

"But what if I do lose control and hurt you?"

"I'm an alpha too—I can take care of myself, and if you were to hurt me, I'd tell you and you'd stop. I know that. So stop worrying." Denton smiled and pulled him closer. A little later, they separated with mutual shivers, and Denton tugged him back into his strong arms. "This is part of the trust thing we were talking about. I trust you, and you need to trust me. As shifters, we are hybrids—one person with two outward and inward aspects. Both the wolf and man are part of us. That means at certain times one part of us will be stronger than the other. It's the full moon, and our wolves are strong and close to the surface."

"I know all that. But...."

"You have a strong wolf, and sometimes he's going to make insistent demands." Denton kissed him. "Stop worrying and remember this: control or not, you blew my mind."

"I did?"

"Oh yeah, and if we don't get up and wash, we're going to stick together for the rest of the night."

"I don't want to move," Mikael whispered into Denton's ear. "I want to stay just like this, holding you for the rest of the night."

"I want that too." Denton nuzzled Mikael's neck.

Mikael closed his eyes, filling his mind with the way Denton smelled now, sharp and tangy, and the way he felt against him. There was nothing better. Mikael stroked Denton's chest, sighing softly. This was heaven. Sooner or later responsibilities, packs, and the outside world would push their way in, but for now it was just the two of them.

CHAPTER 10

MIKAEL WOKE in a happy fog just like he had each morning for the past ten days, since the pack-joining ceremony. Outside the open window, an electric saw whined, men talked, and the rhythmic pounding of a hammer reminded him that it was definitely time to get up. Denton rolled over and groaned softly in his ear.

"I need to tell Jerry he isn't allowed to start work until I've at least had coffee. Lots of coffee," Denton said.

"He's excited, and the new house is going up faster than I expected." Mikael sighed. "But damn, the sun is barely up."

A sharp sound blasted through the morning air. The sounds outside all came to a stop. Mikael instantly sat up in bed and then jumped out, his feet barely touching the floor. "Was that a gunshot?"

"Yes," Denton said, tugging up his pants as he raced toward the door. Mikael pulled on pants and raced out behind him.

"Alpha...."

"Everyone in the main house, now," Mikael ordered. "Karl, get everyone inside and find out if anyone is missing. Now." He turned to Denton. "Help with the pups. Make sure they're all okay." He scanned around him, scenting the air. He smelled men and a wolf, one that was familiar. Mikael growled and then turned back.

Pack members all dropped their tools and scampered inside.

"Mikael?" Catherine said.

"Make sure everyone is inside and safe." He turned to Karl. "Is anyone missing?"

"No. Everyone seems to be accounted for," Karl answered.

"Great. Where's Kaiawa?" As soon as he asked the question, he saw him across the yard.

"Catherine, stay here and protect everyone." He saw the disappointment on his sister's face. "I need you to stand in for us. I know you'd rather go with us, but you're needed here."

"All right," Catherine agreed. Mikael slipped his hand around the back of his sister's neck, cradling her head, and smiled at her.

"I know you'll take good care of everyone."

"What about me?" Christopher asked.

Mikael paused and then motioned for Christopher to join him. Another shot rang out, followed quickly by a second.

"What are they doing?" Christopher asked.

"Issuing a challenge," Mikael answered. "We're upwind right now, so let's be careful and silent." Mikael stripped quickly and shifted. He was furious and knew he needed to calm down so he could think clearly and rationally. The others followed suit. *Be careful and as quiet as possible. Stay close and always know where the other pack members are. It's Anton and three humans. We need to see what they're up to. Stay safe at all costs.* Mikael raced into the woods, staying close to the ground. Mikael followed the scent, winding through the trees as the scent got stronger and stronger.

He paused and bared his teeth but made no sound at all. These men had no idea what they were doing. They tramped through the woods, making a great deal of noise. However, Anton was nearly silent. Mikael could only follow him by his scent. But he was definitely there. Mikael wished he knew what Anton was up to. He had to know that they would hear them. It felt like a trap, and he cautioned each of his pack members. They couldn't answer him, but when he turned and looked back, they all signaled that they understood.

Mikael paused and listened. Anton and his men had gone silent. That was a sign that they were expecting something. However, Mikael didn't need to hear them; he could smell all of them. There was no fear. In fact, he smelled confidence.

"You said we'd be able to shoot wolves," Mikael heard. "Are you sure they're really out here? We've been going for a while, and there's been no sign of them."

"It would have helped if one of you idiots hadn't fallen and panicked. Your shots scared off our prey. Just be quiet and don't move. They'll give themselves away, and then we'll find them." Anton sounded so fucking sure of himself. "Move quietly and stay alert." Mikael heard their soft steps on the forest floor. Shit, they were heading toward the compound. Mikael turned to the others and pointed out their direction. They were skirting their current position. Mikael headed back the way he'd come and then circled around into their path, well ahead of them.

Christopher, circle around to their right, Karl, you and Kaiawa take the left. We need to box them in. When you hear me call, join in. He moved closer to Denton. *We're going to cut them off.*

The others took off through the woods, tails and legs flashing before disappearing into the undergrowth. Then he and Denton hurried into position, finding a thicket ahead of where the men were going.

He waited until the others had time to get into place, then motioned to Denton, who raced through the woods. Mikael turned his head skyward and howled his caution and threat. The others joined in instantly, with Denton bringing up the rear.

"We're surrounded," one of the men said, and Mikael heard footsteps. He also smelled panic and the acidic tang of ammonia. At least one of the hunters had wet himself. He dashed to the side and howled again. The others had moved as well, and they picked up the call.

"Fuck you all, I'm getting the hell out of here," another man said, and Mikael heard footsteps racing away from them. Another followed, and he huffed softly as the urine scent receded. Christopher and Karl called again, and the two men ran faster.

"Jackass. 'Let's shoot wolves,' he said. Some vacation…," Mikael heard one of the men say to the other as they ran. The third one was remaining still, but Mikael smelled fear building. He growled, and the others did as well. Mikael knew it wasn't likely they could be seen, and the remaining hunter's fear level shot higher before he too took to his heels.

With all three men running like scared rabbits, Mikael had Karl and Christopher follow them and keep them panicked. *Make them understand the hunter has become the hunted,* Mikael told them. He wagged his tail a few times at how easily the men had been scared off.

Once they were far enough away, he made his way toward where Anton was waiting. *You're a coward,* Mikael told him. *Yeah, I can do it in wolf form too. And I can tell you're scared shitless right now.* His head was beginning to ache, and Mikael knew he would have to start speaking normally soon. *How dare you bring hunters into our territory? I wonder what your pack members would think if they found out you were such a traitorous, worthless pile of crap. Maybe I'll tell them. You can't even see me, and I can talk to you.*

"Come out and face me," Anton said. "Who's the coward now?"

Oh, I'll face you, and so will the rest of my pack members. You aren't going anywhere. Mikael had no intention of fighting Anton here, but he knew he needed to get the man angry. *Anna and her pups send their best, as does Vadim. He's doing well now that he's away from your poison. He also told us plenty about you.* Mikael laughed in his mind, sending it to Anton. *The cool thing is that I can do this anytime I want, and there isn't a fucking thing you can do about it.* That was a lie. Wolves could learn to block this type of communication, but he wasn't going to tell Anton that. *It works especially well on the weak-minded.*

Anton was seething—Mikael could smell anger rolling off him, overpowering the scent of the woods. "I've issued a challenge!"

Mikael moved closer so he could see Anton standing in a small clearing. He was definitely nervous. *I take it things didn't go the way you expected?* Mikael laughed, and Anton looked all around him. *Now what I want to know is why you'd be stupid enough to actually come here alone.* He would have to shift soon because this form of communication was wearing him out.

"How do you know I'm alone?" Anton asked. He, of course, had no idea where Mikael was because he couldn't follow his voice.

I know you're shaking in your boots and that you're about to wet yourself. That would be a sight for your pack members. The great alpha Anton soaking his shorts. Mikael paused. *You're a fraud and a coward. I know it and you know it. Soon everyone will know it, and you'll be left with nothing. That's what I want: to see you reduced to nothing, like you were when you were a kid. A nobody that no one gives a shit about.*

Anton shook, and the stench of anger reached Mikael's nose. "Face me!"

Mikael stayed right where he was, watching Anton shake from head to toe. It was a beautiful sight. It seemed he had hit the target dead-on.

"You want to know why I came with just hunters? Because there's no way you can take me, even with your entire pack."

Mikael stayed still. He wasn't falling for the bait.

"I heard you formed a new pack. That will only make it easier for me to take over the entire territory at once."

Mikael had had enough. He shifted and stepped to the edge of the clearing. "That's what you think," he said calmly. "You know, you ought to learn to control your anger." He smiled. "If your face gets any redder, your head will explode." On the inside, his stomach was a bundle of nerves, but he wasn't going to let it show.

Anton stepped closer to him, and Mikael shifted his hand in a split second as a reminder of just how dangerous he was. Anton stopped and glared at Mikael. "I challenge the alpha of the combined Evergreen and Yellowstone packs to a fight to the death." Spittle flew from Anton's mouth, and Mikael thought he might start foaming at any moment. "I expect—"

"You get nothing. Your challenge has been issued, and I will set the terms. We will meet right here in two days. You can bring one beta and one other wolf. No one else."

"You will bring—"

Mikael raised his hand. "I set the terms. You get no say." He didn't have to raise his voice. "You're sick, and I'll have no part of it. We'll be here, and we'll bring one beta and another witness. That's it. Now leave my territory. I will see you in two days at exactly noon." Mikael met Anton's gaze, refusing to back down. "You've been warned. If you are still here in thirty seconds, we will attack and tear you apart. There's no mercy for trespassers."

Mikael waited, and eventually Anton turned and left the clearing. Mikael shifted and stood guard. He knew Anton was being followed at a distance, but he kept all his senses on high alert, scenting the air until Anton's noxious odor faded away.

After a while, the others returned, trotting happily into the clearing. Mikael nuzzled Denton, checking him over. He knew there wasn't any reason to believe that Denton had been hurt, but his wolf needed to know his mate was okay. Denton seemed to be doing the same thing. As soon as Mikael was satisfied, he turned and raced through the trees toward the compound with the others behind him.

"You were awesome," Christopher said as soon as he shifted and began dressing.

"What did you tell him to get him to challenge you?" Denton asked. Mikael instantly moved between his mate and the others. He hated the idea of anyone but him seeing Denton naked.

"Relax. I'm not after your mate," Christopher told him. "Though you are a lucky wolf." He smiled, and Mikael lifted his lip to bare his teeth. He hadn't known his younger brother was interested in men. Not that he cared, of course, but he better be keeping his hands to home, and eyes, for that matter.

Denton pulled on his pants, and Mikael relaxed once Denton was covered. "I used his ego and pride to goad him into it."

"I take it he can't do the mind-talking thing the way you can." Denton pulled on his shirt and handed Mikael his.

"No. He's a huge brute, but there's no real intelligence or deep thinking there. He desperately wants to be important, and he'll do anything to accomplish that, so I used that against him."

"He smelled awful," Catherine said.

"That's the darkness in his soul. It's eating away at him and taking over. I think it's poisoned his mind." Mikael sighed. "That isn't going to make him any easier to beat." The Mother had said that together he and Denton could defeat him, but a challenge was one-on-one, and anything else wouldn't be appropriate.

"Probably not, but you can do it," Christopher said. "You're the strongest wolf I've ever met."

"Thanks," Mikael said. Fighting wasn't his first choice. He believed in solving problems in other ways, with fighting as a last resort, but he had no choice. Anton's threat had to be removed, or his pack would never be safe. He'd brought hunters into their territory with the promise that they would be able to shoot a wolf. The bastard! Anton had sent men to set the fire that destroyed Denton's pack compound. He'd created a huge gap in the landscape, killing off plants and trees that had grown for generations. Fire was a normal part of the cycle of life, but setting one on purpose certainly wasn't.

"Finish getting dressed," Denton told him.

Mikael pulled on his shirt and turned to the others. "Make sure everyone is okay. I don't want anyone leaving this general area until after the challenge. We need to keep each other safe."

"You got it," Christopher told him and began mustering the others away.

Karl hung behind and stood with him and Denton. "Are you really okay with this? I saw that guy and…. It's not that I don't think you can take him. It's that I don't know what he's going to pull. But there will be something. He won't play fair, I know that. He challenged you, and he'll do anything to win. You need to figure out how to counter whatever he tries."

"That's what I'm afraid of. He's going to try to weaken me or attack the pack in some way, so we all need to be on the lookout and vigilant. If he tries anything, we'll be ready." Mikael clapped his brother on the shoulder and then went through the main compound, smiling and doing his best to reassure each pack member. Inside the main house, he greeted Anna and the boys before heading right up the stairs to his studio.

"What do you need?" Denton asked from behind him, closing the door.

"I think I need to be alone," he whispered.

"That's where you're wrong. The last thing you need is to be up here alone stewing over what you think could happen."

"I'm not a child, and I know my own mind."

"Neither am I." Denton stalked over to him. "This whole 'alpha going it alone' crap is going to stop right now. We're doing this together, and that's all there is to it. So you're going to tell me what's got you rattled, and don't say it's nothing, or so help me, I'll…."

"Okay, I get your point. I'm used to doing some things on my own, but I don't know how I feel about this." Mikael turned away to look out over the land. "I'm scared, okay?" he whispered. There wasn't another person on the face of the earth he could have admitted that to. Not his brothers, sister, or even his mother, and certainly not to another pack member.

"Jesus," Denton said softly. "Do you think you're alone? When I fought my cousin for the alphaship of Evergreen, I was scared shitless. Not about whether I'd win or lose but about what would happen if I won. I'd be the leader of the pack, and I'd have to take on the responsibility."

"This isn't the same. If I lose, then you and everyone else will be at Anton's mercy." Mikael turned to him. "This isn't about who will lead a pack, but about the survival of our family. If I lose, our pack will cease to exist. Anton will come in here, and their lives will be as much a living hell as Vince's. He'll take over everything."

"You don't think I know that?" Denton touched his shoulder. "You're the strongest wolf I've ever known. And not just physically. You use your senses to see what people are feeling and how they might react. That's more powerful than your physical strength." Denton pressed against his back and wound his arms around Mikael's waist. "I know what's in your heart. I feel it each time we're together. I love that you're willing to look inside and try to figure things out. It's part of what makes you a remarkable person. And it's why I love you."

Mikael leaned back into Denton's embrace. He had to get a handle on the nervousness that swirled through him. He hated feeling that way. He needed to be confident and sure of himself. He'd done what he had to; he knew that. It was his job—*their* job—to keep their pack safe. "You have to promise me that if things... don't work out... that you'll watch over the rest of the pack. Anton thinks that if he wins, he'll take over the pack. You have to stop him."

"You know I will. But it would only be a matter of time before he took me on."

"I know." Mikael stepped out of Denton's embrace and walked over to the metal filing cabinet in the corner. He pulled one of the drawers open and took out a gun. "Use that and shoot him. I don't care if it's unsportsmanlike or breaking every rule our kind has—you shoot him until he's as dead as his soul already is." Mikael shook with anger and resolve.

"If you die in this fight, so help me, I'll figure out a way to resurrect you, and then I'll kill you myself." Denton slammed the drawer closed with a bang that sounded as though the gun had gone off. "Stop talking like that. You're going to tear that asshole apart, and you know it." Denton's eyes lit with fury. "I just found my mate, and if I lose you now, I swear to God, I'll... I'll...." Denton stomped toward the door and then turned back around. "Fucking hell, I'm so mad at you right now I could spit quarters." Denton barreled back to him, crashing into Mikael, sending them both to the floor. "You are not allowed to lose, so get that through that thick head of yours, all right?"

Mikael nodded and chuckled. "Okay."

"I'm here and so is your entire pack." Denton got up and walked to the southernmost window. "See what they're doing?" The new house had been laid out, and footings were being created. "That's because of you. My old pack and your old pack—they're all working together. Do you have any idea how hard it is to merge two groups of wolves? But you did it without anything more than the occasional raised voice that's quickly dealt with by someone else. So if you think that just anyone can step into your shoes, you're crazy. I was a decent alpha to my pack, but you are a great one." Denton turned to him. "And I get to be selfish. I've known you a few weeks, and already I can't figure out how I'll live without you. I've seen the haunted grief that crosses Anna's face when she remembers she's alone."

"What else can I do?" Mikael asked.

"That's just it. You're doing the right thing, but your attitude is defeatist, and I will not have that."

"It's not. I figure if I make plans for the worst, then it won't happen." Mikael stood next to Denton. "I have to think of every eventuality."

"But not that one. You aren't allowed to make those plans because it just will not happen. It cannot happen," Denton told him, the heat gone from his voice, replaced with a soft plea. "It's not allowed."

"That's easy enough to say. And you know I will fight with my last ounce of strength for this pack and for you." Mikael drew Denton to him. "My entire life is here with you and this pack." He stood with his arm around Denton for a while. "Come on, I'm sure they could use two more hands." He turned and nuzzled Denton's neck.

"Am I losing my appeal already?" Denton asked. He'd obviously been expecting more of a workout.

"You never will. When you're old and going gray, you'll still be the sexiest wolf I know. But by now the pack will have heard what happened, and if we don't reassure them, they'll begin to worry, and that isn't good for anyone."

"I suppose not." Denton leaned close and kissed him hard. "That's a reminder of what's coming later."

Mikael's breath hitched for a second, and he regretted what he'd said earlier. He wanted nothing more than to take Denton to their bed and pound him into the mattress. His wolf was already raring to go. But at the moment there were more pressing things than sex. Mikael took Denton's hand. His mate being with him was enough for now. The two of them would have all night together, and Mikael would make the very most of it. His wolf was not at all happy, though. "All right, let's go. But I am warning you: if you so much as take off your shirt, I'll drag you into the nearest cabin and take you right there on the floor."

"The same goes for you," Denton warned, and Mikael grinned before leading him toward the stairs. He pulled open the door, and they descended the steps in a hurry, their feet heavy on the treads. They passed Mikael's mother and Anna in the great room, speaking quietly. They'd been doing that more and more. Mikael hoped it was helping Anna with her grief and loss. His mother had also been through the loss of a mate. They looked up as he passed and acknowledged them, but he and Denton continued on outside.

"Alpha Mikael," Alexi and William called as they ran up to him, carrying hammers.

"We're helping," Alexi said.

"Come see. We pound nails really good." William grinned and led them over to the side of the building site. There, a scrap log had been set up with nails that had been pounded into it. Most of them were bent beyond recognition, but a few of the nails had been pounded in properly.

"You certainly have," Mikael said as the two boys stared at him proudly. "You'll be builders soon enough." Each of the boys showed him what good "pounders" they were, and both drove the nails in properly. Mikael told each of the boys how well they'd done and was about to see if he could be of any help when Misha ran over to him, wiping his eyes.

"Maria says you're going to fight the bad wolf that killed Daddy," he whimpered. Mikael lifted him into his arms, and the pup curled up against him, crying. "I don't want you to go like Daddy did."

Alexi dropped his hammer and ran off toward the main house as fast as his legs would carry him. He shifted when he got halfway there and ended up tangled in his clothes. Denton helped him out of them, and then the pup raced to the house.

"It will be okay. Someone needs to take care of the bad wolf," Mikael said. "That way he won't be able to hurt anyone again."

"But why do you have to do it?" Misha asked. "Let someone else do it. I don't want you to get dead." His little body shook in Mikael's arms.

"I'm going to be fine," Mikael soothed. He wasn't sure what else to say. When Denton returned, he lifted William into his arms, and they made quite a parade as they soothed the upset pups. Anna and Mikael's mother met them at the door. Anna took Misha, and his mother lifted William from Denton's arms.

"They'll be fine," his mother said, but Mikael knew she was worried as well. When he returned to the work site, he could feel that same worry all around him. The men kept working, but they were unusually quiet, talking about the work to be done rather than the usual laughter and chatter that went on. Mikael knew it wasn't that they doubted his abilities. They had just all been through so much that the threat of more put everyone on edge.

"It's likely to be a difficult few days, and the pack is going to be edgy," Denton told him quietly.

Mikael nodded. "Look, guys," he said loud enough for everyone to easily hear him. "I know there's a challenge in a few days, but we can't let that run our lives. We have work to do. Anton challenged the alpha of our pack, and the challenge was accepted. It's in line with what the Mother explained to me. All we can do for now is pray for her blessing and continue with our work."

"But what if…," Jerry began and then stopped. "You're right."

"Thank you. I know it sounds unusual, but your positive energy and attitude will help me."

"Can we go to the challenge with you?"

"No," Mikael said. "Do you remember the stories of the dark wolf we were all told as children so we'd behave? I believe those stories have some truth to them."

"Alpha, are you saying that Anton can use fear somehow?" Stan asked, setting down his plane.

"There's a lot I don't know. But if the stories have a basis in truth, then why take the chance? So let's worry less about what's going to happen and see what we can do to get this house built so we aren't all packed together like sardines this winter."

Stan turned to the others, and Mikael heard some snickering. Mikael growled, and Stan stepped forward. "It seems you and Alpha

Denton tend to be a little loud and, well, there are a few people who would like to be able to sleep." He glanced at Kaiawa, who was doing his best to try to disappear.

"Is that so?" Denton chided the beta wolf.

"Maybe there are a few things we don't need to hear go bump in the night, like a dang headboard against the wall, over and over again." Kaiawa smiled, and Mikael snapped his teeth at him before grinning.

"We need to find Kaiawa a mate," Denton said.

Kaiawa shook his head hurriedly. "I just need a good night's sleep once in a while," he said grumpily and then turned and went back to work.

"You were a little loud last night," Denton said to Mikael.

"Me?" Mikael lunged, and Denton dodged him and ran across the compound. Mikael took off after him and easily caught Denton in his arms. "I'm not the one who screams his—" Mikael stopped when he realized the entire pack was watching him. He growled and moved Denton behind him.

"No one is going to take your mate from you," Catherine said as she stepped into the group. "Sheesh. And for the record, we could all use a little peace and quiet every once in a while. We are wolves, you know, and there's only so much we can ignore, especially when you have the windows open."

"Okay, fine," Mikael conceded and turned to Denton. "Aw, hell." He took him in his arms and kissed him hard right there. "We'll start being quiet... eventually." He and Denton smiled as the others laughed. They clearly didn't believe him, and that was just fine, because Mikael had no intention of dampening his or his mate's pleasure. Instead he would try to remember to close the windows at night. "What do you need us to do?" he asked Jerry, and then he released Denton so they could get to work.

THE TRICK to keeping both his and his pack members' minds off the impending challenge seemed to be keeping busy. The next day he kept everyone focused on getting as much done on the new house as possible. Logs were brought in and stripped of their bark in preparation for becoming part of the walls. The foundation still needed to set, but

Mikael figured getting ahead was never a bad thing. By the end of the day, he was tired but invigorated. They had accomplished a lot as a team and as a pack.

"Okay, boys," his mother said as they were finishing up for the day. "Everyone come inside and fill a plate. I have enough food for a small army, so it's a good thing we have one." She smiled, but Mikael could sense her nervousness; it seemed to be just under the surface. If he were honest, it was for him as well. He put his tools away and helped the others before going inside.

Every seat was filled with pack members. The great room and kitchen were stuffed with people, all eating. It was good, and he liked having everyone around him. He just hadn't realized how big the pack had gotten. Either that, or the house had shrunk. His mother had plates made up for him and Denton, and two places opened up at the dining room table. They sat down, and Mikael listened to the conversation but didn't join in. He wasn't really in the mood for talking. What he wanted to do was go up to his studio and be alone, but that wasn't the right thing to do at the moment.

"You know they'll forgive you if you want to leave," his mother whispered in his ear. "Just finish your dinner." His mom was still such a… well, mother. Mikael ate, barely tasting his food, then stood and shared a glance with Denton before quietly walking out of the noisy room and up the stairs. He didn't stop until he'd reached his studio, and then he closed the door, shutting out most of the sound from below.

Mikael went right to one of the blank canvases he'd prepared and placed it on the easel. Then he grabbed pencils and got to work. He had an image in his mind that he wanted to transfer to the canvas, and doing a drawing first was the fastest way for him to get started. All his worries and concerns receded to the background as he sank into his work. His mother had often said the house could fall down around him when he was working, and he wouldn't know it. There was now proof, because he didn't hear Denton come in, and he didn't realize he wasn't alone until he felt Denton's lips on his neck.

"Come to bed," Denton whispered. "Pretty much everyone has left, and I think it's time I did my very best to make you forget all about tomorrow."

Mikael set down his pencil and stood up. Denton moved into his embrace and kissed him. Denton removed Mikael's shirt and dropped it to the floor, the first of a pile of clothes, and then they joined them.

"When things get bad, remember the happiness we have together. That will always see you through," Denton said.

"Are you being prophetic?" Mikael asked, licking the base of Denton's neck before sucking up a mark.

"No, just truthful," Denton responded. After that there was very little talking but plenty of other wonderful sounds. Thank goodness the windows were closed, because tonight was between him and Denton. This could possibly be the last time he and Denton were together. The thought made his heart ache and his wolf possessive as hell. When they came together, his wolf couldn't be denied, and Mikael howled their coupling to the ceiling as he rode a wave of intense passion unlike anything he had ever felt before. Denton followed right behind, and Mikael re-marked his mate as his forever.

"You know, we could just go to bed," Denton whispered a while later as Mikael crushed Denton to him. They hadn't moved at all, and there was a very good chance that they were going to end up stuck together.

"I don't want to move, because then...."

Denton stroked his cheek. "You know I'm going to be with you always, no matter what. And you are the strongest and smartest wolf I know." Denton placed his forehead against Mikael's. "I bet Anton is shaking in his boots right about now, trying to figure out how in the hell he can get out of this because his ego bit off a lot more than it can chew." He moved away and got to his feet. Denton took Mikael's hand and led him out of the studio and down to their room. He pulled down the covers, and Mikael crawled into their bed. Then Denton got in and curled next to him. It took a while, but Mikael eventually fell to sleep.

MIKAEL HAD planned to spend the morning clearing his mind to get ready for the challenge, but instead he spent it with the pups. Then he, Denton, and Karl left the compound and walked through the trees toward the clearing. He scented the entire time and kept track of where Anton was. He remained upwind. He smelled the three wolves: two normal plus Anton's almost putrefied scent stinking up everything around him.

"You didn't back out. These are the last two packs I need to defeat to rule over the territory," Anton said as soon as the three Old Faithful pack members stepped into the clearing. He had an air of confidence as he stepped away from his men. Anton was big, and there was strength under his clothes, but his eyes and face still had a sunken look.

"Of course not. But I expected you to," Mikael said confidently. He pulled off his shirt and handed it to Karl. His shoes and pants were next. Then Mikael stood naked and watched as Anton ripped his own clothes away, letting them fall to the ground in tatters. "When this is over you won't need them anyway, I suppose."

He saw anger rise in Anton's eyes but kept his cool. Anton leaped at him and shifted in midair into a huge wolf. Mikael stepped out of the way and let Anton's momentum carry him, then lashed out as he passed. He'd seen Anton fight and knew he went straight at his opponent like a bulldog, all strength and power. Anton landed and leaped again. Mikael shifted and captured Anton's rear leg in midair, clamping down hard.

Anton whirled and snapped, trying to get hold of Mikael's neck, but he missed. Still, his claws raked over Mikael's side as Mikael bit down harder, tearing open the leg before releasing it. Mikael stepped out of the way and growled as Anton landed on the ground and turned back to him. Anton was limping, which was good, but the growl that came out of him seemed to come from the depths of hell. Mikael knew he was using it for intimidation, and he got ready for the next charge, which came within seconds. Mikael dodged and raked Anton down the side. It didn't seem to faze him, and Anton attacked again and again.

Mikael knew Anton was using an immense amount of energy, but he didn't see any sign of him flagging. Mikael jumped away from the latest attack, but Anton was ready and circled in midair. He bit at Mikael's side.

Mikael twisted, biting down on Anton's ear. He bit and twisted until the skin ripped, and his mouth filled with foul-tasting blood. He released and bit again, clamping down on the side of Anton's face. Anton let go of him and came at him once again. Mikael's side hurt like hell, but he fought with everything he had.

They circled each other for a few seconds, and Mikael used the breather to get oxygen into his lungs. He saw when Anton was about to lunge and stayed still before dodging once again. *What the fuck is going on?* he sent to Denton. *He should be tired as hell.* Mikael's energy was flagging. After dodging yet another attack, Mikael glanced at the two wolves who'd come with Anton. They looked like hell, like they were about to collapse. *Take out the other two,* he sent to Denton and Karl as he jumped out of Anton's way yet again.

He saw a flash of fur as Karl raced around the edge of the clearing. He paid no attention to what happened next, but Anton's next lunge lost some of its power. When Anton landed, Mikael attacked, not giving him any chance to recover. He landed on Anton's back, going for his neck. Anton bucked Mikael off his back, and Mikael managed to land on his feet somehow. He felt shaky and blinked a few times to clear his head. He had searing pain in his side, and one of his legs had been raked by Anton's claws. He was bleeding from multiple places, and he knew he didn't have much strength left. He had to end this now, but he wasn't sure how the hell to do that. His plan had been to let Anton wear himself out, but that was failing miserably. He was the one getting worn out.

Take what's offered.

Mikael wasn't sure where the voice came from, but within seconds a surge of energy welled up inside him. When Anton lunged this time, he leapt away and crouched, suddenly hyperalert and ready for anything. Mikael turned and pounced once again, knocking Anton off his feet. He went for Anton's throat, clamping his jaw around the tender flesh and tearing into it.

Anton tasted terrible, the blood foul. Mikael wanted it out of his mouth, but he didn't stop, ripping into the flesh, tearing deeper and deeper, shaking his head until he felt no more movement. Then and only then did he let up and step away. Anton lay on the ground, still and covered in blood. Mikael watched for any sign of life but saw nothing. He then turned his head to the sky and let loose a howl of victory. He heard the other pack members pick up the cry in the distance and carry it on until a symphony of voices reached his ears.

However, one voice was silent. Mikael turned to Denton and saw him on his knees, looking down at the ground. Mikael shifted. "Karl, get over here," he called and hurried to his mate, just as Denton fell forward onto the grass. "What the hell is going on?" He crouched on the grass and saw that Denton was breathing, but just barely.

"I don't know. But he doesn't look so good," Karl answered.

Mikael cradled Denton's head in his arms. "Can you talk to me?"

"I prayed and she answered," Denton gasped.

"You did what?" Mikael asked, stroking Denton's cheek.

I told you that it would take both of you to defeat Anton. The voice said again, and Mikael looked all around but saw nothing. *Don't you know my voice by now, Mikael?* He wondered if the others could hear her, but they didn't seem to. *He offered to give you his strength, and I allowed it.* Denton slowly sat up, and Mikael breathed with relief. *I didn't offer more than he could give, but I had to do it quickly.*

"He could have died," Mikael said, and the others looked at him like he was off his rocker.

After all I went through to get you a mate and then get you two stubborn pains in the…? Let's just say I would never do that. He heard laughter that faded away.

"Who are you talking to?" Karl asked.

"Never mind." He drew Denton to him. "Are you all right?"

"I should be asking you that. I wasn't the one fighting that thing," Denton said. "He was pulling strength from the men he brought with him. They looked weaker and smaller as the fight went on, and I knew I had to do something to help. So I offered you my strength through the Mother. Then I saw you win the fight, and I couldn't stand any longer."

"Thank you," Mikael whispered. "And promise me you'll never scare me like that again." Seeing Denton on the ground like that had nearly stopped his heart.

"What do you want me to do with that mess?" Karl asked, tilting his head toward what was left of Anton and the other wolf that he'd taken out. "The last one ran for it, but he won't get very far."

"Start a fire and burn these two. And see if you can find the one who got away. He must be in as bad shape as Denton." Karl looked at him as though he were crazy. "They didn't have much choice about coming with Anton, if what I understand is correct. So see if you can help him."

Karl took off, even though he obviously thought Mikael wasn't thinking clearly, and maybe he wasn't. Mikael turned back to Denton, who slowly sat up. "What are you doing?" Mikael asked.

"It doesn't seem right for me to lie here when you were the one who did the fighting," Denton whispered.

Mikael drew Denton to him. "Never think that. We fought together, because I couldn't have won without your generosity. She told me it would take both of us, but I didn't understand what she meant." He held Denton to him and waited for Karl to return. He wished his energy would return, but it seemed exceedingly slow to do so.

"You know you should get dressed again. I hate it when others see my mate without his clothes, because you're mine." Denton stroked his cheek.

Mikael leaned close and kissed him tenderly. Part of him wanted so much more than a kiss, but the body was weak even if the spirit was willing.

"I found him," Karl said as he approached with another wolf, who looked near death. He could barely walk, and when Karl settled him on the ground, he nearly fell over. Karl pulled out his phone and by some miracle must have gotten a signal. He called back to the compound, and apparently help was on the way.

Mikael dressed and sat with Denton until several pack members arrived. Catherine took charge and soon had a fire blazing in the center of the clearing. Anton and Clyde, his dead beta, were placed on the fire, and everyone stood upwind because the smell from Anton's body was enough to sear their noses.

"He was foul through and through," Mikael whispered from where they sat on a fallen log, watching the flames.

"What was wrong with him?" Denton said.

"His soul was eaten away. The Mother sustains us, but the darkness, well, it's a cruel master, and it demands our very souls. Anton was doomed as soon as he turned there to get what he wanted."

"But what was his purpose?" Denton whispered. "There had to be more to it than just power. He didn't do anything with it other than try to get more. There has to be something he wanted or that the dark powers wanted from him."

Mikael nodded. "Maybe we'll find out eventually."

Karl added more wood to the fire, and it blazed high into the air, burning hotter and hotter. The remains of the two wolves were quickly consumed, and then Catherine let the fire die. Mikael and Denton sat and watched until there was little left but smoking embers.

"Go ahead and make sure everything is out," Mikael told the others. Buckets of water were poured on the ashes to extinguish the flames, and Mikael said a prayer of thanks to the Mother. Then he and Denton got to their feet. They shakily turned away and began a slow walk back to the compound with the others.

"What do we do with him?" Karl asked, tilting his head to the man still sitting on the ground.

"Bring him with us and get him something to eat." Mikael realized that somehow he had to rebuild what Anton had ripped apart. But for now, all he wanted was food, his bed, and his mate. Everything else could wait.

In the compound, a celebration of sorts was already in full swing. Everyone patted Mikael on the back, and his mother was apparently cooking up a storm already. Everyone was thrilled about his victory. "I want to go upstairs," Mikael whispered to Denton and then turned to all the others. "Thank you for your confidence in me. Anton was defeated, but there's still a lot of work to do. We are the only pack in this area of the country that survived Anton's grab for power. For that we can thank the Mother. But we have a lot to do, so I'll ask that the celebration be kept in moderation."

The others all bowed their heads in respect as Mikael and Denton walked toward the main house. Inside, Mikael greeted his mother.

"Your father would be so proud of you," she said

"I did what I had to do to keep the pack safe. That's all. There isn't any glory in it," Mikael told her. "Dad always said fighting was the last resort."

"Yes, he did," his mother agreed. "But he also taught you to be strong and that there were times when it was necessary."

"True. But I really don't want to celebrate that. So please...." It seemed wrong to be celebrating the fact that Mikael had just killed someone, even though it had been necessary for the pack's safety. "We're going upstairs."

"Should I bring plates up for you?" she asked, looking concerned.

"That would be nice. Thanks." He kissed her on the cheek and then followed Denton up to their room.

The sun blazed in through the open windows. It seemed brighter and the air fresher than before. Maybe it was because he felt freer than he had since his father's death. Mikael walked to one of the windows, sighing as he peered out. Denton slid warm hands around his waist, working them under his shirt. Damn, that felt good. It was a simple, very gentle touch.

"You do realize that since you defeated Anton, you took over everything he controlled," Denton whispered into his ear.

"I don't want that," Mikael sighed. "I just want to lead my pack and live here with you. Nothing else is important." Thankfully, Denton didn't argue with him. But the more Mikael thought about it, the more he realized he had a lot of work ahead of him. Anton had destroyed the entire pack system that evolved after all those years of hiding. Now it would have to be rebuilt, and he would be the one responsible for doing it.

"You know you're not alone," Denton whispered as he leaned his chin on Mikael's shoulder. "You have me and your entire pack to help you. And if you want my opinion, I think your brother Christopher might turn out to be the surprise element in all of this."

"I always want your opinion." Mikael turned. "Why Christopher?"

"Your brother hasn't been able to fit into the pack. You've been busy, but he's still very much an outsider."

"That's just because he's been away."

"No. It's because your brother is more like you than you realize. I think he's an alpha, but no one ever gave him the chance to realize his potential. He stays away from the others most of the time and isn't shy about taking a leadership role when given the chance. So help him. Teach him to be a good leader, and he might be part of the solution you're looking for."

Mikael wasn't so sure, but he trusted Denton. "I'll talk to him."

Denton squeezed lightly and sucked on his ear. Mikael figured the talking was over for now, and that was perfectly fine with him. Denton gently led him away from the window, and of course Mikael followed.

"Where are we going?" Mikael chuckled.

"I was thinking about taking you to bed, but the last thing I want is for your mother to walk in, so we're going up to the studio."

"Why?"

213

"It's quieter there, and I love looking out those windows." Denton took his hand, and they quietly left the bedroom and went up the stairs. In the studio, Denton closed the door and followed him over to the window.

"I hate looking down at that scar, knowing what caused it," Mikael said, looking toward the horizon and the scorched patch where once there had been lush forest.

"It's all right. The Mother has already set to work there. Once the rains come, seedlings will sprout, and next spring the area will be covered in green. New trees will grow and race upward toward the light. Her light. Yeah, I'm angry as hell that Anton burned us out, but look what came out of it: a new pack, new life"—Denton motioned toward the window—"and a new chance for all of us."

"It's a high price to pay," Mikael whispered.

"It is, but have you ever considered that it's worth it? That you're worth that price?" Denton touched his chin, and when Mikael turned, he kissed him. "I'm beginning to realize that you're an amazing man and worth any price to have you in my life."

Mikael turned back to the window and leaned back into Denton's embrace, letting him be the strong one right now. He was worn out. His side and leg still ached. The wounds had started healing, but the residual effects could still be felt and probably would still be for a few days yet. "So what do we do first?"

"Well…," Denton whispered. "You rest and get your strength back, you and I celebrate your victory in a very special way, and then we take each day as it comes."

"I'm going to have to go around and visit the various packs to see what kind of mess they're in. Maybe there are wolves who can take over leadership of the groups now that Anton is gone." Mikael sighed. This was going to be a huge job. It was likely that anyone who could possibly challenge Anton had either been eliminated or cast out.

"Possibly. But I think you can take some time." Denton licked his shoulder, and Mikael's breath rumbled in his throat. It came out as a growl but a contented one. His pack was safe and secure, and he had his mate to spend his life with. Nothing else really mattered at the moment. Mikael turned away from the windows and drew Denton into his arms. A knock on the door stopped him.

"Yes, Mother," Mikael called.

"I have lunch ready for you. I can bring it up, but the others are all asking for you."

"Thanks, Mom. We'll be down in a few minutes," Mikael called through the door. "We better go on down and see what they're up to. However, once this is over and everyone leaves, you and I get to spend some mate-on-mate quiet time."

Denton scoffed softly. "Since when is that kind of time quiet?" Denton made no effort to move away. "Not that I'd change a thing. Together we have something special. I never imagined I'd find someone who felt so right. I always figured that because I like men there wasn't going to be a mate out there for me, so I never really looked." Denton sucked at the base of Michael's neck, and Mikael stretched to give him better access.

"Am I going to have marks?" Mikael asked.

"Probably. I want everyone to know you're mine."

Mikael chuckled. "I somehow doubt there's anyone who doesn't know that you're mine and I'm yours. I think we get more than our fair share of curious looks, some maybe even a little jealous." He liked the jealous part. Mikael was proud of his mate—he was special.

"You know, if you two take any longer, lunch will be over," his mother said, her voice drifting through the door. Mikael smiled and kissed Denton possessively, a preview of what was to come. Then they parted and Mikael took Denton's hand. Together they went down the stairs to face their pack celebration and whatever else would be coming their way. Mikael knew that together they could indeed accomplish anything.

EPILOGUE

"YOU KNOW, if you keep scowling like that, your face is going to stay that way," Denton told him. "We're almost home." Denton drove on, and Mikael closed his eyes, feeling exhausted but grateful. They had been gone too dang long. It had only been a week, but it had seemed much longer.

"Thank God. If I see one more wolf almost grovel to me when they realize I'm the one who defeated Anton, I'm going to scream."

"In the core of his authority, Anton had a long time to build his power base, and he obviously lorded it over others."

"I know, but...." Seeing wolves so beaten down that they almost seemed like slaves had been heartbreaking. At least Gregor's old pack had been relatively easy to reconstitute, along with a few others where the challenge and takeover had been recent. Anna and her pups had stayed. The renewed packs had elected alphas to lead them and seemed to be moving forward. However, much to Mikael's chagrin, they had recognized him as Supreme Alpha.

"Have you decided what you're going to do?" Denton asked.

"Not yet."

"You need to decide pretty quickly, otherwise they'll end up fighting among themselves," Denton reminded him.

"I know. But with little left but scattered wolves, most of them are too scared of their own shadows to lead. Anton pulled any sort of leadership potential out of those packs and centered it all with himself and his men, most of whom were yes-men and not really any sort of leaders themselves. I need a chance to be home with my own pack, where I can think." He'd seen so much pain and the results of so much abuse.

One of the good things was that he'd met up with Vince, the shifter who'd started the fire at the Evergreen compound, and his family. They had been relieved to hear about Anton's death, and for now, Vince was standing in as alpha. Mikael knew it was temporary, but he also knew that Vince had a decent heart and would be a good leader; he'd started the fire under coercion. Mikael needed to come up with a plan; he'd told Vince he'd visit again in a week. But he'd left Vince with enough things that he and his pack needed to do to keep busy, including repair of all the buildings that had been simply left to the elements because Anton hadn't cared about anything or anyone other than himself, and with winter approaching, there was a lot to do.

"We'll talk about it tomorrow when you're not so tired." Denton squeezed Mikael's thigh, and he smiled. Nothing was as welcome as his mate's touch.

"Thanks. I never signed up to be some sort of supreme wolf leader. All I want to do is protect our family and keep them safe."

"I know. But that's what you are. Through no fault of your own, you are Supreme Alpha."

The way Denton said the last part made him smile. At least his mate wasn't going to change the way he acted around him. That was such a good thing.

"Not me. Us. We're in this together. For however long it takes." The thought made Mikael tired. How was he going to do everything that was expected of him? "I need you more than ever, because there is no way I'm going to survive this alone."

"You don't have to—you know that."

Mikael sighed and reclined his seat as far back as it would go. "How much longer until we're home?"

"You sound like Alexi," Denton teased. "And we're almost there. If you opened your eyes, you'd see that."

"I'm too tired," Mikael mumbled as he felt the car turn and then speed back up again.

"I'm going as fast as I can. We'll be home soon, and tonight we can sleep in our bed. Tomorrow I'll make sure everyone stays away, and you can paint to your heart's desire."

"God, I love you," Mikael whispered.

"Hey, I know you well enough to know that all the strength and patience you show comes from deep inside you. And that innate goodness needs to be recharged and nurtured. You do that with your painting. It restores your soul. So while we're at home, I intend to get you as much of that time as I can, because you're going to need it."

Mikael yawned. "Thank you."

"Go to sleep if you want," Denton said, and Mikael let go of the cares and frustrations that had plagued him for much of the past two weeks. He was almost home, and his spirit felt it. He dozed off and awakened when they slowed and made the turn onto the drive to the compound. He blinked a few times as he put his seat up. He loved that nothing was visible, and then there it was—the main house, his home at the end of a tunnel of green.

"The alpha's back," Alexi called as he raced out of the house and up to the car, pulling open the passenger door as soon as Denton came to a stop. Misha and the other pups were right behind him, surrounding Mikael with gentle energy as soon as he stepped out of the car.

"We missed you," Misha said, and Mikael lifted him into his arms for a hug. "We had a new baby," Misha announced.

"You were supposed to keep that a secret," Maria scolded. Before anyone else could scold Misha, Mikael headed inside with the pups following. Carol and Jerry met him in the great room, Carol holding a tiny bundle.

"It's a boy," she said proudly, and Mikael met both her and Jerry's grins.

"We named him Dmitri," Jerry told him.

"I wanted to name him after you, but Jerry suggested we name him after your father."

Mikael swallowed hard. "That's very special," he whispered as he looked down on the sleeping baby, sniffing slightly. "He's healthy and strong. He'll be a fine addition to our family."

"Thank you," Jerry said.

Mikael smiled and moved through the crowded house, greeting each person in turn. It was so good to be home. He shared a handshake with Karl that turned into a hug, and then he hugged Catherine and Christopher in turn. His mother received a kiss, and a plate was shoved into his hands, along with a fork.

Mikael took a seat in the great room, and his pack members settled around him, telling him about the new building and how close it was to completion. They were also stockpiling supplies for more duplexes, which Jerry wanted to get started on right away. That way every family would have a home, and Anna and the boys could move out of the main house. Not that Mikael minded, but it would be nice to have a little room again.

"That's great," Mikael said with a smile and began to eat. His mother's cooking was like a tonic—it both smelled and tasted like home—and he felt so much better after he'd eaten. With his belly full, he sat back with Denton next to him and just listened to the sounds of home. His eyes grew heavy, and he dozed off, leaning on Denton.

When he woke, the house was quiet, and he'd curled up on the sofa, his arms around Denton's waist, head against Denton's chest. "How long have I been like this?"

"Everyone left half an hour ago, and you curled up and went right to sleep."

Mikael yawned and sat up. "It's quiet." He stood up and stretched his back. "It's been so long since I've actually heard quiet." He stretched, reaching for the ceiling, and then let his arms fall to his sides. He was still tired but felt somewhat better. "Let's go see the progress they've made."

"It's almost dark, and everyone is settling in for the night. I'd suggest a run, but I think you'd fall asleep halfway through it, so how about we go upstairs and take advantage of the silence?" Denton took his hand and turned out the lights, leading him through the house and up the stairs. Instead of stopping on the second floor and their bedroom, Denton continued up to the third floor and into his studio.

"This is my favorite room in the house," Mikael said as he wandered to the wall of windows, looking out as the last of the sun dipped below the horizon and the blues and purples of evening began spreading over the sky. The first stars came out as he stood hand in hand with Denton—his love, his mate, and his life. Mikael breathed a soft sigh.

"What's that for?" Denton asked in a whisper.

"I'm happy. Regardless of what still lies ahead of us, I'm happy." He turned to Denton and kissed him as more stars dotted the night sky. Together they sank down to the floor and broke the silence of the night with the sound of their joy.

DIRK GREYSON is very much an outside kind of man. He loves travel and seeing new things. Dirk worked in corporate America for way too long and now spends his days writing, gardening, and taking care of the home he shares with his partner of more than two decades. He has a master's degree and all the other accessories that go with a corporate job. But he is most proud of the stories he tells and the life he's built. Dirk lives in Pennsylvania in a century-old home and is blessed with an amazing circle of friends.

Facebook: www.facebook.com/dirkgreyson
E-mail: dirkgreyson@comcast.net

As former NSA, Dayton (Day) Ingram has national security chops and now works as a technical analyst for Scorpion. He longs for fieldwork, and scuttling an attack gives him his chance. He's smart, multilingual, and a technological wizard. But his opportunity comes with a hitch—a partner, Knighton (Knight), who is a real mystery. Despite countless hours of research, Day can find nothing on the agent, including his first name!

Former Marine Knight crawled into a bottle after losing his family. After drying out, he's offered one last chance: along with Day, stop a terrorist threat from the Yucatan. To get there without drawing suspicion, Day and Knight board a gay cruise, where the deeply closeted Day and equally closeted Knight must pose as a couple. Tensions run high as Knight communicates very little and Day bristles at Knight's heavy-handed need for control.

But after drinking too much, Day and Knight wake up in bed. *Together.* As they near their destination, they must learn to trust and rely on each other to infiltrate the terrorist camp and neutralize the plot aimed at the US's technological infrastructure, if they hope to have a life after the mission. One that might include each other.

www.dreamspinnerpress.com

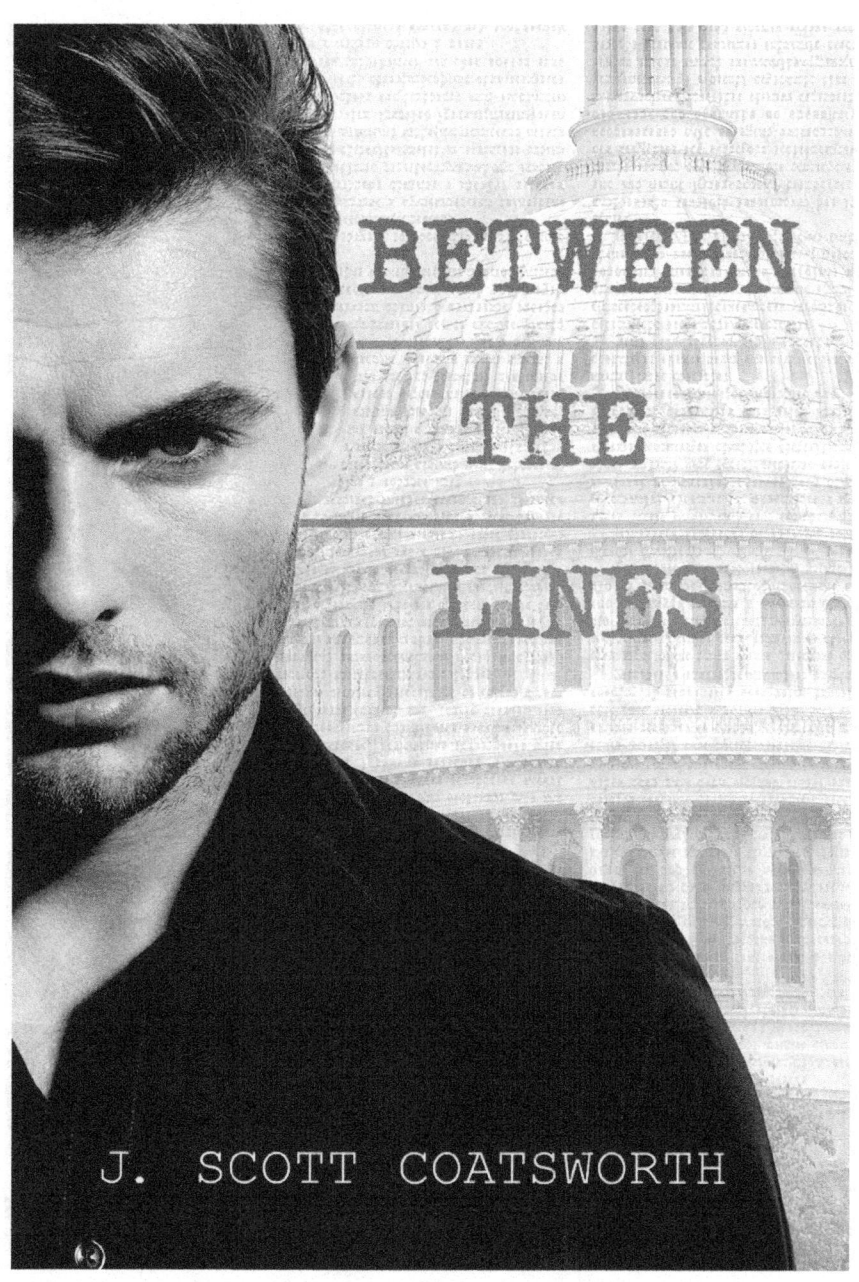

BETWEEN THE LINES

J. SCOTT COATSWORTH

www.dreamspinnerpress.com

RAVON SILVIUS

FRESHMAN
BLUES

www.dreamspinnerpress.com

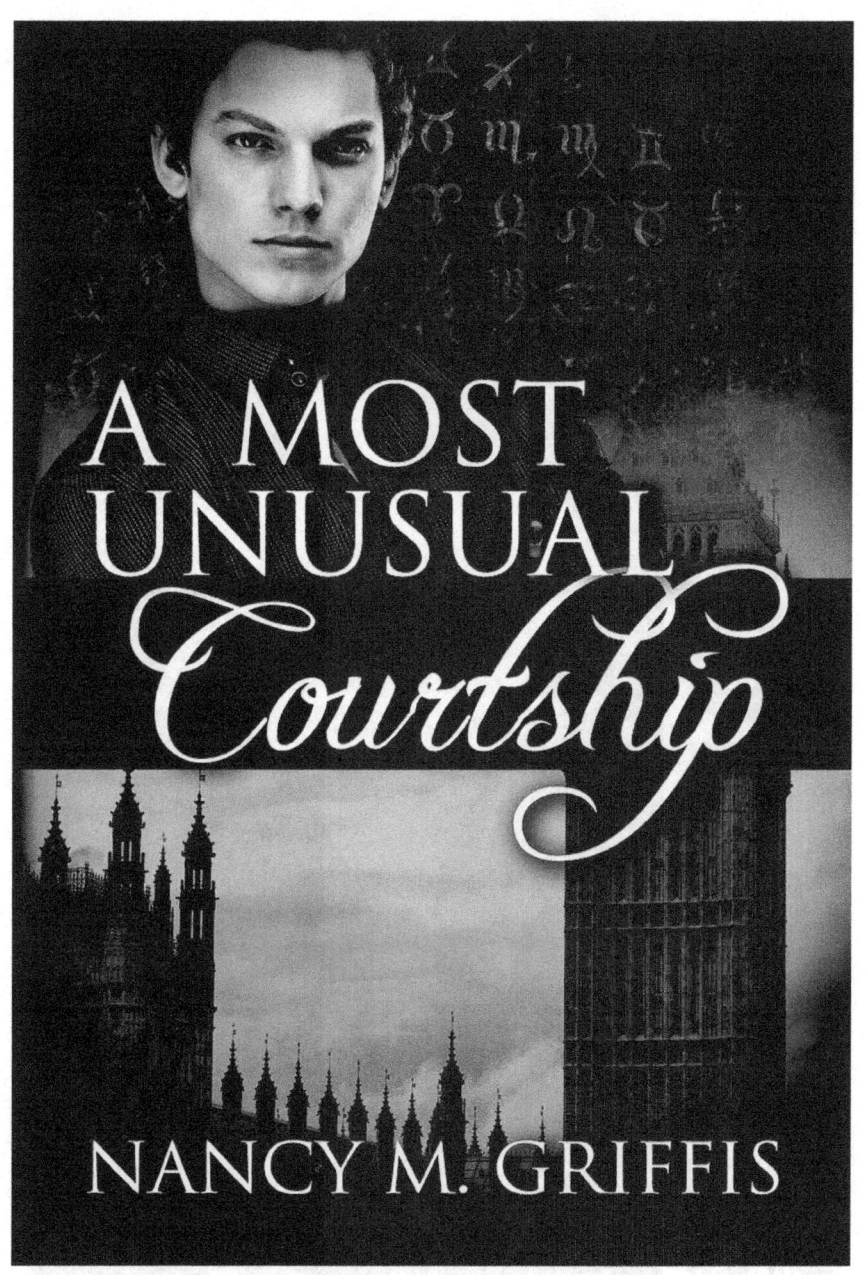

A MOST
UNUSUAL
Courtship

NANCY M. GRIFFIS

www.dreamspinnerpress.com

Made in United States
Orlando, FL
22 March 2026